SUICIDE
MISSION

SUICIDE MISSION

WILLIAM W. JOHNSTONE
with J. A. Johnstone

PINNACLE BOOKS
Kensington Publishing Corp.
www.kensingtonbooks.com

PINNACLE BOOKS are published by

Kensington Publishing Corp.
119 West 40th Street
New York, NY 10018

PUBLISHER'S NOTE
Following the death of William W. Johnstone, the Johnstone family
is working with a carefully selected writer to organize and complete
Mr. Johnstone's outlines and many unfinished manuscripts to
create additional novels in all of his series like The Last Gunfighter,
Mountain Man, and Eagles, among others. This novel was inspired
by Mr. Johnstone's superb storytelling.

All Kensington titles, imprints, and distributed lines are available at
special quantity discounts for bulk purchases for sales promotions,
premiums, fund-raising, educational, or institutional use. Special
book excerpts or customized printings can also be created to fit specific needs. For details, write or phone the office of the Kensington
special sales manager: Kensington Publishing Corp., 119 West 40th
Street, New York, NY 10018, attn: Special Sales Department; phone
1-800-221-2647.

PINNACLE BOOKS and the Pinnacle logo are Reg. U.S. Pat. & TM
Off.
The WWJ steer head logo is a trademark of Kensington Publishing Corp.

ISBN-13: 978-0-7860-3134-4
ISBN-10: 0-7860-3134-4

First printing: October 2013

10 9 8 7 6 5 4 3 2 1

Printed in the United States of America

First electronic edition: October 2013

ISBN-13: 978-0-7860-3135-1
ISBN-10: 0-7860-3135-2

BOOK ONE
THE NEW SUN

CHAPTER 1

Odessa, Texas

Yeah, the redhead had some miles on her, William "Wild Bill" Elliott thought as he studied her along the length of the bar. But hell, if you added up the miles on him, you could go all the way around the earth a dozen times.

From the jukebox, George Strait warbled about making it to Amarillo by morning. Bill had always liked that song. It was melancholy as all get-out, but most of the time that matched up with his mood just fine.

The redhead laughed at something the bartender said, lifted her drink, and took a sip of it. Bill watched her from the corner of his eye now. He didn't think she was a working girl, but sometimes that was hard to determine, even for a man of the world like him.

That thought made his lips quirk in a self-mocking smile under the thick mustache. He was a man of the world only in the sense that he had seen just about all of it at one time or another. In his heart he was still just an ol' country boy.

Even at his advanced age, sometimes when he talked to good-looking women he had a tendency to scuff a booted foot on the floor and had to fight off the impulse to say "Shucks, ma'am."

He lifted his mostly empty mug and downed the rest of the beer. The night wasn't getting any younger and neither was he. He slid the mug across the hardwood and stood up from the stool.

She saw him sidling toward her. Yeah, she did. Gal like that wouldn't miss a trick . . . so to speak. With that tight little body and that mass of auburn hair, she'd probably had men sniffing around her since she was fourteen. Her green eyes said she'd seen it all and been impressed by very little of it.

Bill stopped beside her, rested his right hand on the bar, nodded at the empty glass in front of her, and said, "Buy you another of whatever it is you're drinkin'?"

She studied him as blatantly as he had studied her. In boots, jeans, and pearl-snapped shirt, he looked like an aging cowboy. His rumpled thatch of hair had started going silver at a relatively young age, and so had his mustache. He'd been told more than once that he ought to shave off that porn 'stache, but he'd been wearing it a long time and he liked it.

He'd never been one to do something just because somebody told him he ought to, either. That stubbornness had gotten him into trouble on plenty of occasions.

The redhead must have found what she saw tolerable, anyway. She said, "Sure, I'll have another," and nodded to the bartender, who picked up a bottle and splashed more liquor into the glass. The red-head went on, "Thanks . . ." and the way her voice trailed off told him she was waiting for him to supply his name.

"Bill," he said. "Bill Elliott. Sometimes they call me Wild Bill."

"Because . . . ?"

Hell, darlin', you're old enough to remember Wild Bill Elliott, the cowboy movie star.

Bill thought that but had sense enough not to say it. If she wanted to pretend she didn't know, that was fine. Or maybe she really hadn't ever seen any of those movies. Not everybody had grown up watching B-Westerns like he had.

"I guess I get a little wild sometimes."

"I'll have to keep that in mind." She smiled as she sipped the fresh drink.

The bartender asked Bill, "Something else for you, friend?"

"Yeah, I'll have another beer."

"You got it."

As the bartender drew the beer, Bill said to the redhead, "You didn't tell me your name."

"It's Sheila."

"Pretty name for an Irish colleen. It suits you."

"Thank you. I don't think I've seen you in here before, Wild Bill."

"That's because I've never been here. I'm just passing through Odessa."

That was his not-so-subtle way of telling her that if anything happened between them, it wouldn't be permanent. His home, if you could call it that, was back in Tennessee, but he didn't spend much time there anymore. There was a deep-seated restlessness inside him that kept him on the move most of the time. That restless nature and a love of excitement had led him into the line of work from which he now considered himself retired.

"You need somebody to show you the town?"

The only part of town he really wanted to see was the inside of his motel room, preferably with her in it, but he'd been raised to be a gentleman, so he said, "That would be mighty nice—"

A heavy impact against his shoulder knocked him against the bar. He caught himself, turned so quickly it was hard for the eye to follow his movement, caught hold of the arm of the man who had bumped into him, twisted it behind the man's back, and put his other hand on the back of the man's neck so he could drive his face down into the bar. The man didn't even have time to yell before his nose broke. Stunned, he went limp and collapsed on the sawdust-littered floor.

The whole thing hadn't taken more than a couple of heartbeats.

Bill stepped back away from the bar, giving himself room to move if he needed to. His gaze darted around the smoky room, assessing potential threats.

Sheila sat on her barstool, her mouth open as she gaped at him. The bartender looked equally surprised. So did the three men who stood a few feet away. From the looks of them, they worked in construction or in the oil and gas fields, like the man who lay on the floor at Bill's feet.

One of the trio recovered his voice and said, "What the hell did you do to Steve?"

"He bumped into me . . ." Bill started to say, his voice

trailing off as he realized how lame that sounded, especially compared to his reaction to that bump.

He could tell these men that enemies had tried to kill him hundreds of times, all over the world, and that his instincts were trained to react swiftly and violently to even the slightest hint of danger. That was the only thing that had kept him alive this long.

They wouldn't understand that, though. Like most people, they went about their daily lives without ever facing any real threats. And the only reason they could do that was because of the work of men like Bill Elliott, soldiers in the shadowy war that truly shaped the world.

A war from which he had withdrawn, he reminded himself.

"I'm sorry," he said. "Reckon I didn't think. Let's help your friend up, and I'll buy all you fellas a drink—"

"The hell with that," one of the other men said. "Get that crazy old codger!"

That was exactly what Bill didn't want to happen. He bit back a curse directed at himself for provoking this incident. If he was going to live in the real world, the normal world, the mundane world, he couldn't let a drunk bumping into him in a bar cause a fight.

That resolve was for the future, though. Right now, like it or not, he had a fight on his hands.

The bartender yelled for them to take it outside or he'd call the cops, but Steve's three friends ignored him and charged Bill.

If they had been facing just about anybody else in a bar fight, three-against-one odds would have been overwhelming. To Bill's eyes, though, they seemed almost to be moving in slow motion, and they were practically falling over their own feet as they attacked.

A side kick swept one man's legs out from under him and sent him crashing to the floor. The same motion bent Bill low enough so that a roundhouse punch went harmlessly over his head. He drove his stiffened right hand into that man's belly and brought up his left fist in a blow that landed on the man's jaw and snapped his head back. He folded up, too.

The third man actually got a punch in, which made Bill worry that he was slowing down. The man's knuckles grazed the side of Bill's head. He grabbed the man's arm, twisted, and with a perfect hip throw sent the man flying through the air to slam down on top of an empty table. The table was sturdy enough that it didn't collapse. The man lay on top of it, groaning.

Again, the whole thing had happened almost too fast for the eye to follow.

The bartender had a cell phone pressed to his ear. Bill figured the man was calling the cops, as he had threatened to do. The other dozen or so customers in the bar just stared apprehensively at him, like they would with a dog they suspected of being rabid.

Well, maybe they weren't so far wrong at that, Bill thought.

Sheila hadn't budged from her barstool. Bill looked at her and said, "I reckon you're gonna take back your offer to show me around town, right?"

"I . . . I don't think that would be a good idea."

"You're probably right."

She summoned up a weak smile and said, "I can't

say you didn't warn me. You told me you could get a little wild."

"It happens more than I'd like." He took out his wallet and tossed a hundred-dollar bill on the bar, telling the bartender, "That ought to cover the drinks and your trouble."

"Wait a minute," the man said. "You can't just beat up my customers and then walk out of here. The cops are on their way."

Bill knew he could still call a number in Washington and make any legal trouble with the local authorities go away, but he didn't want to do that. He didn't want to owe any favors to anybody in that damned town where so much of what was wrong with the country had started.

Instead he said quietly to the bartender, "You don't want to try to stop me."

The man looked plenty tough. Anybody who tended bar in a town like Odessa had to be. But he swallowed hard and settled for saying, "Don't ever come back in here again."

"You don't have to worry about that."

Nobody got in his way or tried to stop him as he walked toward the door. But Sheila called after him, "Goodbye, Wild Bill."

He looked back and drawled in his best cowboy voice, "So long, ma'am."

As he got into his pickup and drove away, he told himself sternly that he was going to have to learn how to control those reactions. He had walked away from the sort of life where somebody was trying to kill him all the time. Those days were over.

He was through with them, and he was never going back.

CHAPTER 2

The foothills of the Hindu Kush

Tariq Maleef fingered the knife thrust behind his belt as he watched the truck bounce along the rutted road toward him and his companions. This rugged, mountainous area was mostly barren of vegetation, and the truck's gray body, as well as the brown canvas cover over the back, made it blend in with its surroundings.

Tariq's dark, keen eyes followed it easily, though. He had spent much of his childhood here, before being sent to Saudi Arabia and then to England for schooling, and the blood of the wild hill men flowed in his veins.

The big knife was the only weapon he carried, although his companions were armed with an assortment of AK-47s, AR-15s, MAC-10s, Glocks, and Sig Sauers. Tariq fully appreciated modern weaponry, but he was enough of a primitive to relish the feel of a blade in his hand, too.

He was in his thirties, a compact, muscular man with a shaved head and a neatly trimmed goatee.

He wore jeans, a khaki shirt, and a leather jacket that felt good when the chilly winds blew down out of the mountains. His friends were dressed much the same, with none of the traditional robes and headgear in sight. They were the new breed, the ones who could tolerate the garb of the hated West and blend in with their enemies.

Their jeeps were parked over the ridge behind them. As far as anyone could tell by looking, they might as well have been dropped from the sky into this empty wasteland.

The truck was close enough now that Tariq could hear the rumbling growl of its engine. His pulse quickened. With every foot of ground the truck covered, his dream came closer.

Finally, the truck ground to a stop about twenty yards away from the group of a dozen men. The sun's reflection on the windshield made it difficult to see, but Tariq knew there were two men in the cab, the driver and one other.

Dolgunov.

Tariq's father had been a *mujahideen*. More than three decades earlier, he had fought a war against men like Dolgunov. Tariq had been only a boy at the time, but he recalled vividly how proud he had been that his father and men like him had brought the proud Soviet army to its knees and sent it crawling home in defeat.

Now circumstances forced him to deal with the Russians and that necessity rankled, but Tariq reminded himself that Dolgunov was *Mafiya*, not military, although the man and the organization he worked for had connections within the Russian army. Otherwise he would not have been able to get his hands on the item he was delivering to Tariq and his friends today.

After a long moment, the passenger door of the truck's cab opened. A tall, blocky, blond-haired figure stepped out. Tariq recognized Dolgunov. The two of them had met several times in the past, feeling each other out to see if they were trustworthy.

Of course, no one really trusted anyone else. One's brothers in the cause, perhaps, but that was all.

Dolgunov gestured curtly, and the canvas cover on the back of the truck was pulled aside to reveal a .50 caliber machine gun mounted so that it could fire over the top of the cab. The gun could be swiveled on its mount so that its bullets would rake the entire group of men facing it.

Tariq sensed some of his companions stiffening, but he spoke a low-voiced word of assurance. Given the stakes of this transaction, he wouldn't have expected Dolgunov to show up without taking some precautions.

"Tariq, my friend," the Russian called. "Come, and bring two of your men with you."

Tariq motioned to a pair of his men and started walking toward the truck. At the same time, several more Russians carrying automatic rifles climbed out of the back of the vehicle and arrayed themselves behind Dolgunov, who strolled forward to meet Tariq.

The two leaders shook hands when they met. Dolgunov was several inches taller, but Tariq didn't feel intimidated by the man. No infidel could ever make him feel intimidated.

"Are we ready to conclude our transaction?" Dolgunov asked.

"As soon as I see the merchandise."

"Of course. Come with me."

The armed Russians stepped back as Dolgunov and Tariq went to the rear of the truck. Just inside the back of the vehicle sat a heavy-looking metal case. Dolgunov unsnapped the two catches and opened the lid.

Tariq leaned forward to look at the metal cylinder that was fatter on both ends and in the middle. It sat in a cushioned recess in the case that was obviously made for it. A small control panel was built into the cylinder.

Tariq crooked a finger at one of his men and said to Dolgunov, "My friend Assad will authenticate it."

"Of course. With this much money involved, you have to be sure of what you're getting, eh?"

Tariq didn't care about the money. All that mattered was that the device be capable of doing what he wanted it to do.

As Tariq and Dolgunov stood by, Assad examined the cylinder and the case closely. Tariq began to grow impatient, but he controlled it. This was a vital step.

After what seemed like an eternity, Assad stepped back and nodded.

Tariq slipped a compact satellite phone from his pocket and punched a number. When a voice answered, he said simply, "Yes." Then he broke the connection, put the phone away, and told Dolgunov, "Give it a minute, then check with your people."

Dolgunov didn't have to make the call. Someone

called him less than a minute later. He took out a similar sat phone and spoke into it in Russian. A pleased smile broke out on his face. He pocketed his phone and told Tariq, "The funds are in the Swiss account, as arranged. Our business is done."

"As soon as I take possession of the device."

Dolgunov made an expansive gesture.

Assad and the other man lifted the case from the truck and carried it toward the ridge. They disappeared over it.

Still smiling, Dolgunov said, "As the Americans say, a pleasure doing business with you."

Tariq replied, "As the Americans say, go to hell, you Russian bastard."

Dolgunov's smile vanished. He opened his mouth to say something, but before any words could emerge Tariq's knife flashed in his hand as a blindingly fast stroke opened Dolgunov's throat almost to the spine. Blood spurted several feet from the gaping wound and splashed onto the sand. Dolgunov collapsed.

Tariq threw himself to the ground as the rocket fired from a nearby hilltop streaked through the air and slammed into the truck, engulfing it in a ball of fire. Tariq felt the heat and the concussion and knew he should have been farther away, but he had wanted to be close enough to Dolgunov to see the horror in the man's eyes as death claimed him.

The force of the blast knocked the other Russians to the ground. Tariq's men opened fire on them before they could gather their wits about them. The streams of lead shredded them, chopping them into bloody heaps of flesh that barely looked human. Tariq didn't raise his head until it was all over.

Then he stood up, brushed himself off, and turned away from the carnage. The men Dolgunov worked for would be upset about this, but they had gotten their money, after all. That ought to be enough to mollify them. In the end, they would consider the deaths of Dolgunov and the other men as just part of their overhead, another cost of doing business.

A few minutes later, with the suitcase nuke secure in one of the jeeps, Tariq and his fellow warriors drove away, leaving a column of black smoke from the burning truck climbing into the sky behind them.

CHAPTER 3

Ciudad Acuña, Coahuila, Mexico

Alfredo Sanchez pushed the steel-framed glasses he wore back up his nose. They had a habit of sliding down, and he had thought more than once about getting contacts.

He liked the glasses, though. He liked being able to take them off and have the world go soft and blurry around him for a moment. It was harder to see the ugly things that way. Life was reduced to a collage of bright colors, at least temporarily.

But then he had to put the glasses back on and see the truth again.

At the moment, the truth was that Pablo Estancia was a stupid fool.

"You brought them here?" Alfredo asked. His voice was cool and flat, revealing none of the inner turmoil he felt. He never revealed his true feelings unless it was absolutely necessary.

Pablo's heavy shoulders rose and fell in a shrug.

"I thought you would like to question them

yourself, amigo," he said. "With so many important
things coming up . . ."

Alfredo ignored that. He knew that Pablo was
just fishing for information. He considered himself
an important man in the cartel and resented it
whenever anything was kept from him.

Pablo *was* important. Through a combination of
brute force and animal cunning, he kept the pipe-
lines of drugs and illegals moving smoothly in this
area. But his abilities were limited to that. He had
nothing to do with strategy and planning. Certainly
not when it involved an operation as large and important as the one that Alfredo had put together.

"Since they're here, I'll talk to them," Alfredo
said. "Bring them in."

Pablo nodded and left the room, which was large
and well-furnished, like all the other rooms in this
villa. An enormous flat-screen TV dominated one
side of the room. The opposite wall was glass, revealing a courtyard with a pool surrounded by a
tiled patio.

Normally the lights around the courtyard would
be on so that Pablo could frolic in that pool
with the drug-addicted *putas* he preferred. Those
women might be young and still beautiful, not yet
showing the ravages of the poison they put in their
bodies, but they were still whores, Alfredo thought,
and they were prime examples of just why Pablo
couldn't be trusted with anything too important.

Sometimes in the past when Alfredo had visited
the villa, one or more of the women had tried to
entice him. After all, he was slim, elegantly dressed,
and with his dark hair he was handsome even when
wearing the steel-framed glasses. Because he hadn't

succumbed to their charms, they had talked about him behind his back and proclaimed him to be a homosexual.

That was nonsense, of course. Alfredo enjoyed the company of women, but only the *right* women. There was a professor of antiquities in Mexico City . . . a diplomatic liaison . . . a lawyer . . . women who were intelligent enough to carry on a conversation and refined enough for an important man to be seen with.

So let the whores make their scurrilous comments about him. They were unimportant, not worth caring about.

Pablo came back into the room, trailed by five men. Two of them stumbled as they walked because they had black hoods over their heads and couldn't see where they were going. The other three prodded them along with machine pistols.

"That's far enough," Alfredo told the three guards. He gestured, and one of the gunmen pulled the hoods off the prisoners' heads.

Their faces showed the marks of the beating they had endured. Their mouths were bloody, their eyes swollen almost shut. Bruises discolored their features. Smears of blood had dried on their skin.

One of the men was Hispanic, the other black. They looked terrified but also stubbornly defiant, meeting Alfredo's speculative gaze without looking away.

"You're certain they are who you say they are?" he asked Pablo.

"The information is trustworthy," Pablo said. He pointed to the Hispanic prisoner. "This one is Border Patrol. The other works for the DEA."

Alfredo smiled coolly and said, "I wasn't sure the Americans even had a border patrol anymore. What purpose does it serve when the funding is cut to the bare bones because the President wants more and more illegals in the country so they can vote for him?" He turned his gaze to the black prisoner. "And why enforce the drug laws? Sooner or later all drugs will be legalized in your country, because that's what the voters want, eh, amigo?"

"You'd better hope that day never comes," the man answered. "When it does you're out of business."

"A good point," Alfredo admitted. "But until that time, we all still have our parts to play in this little drama."

"Life isn't a *telenovela*," the Hispanic prisoner snapped.

Alfredo raised his carefully barbered eyebrows and said, "If it were, it would be so much more entertaining, wouldn't it? All the men would be handsome, all the women gorgeous." He clasped his hands together behind his back. "Tell me what you know."

The two men stared sullenly at him and remained silent. After a moment, Alfredo nodded to Pablo, who barked an order. One of the guards lowered his machine pistol, pulled a blackjack from his pocket, and smashed it into the back of the Hispanic prisoner's right knee. Despite his obvious determination not to, the man cried out in pain and fell to the floor as that leg folded up underneath him. The guard struck again with the blackjack, this time shattering the man's kneecap.

Howls of agony filled the room until the guard

put his foot on the prisoner's throat, choking off the sound.

"Do you know how many bones there are in the human body?" Alfredo asked. "No, of course you don't. But there are hundreds, and every one of them can be broken. It would take many hours to break all of them . . . but it can be done. It will be done unless you tell me what you know about El Nuevo Sol."

The DEA agent shook his head and said, "I don't have any idea what you're talking about."

His eyes told a different story, however. Alfredo could tell that the man had at least heard the phrase before.

"This is the last chance," he said softly.

The prisoner just stared at him.

"The last chance for your friend, I should have said," Alfredo went on. He nodded to Pablo again, then turned his back and took off his glasses. He took a fine linen handkerchief from his shirt pocket and began polishing the lenses as more screaming began behind him.

It took hours, as Alfredo had said, and the Hispanic Border Patrol agent died before they were finished. The DEA agent would be permanently crippled if he lived, which was highly doubtful. But when the questioning was finished and Pablo came to the guest room where Alfredo was staying, he had the information they needed.

"I want to hear it for myself," Alfredo said.

"I think he's still conscious," Pablo said. "But we should probably hurry."

They went back to the room next to the court-yard. The floors here were tile, too, like the patio, and the blood might not be easy to clean from them, but that wasn't Alfredo's worry. He hitched up his trousers slightly so that he wouldn't ruin the line of them as he knelt next to the broken heap of humanity that had been the DEA agent.

"Tell me what you know about El Nuevo Sol."

"Just . . . just rumors," the prisoner gasped. "Something big in . . . in San Antonio. We were on the trail . . . of a man named Chavez . . ."

Alfredo's face was unusually grim as he glanced up at Pablo. Chavez was one of the cartel's computer experts . . . if the prisoner was talking about the same Chavez, which seemed likely. He had handled many of the details of communications with the cartel's partners in this operation, routing the emails through so many anonymous digital pathways that no one could ever trace them.

But in order for that to be possible, Chavez had to be privy to a great deal of sensitive information.

"Is he here at the villa?" Alfredo asked.

Pablo looked distinctly uncomfortable as he said, "He works out of his own place. He has an apartment over the club where his girlfriend works. She's a, uh, stripper."

"Bring him here," Alfredo ordered. "We need to find out if he's had any contact with these men."

"Chavez would never betray us."

"You'll pardon me if I don't take your word for that, Pablo. I want to talk to him myself."

"Of course, of course, Alfredo, right away." Pablo made a sharp gesture to his men. "Take care of it! Find Chavez and bring him here."

Alfredo looked down again at the DEA agent,

who was gasping for air through his broken mouth and nose.

"What is El Nuevo Sol?"

"I . . . don't . . . know."

Alfredo believed him. And so there was no more point in keeping the man alive. Alfredo took a small .25 caliber semi-automatic pistol from his jacket pocket, placed the muzzle against the DEA man's right eye, and pulled the trigger. The little bullet wasn't powerful enough to penetrate the skull, so it just bounced around inside the prisoner's head, scrambling his brain and making him twitch like a broken puppet for a moment before he died.

Alfredo stood up and handed the pistol to Pablo. Even though only one shot had been fired from it, he didn't want to put it back in his pocket.

"Clean that," he said. "While we're waiting for Chavez."

CHAPTER 4

Martin Chavez sipped his drink as he watched the nearly naked young woman contorting on the stage in time to the loud, pounding music.

Catalina was a better dancer and more graceful than any of the other women who worked here at the Paloma Azul. Her body was slim but curved where it should be, with enticing hips and firm, high breasts. Her long brown hair swirled around her shoulders as she moved, alternately concealing and revealing the dark brown nipples that crowned those breasts.

Pride filled Marty as he watched Catalina dance. It wasn't every man who could say he had a girl-friend so sensuous and so beautiful.

Especially when he was a little overweight, near-sighted, and spent most of his time hunched forward in a chair, staring at a computer screen.

His phone chimed. He couldn't actually hear it over the music, of course, but he felt it vibrate momentarily in his shirt pocket. He took it out and saw that he had a message from Guadalupe Cerna.

Lupe lived across the hall from him, and Marty slipped him a little money each month to pay him for keeping an eye on his place.

"*Tres hombres,*" the message read. That was all, but it was enough. Three men were upstairs looking for him.

Marty tapped some keys on the phone and accessed the feed from the camera he had hidden in a light fixture at the end of the upstairs hall. He stiffened in his chair. The three rough-looking men were still standing there in the upstairs corridor, talking to each other. The feed didn't have audio, but Marty didn't have to hear what they were saying to know they were upset.

All three men reached under their jackets and took out guns. One of them lifted his foot and drove it against the door, splintering the jamb and making the door fly open.

Marty's eyes widened. Watching three men break into his apartment was bad enough to start with, but the fact that he recognized these men made it even worse.

They worked for Pablo Estancia, the same man Marty worked for.

Marty uttered a stunned curse under his breath. Pablo wouldn't have sent those men to look for him—and in such a violent fashion—unless he'd found out what Marty had been up to.

It had seemed so easy at first. Just hack into the cartel's network, shift a little money here, a little more there, never enough for anyone to miss it easily, and over time he had a substantial amount in an untraceable overseas account.

It was stealing, sure, but when it was just pixels on a screen it didn't really seem like a big deal.

It would be a big deal to Pablo, though. Anything that made him look bad in the eyes of the cartel was a big deal.

The three gunmen had disappeared into the apartment. Marty had cameras set up in there, too, but he didn't think there was any point in accessing them. He knew what the guys would be doing: tearing the place apart looking for him.

And when they didn't find him, they would come back down the outer stairs and enter the Paloma Azul, since Pablo knew that Catalina worked here.

He had to get out.

Now.

The music *boomp-boomp*ed to a halt as Catalina ducked back through the curtain at the back of the stage and vanished. The customers hooted and whistled and applauded, no doubt trying to coax her back out for an encore.

That effort was doomed to failure. Catalina performed precisely the number of sets she was supposed to, and she could time each set down to the second so that she never spent any extra moments on stage. She gave exactly what she was paid for, no more, no less.

Marty put the phone away and stood up. The room was crowded, with men lining the bar, sitting at all the tables, and perched on the stools around the stage. A mixture of tobacco and marijuana smoke filled the air and made the already dim lighting hazy. The spotlight was turned off at the moment and wouldn't come on again until the next dancer took her place in a few minutes. The customers concentrated on their drinks.

That gave Marty a little time to move without anybody paying attention to him. He circled the room, heading for the door that led backstage.

A bouncer named Ontiveros stood there, brawny arms folded over his massive chest. He was a bodybuilder, thick with muscle. He could pick up pale, soft Marty and tear him in half like a phone book.

But he wouldn't because he knew Marty, knew that Catalina was his girlfriend. That puzzled Ontiveros as much as it did everyone else who knew them—why would any woman as beautiful as Catalina have anything to do with someone like Marty?—but he accepted it, as did the others who worked here. He gave Marty a nod and moved aside from the door.

Marty's heart slugged heavily in his chest as he went down the short hallway to the dancers' dressing room. If Pablo wanted to talk to him about some work matter, he would just call and have Marty come to the villa.

The fact that he had sent three of his apes to *fetch* Marty spoke volumes. Pablo was mad about something, and it had to be the money Marty had skimmed from the cartel.

It had been a foolish thing to do. Marty had known all along that it would probably result in his death if he was ever found out, but the temptation had been too strong. He was like everyone else: he wondered what Catalina saw in him. He had to be worthy of her, and the only way he could do that was by being rich.

He stepped into the dressing room and found

himself surrounded by nude or nearly nude female flesh. He was used to it, though, and was able to concentrate on Catalina, who sat at one of the dressing tables in only the G-string she had worn at the conclusion of her set. She was touching up her makeup, but she spared a glance for Marty in the mirror and smiled at him.

"Was I good?" she asked.

He didn't know how she could ever wonder about such a thing. She was more than good. She was spectacular.

"Wonderful," he said, "but we have to go."

Her smile turned into a frown.

"Go? I have two more sets to do."

"Not tonight." He leaned closer to her and lowered his voice. "We need to get out of here. Now."

Her brown eyes widened, and she said, "Oh, Marty, what have you done?"

"Nothing, I—" He couldn't explain it to her, not now. There wasn't time. "We just have to go, okay? You need to get dressed."

Still she hesitated, and he thought that he should have gone out the back door of the club and left her here.

But he couldn't do that, and he knew it. Pablo's men knew who she was. They would grab her, take her back to the villa, try to force her to tell them what she knew about his little scheme . . . which was exactly nothing.

That lack of knowledge wouldn't stop them from putting her through hell and eventually killing her.

He never should have done it, never should have put her life at risk. But it was too late to think about that now. All that mattered now was living through the next few minutes.

"Please, Catalina," he said.

"Oh, all right. But if I get in trouble, it's your fault."

Truer words had never been spoken, he thought.

She pulled on a pair of jeans and a T-shirt. She didn't need a bra. Her feet went into a pair of running shoes. She picked up her bag and asked, "Are we going upstairs?"

Marty shook his head.

"Out the back." He didn't tell her they would never be able to go back to the apartment again. Everything there was lost.

But he had enough money to replace everything. He just needed to get to somewhere with a computer. There was a coffee shop a few blocks away . . .

What they really needed to do, he realized as they went down the hall, around a corner, and out a narrow door into an alley, was get across the border.

Not that the cartel couldn't still reach them there, but it might be a little more difficult on American soil.

He took hold of her arm as they left the alley and turned onto the sidewalk. She stiffened a little and said, "Marty, you're scaring me."

"No need to be scared," he lied. "Everything is going to be all right."

"You act like we're running away from something."

"No, just . . . I want to go over to Del Rio."

"At this time of night?"

"I have to see somebody. It's business."

He had never explained his business to her, but

he was sure she suspected it had something to do with the cartel. Everything in Ciudad Acuña had some sort of connection to the cartel, no matter how slight.

His phone buzzed again. He kept his left hand on Catalina's arm and used his right to take out the phone. The screen displayed an unfamiliar number. It probably belonged to one of the three men who were looking for him. They had stepped into the dimly lit club and one of them had called his number, hoping to hear his phone ring or see it light up.

He ignored it. Keep them guessing. Every minute that went by, he and Catalina were closer to safety.

When he slipped the phone back in his pocket, his fingers brushed a card that was there. It was a business card, but nothing was printed on it except a phone number that someone had scrawled in ink. The card had passed through a number of hands before it came to Marty, along with a message that someone wanted him to call that number. He suspected that it belonged to an American narc or Border Patrol agent. They were always sniffing around, trying to hook up with people on the edges of the cartel in the hope that they could work their way closer to the men who ran it.

Marty had never had any interest in helping the Americans . . . but maybe now they could help him. If he and Catalina could get across the river, he could call that number, maybe set up a meet . . . He would have to be careful, of course, but he had something to trade.

He had a file of cartel financial and organizational information on a flash drive that never left his pocket, along with a lot of intel about the connection between his employers and certain terrorist organizations on the other side of the world. Most of it was encrypted and he didn't know what it meant, but there had been a lot of email traffic over the past few months. Something was in the works, no doubt about that. He could have broken the encryption if he'd taken the time, but he hadn't gotten around to it.

Maybe the Americans would not only protect him but would also pay him to decipher those emails. He might come out of this all right after all, because there was the bridge, less than a block away, and both he and Catalina had work permits that would allow them to cross over into Texas . . .

Behind them, someone shouted, "Chavez!"

CHAPTER 5

Catalina Ramos had been making her own way in the world since she was eleven years old. At first that had meant becoming highly skilled as a thief. Later, it meant becoming highly skilled at . . . other things.

But regardless of what it took, she prided herself on her ability to survive.

It looked like that ability might be about to run out.

Beside her, Marty jerked around and let out an exclamation that was half angry curse and half terrified squeal. He still had hold of her arm. He used that grip to shove her toward the well-lighted bridge over the Rio Grande.

"Run!" he told her. "Get over the river and don't look back!"

He didn't have to tell her twice. Whatever trouble was behind them, she wanted no part of it.

It was pretty obvious that trouble had something to do with the man Marty worked for, Pablo Estancia, and the men Estancia worked for, the leaders of the cartel that moved drugs through this part of the world.

It had always seemed odd that Marty worked for such men. In a different world—across the border, say—his skills with a computer probably would have landed him a good job. But here in Mexico he worked for the cartel, which had its fingers in just about every aspect of day-to-day life.

Catalina stumbled a little from the push he had given her, then caught her balance and broke into a run toward the bridge. Her legs flashed back and forth, moving effortlessly and with sleek grace. She had learned to run during her days as a thief, and she still did as part of her daily workout.

Marty pounded along the pavement behind her, but there was no way he could keep up. His days spent sitting in front of a screen meant that he was in poor shape, easily winded. Catalina heard him huffing and puffing for breath.

Despite what he had told her, she slowed down and looked back. She didn't love Marty Chavez, but he had always treated her decently and she was very fond of him. She didn't want to see him hurt.

That seemed to be what the men pursuing him were bent on doing, though.

There were three of them, and they were closing in fast.

Without thinking about what she was doing, Catalina stopped and turned back.

The street was busy, even at this hour, but no one was going to help Marty. Catalina knew that. In fact, all the pedestrians and the people in the cars going slowly past as they approached the border crossing were making a point of looking away. They didn't know what was going on, and they certainly weren't going to get involved.

So Marty's only chance to get away lay with her.

Catalina never wasted a lot of time pondering a situation. When she had a thought, she acted on it.

Now, as one of the cartel thugs reached for Marty, she left her feet in a leaping kick that sent the heel of her running shoe smashing into the man's jaw.

Since both of them were moving, a lot of momentum was involved. The man's head snapped back sharply. His feet ran out from under him and he crashed to the pavement on his back.

Catalina fell, too, but she caught herself on her hands and rolled, coming back up smoothly on her feet.

"Catalina, no!" Marty cried. "Get out of here!"

He turned and swung an awkward punch at one of the other men. The cartel man ducked and grabbed Marty's arm, forcing it up behind his back. Marty cried out in pain.

"We don't need the whore!" the man holding him said. "Kill her!"

The other man reached behind his back, no doubt for a gun tucked behind his belt and concealed by the tail of his shirt.

Catalina didn't give him time to draw the weapon. Her hand darted into her bag, which was still slung over her shoulder despite her exertions, and came out with a small, needle-pointed stiletto. A flick of her wrist sent it flying at the gunman, who staggered back and screamed as the steel pierced his right eye and buried itself to dig into his brain.

He wasn't the first man Catalina had killed. A pimp in Matamoros who accused her of holding out on him, a client in Piedras Negras who would have killed her, who had probably killed many other prostitutes . . . she had taken those lives to save her own and never lost any sleep over them.

This man's death wouldn't trouble her, either, except for the fact that he worked for the cartel. *That* would come back to haunt her, she suspected, unless she got across the border and ran a long way. She might never stop running.

And even then she might not be able to put enough distance between herself and the cartel's thirst for vengeance.

That was something to worry about in the future. For now she had to stay alive. The stiletto was the only weapon she carried, so she would have to deal with the third man with just her hands and feet.

As she wheeled toward him, she saw that he already had a gun in his hand. He chopped at Marty's head with it, the blow driving Marty to the street as blood spurted from a gash above his ear.

The police on duty at the bridge must have seen and heard the commotion by now, but they weren't budging from their posts. They were paid to check the papers of people crossing the border, and that was all they were going to do.

Catalina threw herself into a rolling dive as the gunman leveled his weapon at her and fired. The shot went over her head. As she came up she kicked him in the belly. She hoped that would knock the gun loose from his hand, but he managed to hold on to it as he stumbled backward.

The shot made people scream and run to clear the street. Up at the bridge, one of the police yelled into a walkie-talkie, no doubt calling for help. It might arrive eventually, but not anytime soon.

Catalina had landed with her toes and finger-tips on the ground, like a runner in a starting stance. She lifted her head, saw the man aiming at her again. She knew all she could do was try to dive to the side, out of the line of fire . . .

Marty surged up from the street just as the gunman pulled the trigger. The bullet struck him in the chest at close range and knocked him backward. His arms flew out to the sides as he fell in an awkward sprawl.

"Marty!" Catalina screamed.

The gunman swung the weapon toward her and fired again, missing wide. She vaulted the body of the man she had killed, and as she did, she snatched the stiletto from his eye. The gunman sent another round at her, but he hurried his shot and the bullet ricocheted off the pavement.

Catalina knocked the man's gun arm aside and buried the stiletto in his throat. She felt the blade grate against his spine as she shoved it as deep as she could.

His eyes were only inches from hers. They widened in pain and disbelief that she had killed him. A mere woman, and a stripper at that. Those were probably the thoughts going through his head as he died.

Catalina jerked the gun from his hand and shoved his collapsing body away, pulling the stiletto from his throat as she did so. The street was empty now, except for her and the four men lying on the pavement. The man she had kicked in the jaw was still alive, moaning softly because she had broken his face.

She shut him up by bending swiftly and cutting his throat.

Then she ran to Marty and dropped to the ground beside him, pulling his bloody figure into her lap and cradling him against her.

"Cat . . . Catalina . . ." he said in a raspy whisper.

"I'm here, Marty. You'll be all right."

"N . . . no. I won't." With a wildly trembling hand, he caught hold of her right hand and pressed something into her palm. Two somethings: a crumpled card and a small plastic oblong that she recognized as a flash drive.

"Take this," Marty said. "Call . . . call the number. Tell whoever answers . . . you have information about . . . El Nuevo Sol."

The New Sun? That made no sense to Catalina. What was it, and how could it help her?

"Be careful," Marty went on. He stopped to cough, and blood trickled from the corner of his mouth. "Don't trust . . . anybody. At least . . . not in Mexico. You need to get . . . across the border."

"No, I need to get help for you—"

"Too late . . . remember this . . ."

He rattled off a long number and made her repeat it back to him. She said it a couple of times and knew that it was etched into her brain. She'd always had a good memory, almost a photographic memory, and he knew that. He had seen her do mental tricks with it many times.

"Don't forget . . ." he told her, and amazingly, he managed to smile. "It's important . . . One of these days . . . you'll thank me."

He coughed again, wrackingly. Catalina clutched

him tighter to her, aware that she was getting his blood on her shirt and not caring.

"Marty, please—"

The sound of several sirens approaching cut her off.

"*Go!*" he whispered urgently. "No time—"

His head fell against her.

She didn't want to believe he was dead. Something unaccustomed welled up inside her. Maybe she had loved him just a little bit after all.

But the danger represented by those sirens crowded out everything else. She eased him off her lap and laid his head gently on the pavement, then stood up. She still had the stiletto in one hand, the gun she had taken from the cartel man in the other. It was an American gun, a .45 caliber semi-automatic, she thought, heavy and ugly. Holding it felt surprisingly good to her, though.

She grabbed her bag off the street where she had dropped it, shoved the gun and the knife into it, and trotted toward the mouth of the nearest alley.

She broke into a run as flashing lights rounded a corner a few blocks away.

By the time the police cars got there and screeched to a stop with their headlights washing over the four bodies in the street, the darkness had swallowed up Catalina Ramos and she was gone just as surely as if she had vanished into the jungles of the Yucatán.

CHAPTER 6

Del Rio, Texas, the next day

Catalina pressed the .45's barrel against the side of the truck driver's neck and said, "Out. Now."

"Holy sh—"

Metal prodded flesh, and he gulped and shut up.

"I don't want to hurt you," Catalina said, "but I need this truck."

He reached for the door handle but paused before he opened it.

"I'll lose my job," he said with a note of pleading in his voice.

"I'm sorry about that," she told him, and meant it. "But I have more to lose."

It had been the longest fourteen or fifteen hours of her life, and while she wouldn't actually shoot this poor hombre, she might be tempted if he didn't cooperate.

Thankfully, he did. He opened the door and slipped down from the cab, pausing to look back at her and ask, "Can you drive a truck like this?"

"I can do a lot of things," Catalina said.

But what she did best was survive. Some instinct warned her and she went on, "Give me your cell phone."

He winced, probably because he'd hoped she would forget about that. He didn't argue, though. Instead he slipped the phone from the pocket of his untucked short-sleeved shirt and tossed it to her.

"You're really gonna leave me out here in the middle of nowhere?" he asked.

"It's not the middle of nowhere. The highway's only a couple of miles away. You can hike there and hitch a ride in less than an hour." She smiled as she scooted over behind the wheel. "You can even borrow somebody's phone and call the cops to report that a beautiful señorita stole your truck. Of course, then you'll have to explain why you were out here with her in the first place. Your boss might understand that, but I doubt if your wife would."

He muttered something under his breath, a prayer or a curse or both, then said, "You're in bad trouble, aren't you?"

"You could say that."

He thought about it and then nodded.

"I won't report the truck being missing for a while, okay?" A sheepish look came over his face. "And I'm sorry I mistook you for a . . . a . . ."

"Never mind, amigo," she said. "That's what I wanted you to think."

He stepped back, and she didn't grind the gears too badly as she pulled out, swinging the eighteen-wheeler in a broad circle and then starting back toward the highway on the dirt road.

When she reached it a few minutes later, she

turned left—south—and headed back toward Del Rio.

That might seem like the wrong thing to do, returning to the city just across the river from where Marty had been murdered and where she had killed three men. She knew cartel gunmen would be searching for her. Her hope was that they wouldn't expect her to double back like this.

If she could stay alive for a while, maybe somebody from the American government could meet her and keep her safe. That was the hope she really clung to.

Wanting someone to take care of her went against the grain for her. She had been taking care of herself for the past fifteen years. But the odds stacked up against her now . . . they were just too overwhelming. She needed help.

She had been numb at first, when she stumbled away from Marty's body. But the animal cunning that was part of her had still been working. She knew she couldn't go to the bridge. The police there wouldn't know what was going on, but they had heard the shots and seen the fight, and they would hold her until they straightened everything out.

She wouldn't have been safe in custody. Too many of the police really worked for the cartel.

So, like an animal, she had found the closest dark hole and vanished into it . . . in this case a squalid alley that led into a maze of narrow streets that were mostly deserted at night. The only people out and about were human predators, and she spent the rest of the night ducking them and staying out of sight as much as possible.

Along the way she had found some washing hanging up in what passed for a backyard and taken a man's faded blue work shirt from the line. She stripped off the bloodstained T-shirt and pushed it down a storm drain. The stolen shirt was big on her, but she rolled up the sleeves and tied the tails in a knot below her breasts, leaving her midriff bare. It didn't look too bad, she thought, and most important, she could move around and fight in it if she had to.

The long hours of mixed martial arts training had come in handy when she tangled with the men from the cartel. Of course, she already knew how to fight and take care of herself from all the years spent on her own, but one of the other dancers had suggested the MMA training to increase her agility and flexibility. It was meant to make her a better stripper, not to save her life, but it hadn't taken long for Catalina to discover that she had a knack for the brutal ballet of an MMA match.

The training had proven lucrative, too, because the proprietor of the Paloma Azul had had the bright idea of staging after-hours bouts between some of his dancers. A lot of men would pay handsomely to watch attractive young women beat the hell out of each other. They liked to wager on the bouts, too, and the club owner got a cut of everything. Catalina, in turn, got a cut of that. She had stashed away a tidy sum . . .

Which, she had realized despairingly, was upstairs in the apartment she'd shared with Marty. She had a very strong hunch that it would never be safe for her to go there again.

Anyway, the men searching for her would sniff

out the money and take it. It was probably gone already, gone for good.

She would just have to start over, she had told herself. It wouldn't be the first time. She had run for her life before and been forced to leave everything behind.

Figuring that the cartel men would be watching the bridge, she hid out until nearly dawn, then joined the throng of women trudging toward the border, bound for their factory and domestic jobs in Del Rio. Catalina figured her clothes were suitable for a factory job. She untied the knot in the shirttails and let the shirt fall loosely around her. She pulled her hair into a ponytail and hoped that and the different shirt she wore might be enough to keep them from recognizing her.

Also, as far as she knew there were no photographs of her in the apartment. She had never liked having her picture taken. So all the searchers would have to go by was her description: a woman in her twenties with brown hair, five-six, athletic build. That would fit many of the women who walked along the street with her. All she could do was hope to blend in.

It took nearly an hour for the long line to work its way across the border, and every minute that went by seemed like a nerve-wracking eternity to Catalina.

No one seemed to be paying any attention to her, though, and since her work permit was legitimate, she had no trouble getting across. Finally she was on American soil.

That made her feel slightly better . . . but only slightly. The cartel had plenty of people working for it in Del Rio, and it was possible that all of them were on the lookout for her.

Also, the bridge had security cameras mounted on it, and for all she knew, the cartel would be able to get the feed from those cameras and study it, looking for her. She knew that Marty had been perfectly capable of doing things like that, and she supposed the cartel had other computer experts who could do the same. They were barbarians, but that didn't mean they couldn't take advantage of modern technology.

No, even in another country, it was only a matter of time until they caught up with her, she thought. She was still doomed, unless she could find someone to help her.

She tied up the shirt again, unbuttoned the top two buttons, and kept an eye on the trucks passing her until she spotted one where the driver was eyeing her with undisguised lust. She waved and smiled at him, and the truck's air brakes hissed as he slowed down and pulled over.

"You need a ride?" he called through the open window to her.

"Oh, no," she said with a coy smile. "I wouldn't want you to get in trouble."

"It won't be any trouble. Come on. I'll help you out . . . and maybe you can help me out." He frowned suddenly, as if something had occurred to him. "You're not a cop, are you?"

She laughed and asked, "Do I look like a cop to you?"

"That doesn't answer the question," he said, his voice hardening.

"No," Catalina said. "I'm not a cop."

He had picked up prostitutes before, she thought. He didn't want to get caught up in any sort of police sting. Well, she couldn't really blame him for that, and she sure as hell couldn't judge him considering some of the things she'd done, she told herself.

He grinned and nodded, motioning for her to get in. She climbed up, opened the door, and slid onto the seat. It was a relief when the truck started rolling again, moving away from the border.

She had already figured out that she couldn't run fast enough or far enough on her own to escape from the cartel. She needed to call the number Marty had given her and get in touch with the Americans.

The truck driver's name was Eddie Velez. He had a wedding band on his ring finger, and he was short and pudgy, with a sweet, innocent, round face. Maybe not so innocent, though, because right away he started trying to sound her out about what she was willing to do in return for the ride he was giving her.

Catalina dodged the questions as best she could, but after ten miles or so when she saw a dirt road leading off to the east from the highway, she said, "Turn in there, Eddie. I'd like to get out and stretch my legs a little."

"You just got in the truck a few—" he began, then stopped short with his eyes widening as he realized what she meant. "Oh! Oh, yeah, sure, Angie."

She had given him the first phony name she thought of, Angie Rodriguez. Under the circumstances, he wasn't just about to ask her for ID to prove who she really was.

Eddie drove for a couple of miles after leaving the highway. The road was pretty rough, but the truck had no trouble handling it. Catalina worried a little that it might bog down in the sand when she tried to turn around, but she would deal with that when and if she had to.

When they were well out of sight of the highway, she'd said, "This is far enough," and Eddie stopped the truck and turned to her with an expectant grin on his face . . .

A grin that vanished when he saw the gun in her hand.

Now she was on her way back. Back into the belly of the beast, she thought, unsure where the phrase had come from or why it had popped into her head.

And all she could do was hope that someone would be able to keep that beast from consuming her.

CHAPTER 7

Sonora, Texas

The cell phone in Bill's pocket buzzed while he was sitting in a diner beside the highway, washing down a cheeseburger and French fries with a chocolate milkshake. An all-American meal for an all-American boy, he had thought when he ordered it. Well, all except for the French fries, he supposed, and he'd decided that the French had long since given up any legitimate claim to them, the same way they'd given up everything else.

No number came up on the phone's screen. That didn't bode well, but it didn't have to mean anything, either, Bill told himself. He considered telling the phone to ignore the call, but in his experience, postponing unpleasant things seldom made them any better in the long run.

He thumbed the button to answer the phone and said, "What the hell do you want?"

"How'd you know it was me?" a familiar voice came back.

"I just figured since I was sittin' here enjoyin' a

good meal, only a real asshole would interrupt it, and that just naturally made me think of you, Clark."

That brought a chuckle from the man on the other end of the call.

"Yeah, we've all missed you around here, too, buddy boy. Where are you?"

"Sonora."

"Mexico?"

"No, Texas."

"Let me look that up . . ."

"I'll save you the trouble," Bill said. "It's about halfway between Odessa and San Antonio. I thought I'd go take a look at the Alamo. I hear they've got all the damage from the battle cleaned up now."

"Well, they should. That was in 18—Wait a minute, you're talking about that big mess a few years ago when *somebody* came up with the bright idea of giving it back to the Mexicans?"

"She who shall not be named," Bill drawled.

"Yeah, well, she wasn't as bad as the guy who came after her, was she?"

"You didn't call me up to talk political history, Clark. What do you want?"

Clark said, "Oh, wait, there's Sonora. I've got it up on the computer now. Well, that's convenient. You're just a hop, skip, and a jump away from Del Rio."

"Two things," Bill said. "Not much of anything in Texas is just a hop, skip, and a jump away from anything else, and the only people who even use that expression anymore are old geezers like you and me."

"Maybe, but the important thing is, you're only about a hundred and fifty miles away from Del Rio. You can be there before tonight without any trouble."

"And why in the hell would I want to go to Del Rio?"

"Because," Clark said, "there's a package there we need you to retrieve."

Bill sat in the diner booth with its throwback red Naugahyde seats for a long moment without saying anything, so long that Clark finally asked him if he was still there.

"I'm here," Bill said. "And I don't do that kind of work anymore."

"Look, this is important—"

"It always is. At least, guys like you claim it is. Everything's a matter of life and death with you."

"That's just the thing," Clark said softly. "By the time a problem gets to us, it usually *is* a matter of life and death."

Bill leaned back and pushed the plate away. He had lost his appetite, which was a damn shame because the food had been good.

"I'm retired."

"You tried that a long time ago. Went back to that little town where you grew up, bought yourself a house, and tried to settle down. Didn't exactly work out, did it?"

That was putting it mildly. Bill never let himself think much about those days, but even now, whenever he heard piano music it sent a little shiver through him.

He had never told anybody about that. All Clark and his other associates knew was that *something* disturbing had happened, something that eventually had made Bill give up his goal of retiring. He had gone back to work for a while, this time not as a freelancer or a government contractor, but as an employee of Hiram Stackhouse, the multibillionaire behind the chain of discount stores that could be found in almost every town in the country.

Stackhouse's security forces were large, well-trained, and well-equipped. Politicians of a certain stripe had been known to complain that Stackhouse might as well be fielding his own private army.

What those politicians didn't know—and probably wouldn't have cared about if they did—was that Hiram Stackhouse was a patriot through and through and only employed his security forces for the good of the country. Without them, in fact, a lot of innocent people would have died in several incidents involving foreign terrorists trying to strike again in American soil.

Bill had played a small part in dealing with one of those incidents, and he had handled other, similar chores for Stackhouse, but after several years he'd had enough of that, too. He had spent most of the time since then traveling.

Until now.

"I refuse to believe you don't have anybody else down here in this part of the country who can handle this job," he told Clark. "How hard can it be to pick up a package?"

"You'd be surprised. There are other people who want what's in that package, too."

This sort of oblique conversation was a habit with

men like him and Clark, Bill knew. His cell phone was a burner; Clark shouldn't have even been able to get the number. And Bill was sure the phone on Clark's end of the line was as untraceable and un-tappable as a tin can with a string tied to it. But that didn't stop them from talking around the real subject.

The "package" was probably a person who had information about something Clark considered vital. Maybe it really was. Somebody else obviously thought so, too, or they wouldn't be trying to get their hands on it. That meant danger was involved, because a lot of times the sort of people they dealt with would kill to keep information from getting out.

All of it was ugly, messy, and dirty as far as Bill was concerned, and he'd had his fill of it. He was about to say so when Clark went on, "The two guys who sent the package our way have dropped off the grid, Bill. You know what that means."

Sure he did.

"And as for the package . . . she's a young woman."

Bill's jaw tightened. It wasn't like Clark to be so straightforward about *anything*. He was really pulling out all the stops in trying to get Bill on board with this operation.

With a sigh, he asked, "You say she's in Del Rio?"

"Yeah, but I'm not exactly sure where. She's going to call again tonight and set up a meet."

"You realize this sounds like a trap of some sort?"

"Of course it does. But Heimdall has picked up some chatter from the sandbox in the past few weeks about something big being imminent. Maybe bigger than 9/11."

"That's what they always say," Bill pointed out. "You know those types over there in that part of the world. They like to think they're the Big Bad and they're gonna be the ones to bring the Great Satan to its knees."

"Maybe. All indications are that the threat is a credible one, though."

"So how does some señorita in Del Rio, Texas, find out anything about it?"

"Don't know, but she mentioned a phrase that Heimdall has picked up a few times. El Nuevo Sol."

"The New Sun," Bill muttered. "What the hell does that mean?"

"Your guess is as good as mine, old buddy-roo. If you pick up this package for us, maybe we'll both find out."

"Hold on," Bill said. He set the phone on the table and closed his eyes. He rubbed his temples and thought.

Heimdall was the name of the computer program that monitored electronic communications worldwide. Earlier versions had had other names, but Heimdall—in Norse mythology, the all-seeing, all-hearing, all-knowing guardian of the Rainbow Bridge between Earth and Asgard—was the most advanced yet. Bill shouldn't have even known it existed.

Everything Clark said just made the situation more ominous. It was easy to dismiss most threats originating in the Middle East. The various terrorist organizations were well-funded, no doubt about that, with oil money flowing to them from their countrymen and, recently, drug money as well from newfound allies in South and Central America. Bill knew for a fact that there were ties between Islamic terrorism and the drug cartels in Mexico. So it was possible that the trail of this New Sun, whatever it was, might stretch from one side of the world to the other and end up in Del Rio.

"Are you finished with that, hon?"

The voice of the waitress broke into his thoughts. He glanced up and saw her standing beside the booth, a carafe of coffee in one hand as she looked questioningly at his plate with the remains of his lunch on it.

"Yeah," Bill said. "You can take it."

"You want a to-go container?"

"No thanks. I don't believe I'll want the rest of it."

"How about a cup of coffee?"

Bill thought for a second and then asked, "Can I get that to go?"

"You sure can. I'll be right back with it, along with your check."

When the waitress was gone, Bill picked up the phone and said, "Del Rio, huh?"

"Yeah," Clark said. "Buy another burner and call me with the number. Then she can call you and tell you where to meet her."

"She gonna have bogeys on her tail?"

"I won't lie to you, Bill. It's possible."

"A hundred grand in my Caymans account."

Clark whistled and said, "That's a little steep."

"No, it's not, and you damn well know it. I thought about asking for five hundred."

"I could just appeal to your patriotism."

"You could," Bill agreed.

A sigh came from the other end of the phone.

"It's not like the old days, is it?"

"Nothin' ever is," Bill said.

CHAPTER 8

Ciudad Acuña

Alfredo Sanchez closed the laptop and sighed.

"This is all your men found?" he asked. He waved a hand at the laptop and the desktop computer on the table in front of him.

"That's it," Pablo replied with a shrug. "Well, as far as the computers go, anyway. They found some money, wrapped up in plastic and hidden in the toilet tank." He laughed humorlessly. "They probably thought about not mentioning that, then decided not to risk it. They know what I would do to them if I found out. The money added up to nearly eighty thousand dollars, American."

Alfredo pursed his lips and nodded.

"That proves Chavez was double-crossing us. He was taking payoffs from the Americans and feeding them information."

As always, Alfredo kept a tight rein on his emotions and didn't allow his face to reveal what he was feeling, but a little worm of panic was wriggling around inside his belly. Chavez might have ruined everything.

"God knows what he might have told them," Alfredo added.

"Maybe the girl knows," Pablo suggested. He placed a stack of photographs on the table in front of Alfredo. "My men found these as well."

Alfredo picked up the pictures and flipped through them. They were all similar, shots taken in a small bathroom while a very well-built young woman undressed and stepped into the shower. Judging by her attitude, she hadn't known that the camera was there.

"This is Chavez's girlfriend?" Alfredo asked. "The stripper?"

"Yeah," Pablo said, and despite the dire circumstances, he grinned. "Doesn't seem possible, does it? What's the gringo word? A nerd like him?"

Alfredo nodded slowly and said, "He had that money hidden, remember? I imagine that was all the girl was really interested in." He came to his feet. "We need to find her."

"You really think she knows anything? You think Chavez would have confided in her?"

"Maybe, maybe not. But he might have told her things, trying to impress her with how important he was. And she might have heard or seen something that could help us, whether Chavez meant for her to or not." Alfredo tapped a finger on the stack of photos. "Find the best shot of her face in these and have copies made. I want them in the hands of all our people in Acuña and Del Rio as soon as possible."

"You think she got across the border?"

"According to the witnesses, she killed three of our men," Alfredo said heavily. "Obviously, they weren't three of our best . . . but I'm not going to put anything past her."

"She's just a dumb stripper and whore!"

"Perhaps, but she's still a potential danger."

Pablo nodded and said, "I'll take care of it, Alfredo."

"See that you do."

Before either of them could say anything else, one of the guards came in, a machine gun cradled in his hands.

"The Arab wants to speak to you, Señor Sanchez," the man said.

Again Alfredo made an effort to not reveal his honest reaction. The man who had shown up at the villa this morning worried him. Alfredo was truly fanatical about only one thing: money. Those who pursued other goals with the passion of a true believer could not be trusted, to his way of thinking.

But he had no choice except to work with this man, so he nodded to the guard and said, "Bring him in."

Tariq sized up the two men as soon as he came into the room. The big, beefy one—Estancia, that was his name, Tariq recalled—was just a thug, dangerous in a physical confrontation, no doubt, but stupid and easily outwitted if necessary.

The other man, though, the slender, handsome one with the sleek dark hair and steel-rimmed glasses, his face was unreadable and completely devoid of emotion. That meant he might be dangerous.

Tariq had been briefed on Alfredo Sanchez and knew that Sanchez was the man the cartel sent to supervise the most sensitive, important operations. Tariq figured he should be careful around Sanchez. They were allies for the moment, but Sanchez was an infidel and not to be trusted.

"Señor Maleef," Sanchez said. "You wished to see me?"

"We have not yet met," Tariq said. Both men spoke in university-educated English, the only language they had in common. "I thought we should."

"I agree completely." Sanchez extended his hand but did not meet Tariq's gaze. "Alfredo Sanchez."

Tariq didn't read anything into Sanchez's failure to look squarely at him as they shook hands. He had been told that was part of the culture in these Latin countries.

"You are in charge of your organization's part of the New Sun?" Tariq asked.

"That's right. And you have brought us what we need to complete the rising of that new sun, the dawning of a new day in the world?"

Tariq allowed himself a faint smile and said, "I have it."

"Secure, I hope?"

Tariq felt a surge of annoyance. Did this man think him a fool? He wasn't going to carry around a suitcase-sized tactical nuclear weapon without taking the necessary precautions.

"Very secure," he told Sanchez. "The detonator

is not armed and will not be until I place it where it's supposed to go."

"Of course. You intend to handle the delivery yourself?"

"When a task is this important, I prefer to see to it myself, yes. Your job is merely to get me over the border and provide transportation to San Antonio."

Sanchez nodded and said, "That won't be any trouble."

It shouldn't be, Tariq thought. While the main business of the cartel was drugs, they also did a thriving trade in illegal immigration. The so-called coyotes who worked for them smuggled thousands of people across the American border every month. One more "wetback" would not be noticed.

Tariq knew he could pass for Mexican. Many of his countrymen could. Some of them had already been smuggled across the border and waited now on American soil, sleeper agents going about their day-to-day lives until the day came when they were needed to strike against the enemies of Islam.

If Tariq had anything to say about it, that day would be soon.

Estancia spoke up, addressing Sanchez as he picked up some photographs from the table where several computers sat.

"I'll take care of this," the big man said.

A look of annoyance flashed across Sanchez's face, so quickly that most people probably wouldn't have noticed it.

Tariq did, though. He could tell that Sanchez would have preferred that Estancia wait until they were alone to mention the photographs. Out of curiosity, Tariq glanced at them. He couldn't tell much about them, except that they were pictures of an unclothed woman.

He loathed these Westerners and their obsession with sex. Whatever this was about, Tariq wanted no part of it, and yet he was concerned. He had to make sure the matter didn't have anything to do with why he was here. He couldn't allow anything to threaten his sacred goal of killing millions of Americans.

"Is there a problem?" he murmured softly.

"What?" Sanchez asked, and it seemed to Tariq he was trying not to show how distracted he was.

"A problem?" Tariq repeated as he gestured at the photographs in Estancia's coarse, sausage-like fingers.

"Oh, no, just a personnel matter."

Tariq thought at first that Sanchez said "a personal matter" and wondered if the shameless woman was his mistress. Then he realized the man had said "personnel." That meant it was related to business, and right now the cartel's most important business was helping Tariq's organization deliver death and despair to the Americans.

"I wouldn't want anything to interfere with our plans," he said.

Sanchez took his glasses off, polished the lenses with a linen handkerchief, and slipped them back on. Tariq recognized that for what it was, a momentary distraction to allow Sanchez to exert an iron grip on his emotions.

"Nothing is going to interfere with our plans, I assure you, Señor Maleef. Everything is set for tomorrow. By the time the sun goes down a second time from now, the world will be changed forever."

"Changed for the better," Tariq said.

"That goes without saying."

Sanchez snapped his fingers at Estancia, who hurried out. Tariq didn't even glance at the man or the photographs he held as Estancia went past him.

He had no interest in the woman in the pictures. When his work on this world was done, there would be scores of beautiful virgins waiting for him in the afterlife. Until then he was fine with his monastic existence. The needs of the soul were much more important than any crude desires of the flesh.

Anyway, he had been too quick to worry, he told himself.

No Mexican slut could pose any threat to the glorious destiny that awaited him.

CHAPTER 9

Del Rio

Bill drove into Del Rio in the middle of the afternoon. He had been here before, which meant he sort of knew his way around, although the border town might have changed some since he had visited it last. Once Bill had driven somewhere, it tended to stick in his mind.

He stopped at a nondescript motel on the edge of town, one of a nationwide chain. He didn't know how long he would be here, but if he needed a room he would have one.

He topped off the pickup's gas tank, too. Here in Texas there could be some long, empty stretches without any gas stations, so it was wise not to let the needle on the gauge drop too far below a half.

And if he wound up with somebody chasing him, he sure as hell didn't want to have to stop for gas.

The new burner phone was in his shirt pocket. All he could do was wait for the "package" to call him and let him know where to meet her. While he was waiting, he turned on the TV in the motel room and changed the station to one of the cable news channels, the only one that could be counted on to broadcast something that bore a distant relationship to reality.

As usual, the people in Washington who possessed the least bit of common sense were still in the minority, while those who didn't know their ass from a hole in the ground—the ones who kept getting elected and reelected by a lot of people who also didn't know their ass from a hole in the ground—kept yammering on about how everything would be just fine if all those filthy rich people would just pay more taxes, "rich" being continually defined downward because even if the government took everything from everybody there wouldn't be enough to make a dent in the flood of runaway spending, and how all the country's problems were still the fault of that guy who'd been in the White House three or four administrations earlier.

After watching for ten minutes, Bill heaved a sigh and changed the channel. He found an old Western movie and left it there with the sound turned low for background noise while he checked his guns.

Before he'd left Sonora he had opened the homemade stainless-steel toolbox and storage chest in the back of the pickup and taken out the locked case that held his handguns. He had picked the Browning Hi-Power to carry in a holster clipped under his shirt at the small of his back and slid a .25 caliber revolver down his boot. The popgun wasn't much good unless you could stick the barrel in somebody's ear before you pulled the trigger, but for that kind of close work it could come in handy. He tucked a .32 behind his belt in the front. His shirt would cover it, too.

Once he was gunned up he felt a little better. Would've been nice to be able to carry a shotgun, too, he thought, but folks tended to look a little funny at somebody who did that. They got nervous in a hurry, too, and Bill didn't like having nervous people around him.

The phone buzzing in his pocket interrupted a stream of inspired gibberish from Gabby Hayes on the TV. Bill muted the sound with the remote and opened the phone, held it to his ear and said, "Yeah?"

"El Nuevo Sol."

The voice on the other end belonged to a woman, all right, a fairly young woman by the sound of it, although you couldn't always tell by that. Bill said, "Go on."

"That's all I know," she said in only faintly accented English. "Except I need help. People are after me."

"What people would that be?" Bill asked in a casual drawl.

"The . . . the cartel. The drug cartel."

"What's your name?"

The woman didn't answer for a moment. Then she said, "You don't need to know that."

"No offense, miss, but if you need my help, then I need to know what I say I need to know."

Again a momentary silence, then, "Catalina."

Maybe she was making it up, maybe she wasn't. Bill didn't really care. He just wanted to establish that he was running the show here. If he was going to help her, she needed to do whatever he said, including answering his questions.

"Where are you, Catalina?" he asked.

"I'm in church."

"The traditional sanctuary for sinners."

Her voice bristled as she said, "Are you here to help me or to judge me?"

That brought a chuckle from him.

"I'm long past the point of castin' the first stone, darlin'," he said. "Which church?"

She told him. It was a Catholic church downtown. That was actually a pretty good choice for a hideout, Bill thought. The cartel didn't care about religion, but here along the border with its heavy concentration of Catholics, even their gunmen would think twice about shooting up such a place.

"I can pretend that I'm saying prayers for a while without anybody bothering me," Catalina went on. "How soon can you get here?"

"Not long," Bill told her. "Fifteen, twenty minutes, more than likely."

"How will I know you?"

Bill described himself, then asked, "And how will I know you?"

"I'll be the woman who looks like she's been running for her life for the past sixteen hours."

"You should probably be a little more specific than that."

"I'm wearing blue jeans and a man's shirt. I have dark brown hair, and it's pulled back in a ponytail. There's nobody else here right now who looks like that."

"All right, I'll find you," Bill said. "In the meantime, there's one more thing you can do."

"What's that?"

"Maybe you ought to do more than *pretend* to pray."

Catalina sat on the pew with her head down, but she occasionally tipped it from side to side and shot glances from the corners of her eyes, studying the other people who went in and out of the church.

At this time of day there were only a few of them, mostly middle-aged and older women, but from time to time a man would come in, too. None of them appeared to be threatening, and they paid no attention to her.

Well, not much attention, anyway. Even drably dressed, with her hair pulled back and the makeup scrubbed off her face in a convenience-store restroom, she was a very attractive woman. Most of the men spared her a second glance and then went on about their business, probably feeling a little guilty at experiencing a moment of lust in such holy surroundings.

Catalina was used to being looked at lustfully, of course. That hadn't bothered her for years. Today, if a man looked at her and *didn't* want to take her to bed, that would worry her.

Because it could mean he wanted to kill her instead.

She had left Eddie Velez's truck in the truck parking area of a big convenience store on the edge of town, walked in, spent some time in the restroom, then bought a bottle of water and a candy bar. When she came out of the store she turned the other direction and simply walked away.

After a few blocks, she had hitched a ride

downtown, then walked around until she found this church. The smells, the hushed atmosphere, the stained-glass windows, all brought back faint memories from her childhood, from the days before she was on her own. That was a surprisingly comforting feeling.

She was ready to get out of here now, though. Every time the sanctuary doors opened, letting sunlight slant into the gloom, she looked around as unobtrusively as possible.

Finally, she saw a tall, lean figure silhouetted against the light in the doorway. The door swung closed, and she couldn't see the man very well for a moment. As he came along the aisle between the pews, Catalina's eyesight adjusted again, and she made out the rough work clothes the man wore. He could have been one of the ranch hands who worked in the area.

Most of them were Hispanic, though, and this man was an Anglo. Catalina looked at the weathered face, the salt-and-pepper hair and mustache, and wondered why the Americans had sent an old man to help her. She needed someone who could take care of himself—and her—not a man who looked like he ought to be retired.

Maybe he wasn't the one the Americans had sent. He might have come here to pray or think and not have anything to do with her or her problem.

But evidently his eyes were keen despite his age, because he slipped into the same pew and sat down a few feet from her. With her heart pounding, Catalina took a chance and said quietly, "El Nuevo Sol."

If he asked her what she was talking about, she could always make some excuse, she thought.

But instead he replied, equally quietly, "The New Sun."

"You are the man I spoke to earlier?" she asked.

"I am if you're Catalina, and I reckon you must be. My name's Bill."

She recognized his voice now. Even though she was still surprised by his age, she began to feel a little better. She still didn't know who the man was on the other end of the phone number Marty had given her before he died, but she figured she had to be dealing with one of the American law enforcement agencies. The Border Patrol, maybe, or the DEA, those were the most likely. But this man who called himself Bill could even be CIA, she supposed.

Although if he was, he was certainly an unlikely-looking spy.

"You need to tell me what you know," Bill went on. "If it's important, more than one person should have the information."

"I know what makes it worthwhile for you to keep me alive," she said curtly. "Take me somewhere I'll be safe, and then I'll tell you what you want to know."

"How can I be sure it's worth riskin' my life?"

Catalina drew in a deep breath through her nose and said, "Because they killed my friend over it."

"Your friend?"

"Martin Chavez. He worked for the cartel, doing things with computers."

"Bunch of thugs gone high-tech," Bill drawled. "Things have sure changed."

"You would know," Catalina said dryly.

A smile tugged at the corners of his mouth under the mustache.

"I'm not quite as much of a dinosaur as you might think I am, señorita. Let's go."

"Where?"

He hesitated before answering, "San Antonio. There'll be a place there where nobody can get to you."

"A CIA safe house?"

"That's more than you need to know." He got to his feet. "Are you comin' or not?"

Catalina started to stand up, but she paused.

"Wait," she said. "I can trust you? You swear?" She gestured at their surroundings. "And remember where we are."

Bill smiled and said, "I give you my word, señorita."

She nodded as she got to her feet.

"All right, then. I'll go with you."

They left the church together. Again, no one paid attention to them. As they stepped out onto the sidewalk, Catalina squinted against the bright afternoon sunlight. Bill touched her arm lightly, just enough to guide her, and said, "My truck's parked over there."

They turned toward a dark blue pickup parked at the curb, and as they did, the doors of a car about twenty yards away opened. The movement caught Catalina's eye, and when she looked in that direction, she saw four men getting out of the car.

Her heart thudded painfully as she recognized two of them as men who had visited Marty at the apartment more than once. The other two were the same sort, soulless cartel gunmen who would stop at nothing to carry out their orders.

She didn't stop to think. She saw the men and turned to run for her life.

CHAPTER 10

Bill bit back a curse as he lunged after Catalina and grabbed her arm. He didn't have to guess what had caused her to jackrabbit. The four mean-looking hombres who'd piled out of that car were pulling guns now as they rushed along the sidewalk.

Catalina was young and strong and fast, but Bill had been dealing with trouble for a long time and knew how to react. He pivoted and used Catalina's own momentum to swing her toward the pickup.

"Get in the truck!" he called to her as his right hand swept behind his back and plucked the Browning from its holster.

One of the gunmen yelled something in Spanish that probably translated to "Kill the old bastard!" Bill didn't bother to figure it out. All he really had to know was that they were pointing guns at him.

In fact, one of the men clutched a machine pistol while the other three held revolvers, so that made him the biggest threat. Bill shot him, the 9mm round sizzling through the air to punch into the gunner's chest.

The man stumbled from the hit. His finger must have jerked the trigger as he fell. Bullets sprayed out of the weapon and chewed into the sidewalk, throwing dust and concrete splinters into the air.

A woman coming out of the church screamed and flung herself back through the doors. Tires screeched as people driving by spotted guns being waved around and either stomped the brakes or hit the gas to get themselves out of the line of fire, depending on where they were.

Bill tracked the Browning to the side and squeezed off two more rounds. The shots made the cartel men scramble behind their car for cover. They returned the fire, but the bullets whined past him.

He turned to see if Catalina had made it to the truck and was surprised when the engine roared and the vehicle lurched away from the curb.

Blast it, she was taking off and leaving him here to shoot it out!

Bill said, "Son of a—!" and sprinted after the pickup. More shots roared from the cartel gunmen.

The truck's tires spun a little on the pavement as Catalina gunned the engine, and that was the only thing that slowed it down long enough for Bill to dive and catch hold of the tailgate. He dropped the Browning inside the bed and hung on for dear life with both hands as the truck began to pick up speed and dragged him along the street with it.

He knew if he let go, the fall might bust him up even if the gunners didn't shoot him. With an effort, he managed to get his feet under him and kicked hard with them at the same time as he used all the strength in his arms to haul himself up. He got a booted foot on the rear bumper and vaulted up and over the rear tailgate.

When he jolted down into the pickup's bed, he felt the impact go through him, shaking him all the way down to his teeth. He lay there catching his breath and getting his wits back about him as Catalina sent the pickup fishtailing around a corner.

After a few moments Bill rolled over and looked around for the Browning. He spotted it and reached over to grip the pistol. He felt a little better once it was in his hand again.

He heard a couple of thuds and knew the sounds came from bullets hitting the tailgate. It was specially reinforced, like the rest of the truck's body, so the slugs didn't penetrate it. He looked up as another round struck the back window. The bulletproof glass starred but didn't shatter.

The sound of the bullet striking the glass right behind her head must have spooked Catalina into jerking the wheel. The pickup's tires shrieked as it veered sharply across the road into the lanes of oncoming traffic. The move threw Bill hard against the sidewall.

Brakes screeched somewhere close by. Metal crumpled in a grinding collision. Since Bill didn't feel the pickup shudder from an impact, he assumed the wreck involved other vehicles trying to get out of Catalina's way.

He braced himself and sat up as the pickup weaved back into the right lane. The car containing the surviving cartel gunmen was about fifty yards back, speeding recklessly after them.

One man leaned from the passenger window in the front, another from the rear window on the other side of the car. They fired their pistols as the driver tried to close in on the fleeing pickup.

Bill didn't figure the car had bulletproof glass in the windshield. Using a two-handed grip, he drew a bead on it and fired four shots as fast as he could.

His hunch proved to be correct. The windshield spiderwebbed from the first bullet, then exploded inward with the second. Bill wasn't sure where the other two rounds went, but judging by the way the car suddenly slewed to the side and smashed head-on into a parked SUV, he figured they had hit the driver . . . which was exactly what he'd intended.

No more shots came from the wrecked car as steam spewed from its smashed radiator. The other two gunmen had to be badly shaken up, at the very least, if they weren't injured or dead.

Bill saw a road sign with an arrow on it indicating that they were coming to U.S. 90. He knew that was the highway that ran almost due east to San Antonio. He tapped on the truck's rear window with the barrel of the Browning and called, "Catalina!" intending to tell her to take the turn.

Instead she twisted on the seat and brandished a gun at him, causing him to fall back and exclaim, "Whoa! Catalina, it's me!"

The pickup swerved back and forth again, tossing Bill from side to side, before she got it under control. He pulled himself up to the window and told her, "Pull over! Let me up there!"

He thought for a second she was going to ignore him, but then the truck began to slow. She steered it to the side of the road in front of a strip shopping center that contained a tire store, a pawnshop, a tattoo parlor, and a consignment store.

Bill worried that as soon as he got out of the back, she might take off and try to leave him again. She was easily spooked, that was for sure.

But that wasn't really fair, he told himself. Most people would panic if somebody started shooting at them. It took naturally steady nerves and plenty of experience to stay cool under fire.

When he was younger he would have just put a foot on the side and jumped out of the back of the pickup. These days he had to be a mite more cautious. He climbed over the tailgate to the bumper and dropped to the ground from there. Then he hurried forward to jerk the passenger door open before Catalina could floor the gas and take off.

The door was barely closed behind him when she did just that. The gun she had waved at him was on the seat beside her. Bill saw that it was a .45, the classic Colt Model 1911A1.

He pointed through the windshield and said, "Take 90 East up here."

She slowed to make the turn onto the highway, then accelerated again. Bill turned to look behind and see if anyone else was following them.

"Are they still back there?" Catalina asked in a tight, nervous voice.

"Don't see anybody chasin' us," Bill said. "How'd you start this truck, anyway?"

She made a scoffing sound and said, "I've been able to hotwire a car since I was twelve years old."

"And get it started that fast?"

"If you dawdle around stealing cars you're liable to get caught."

Bill couldn't help but wonder why she'd been stealing cars when she was twelve, but he supposed the question didn't have any bearing on their current situation.

"It's about a hundred and fifty miles to San Antonio, straight ahead," he told her. "The truck's got plenty of gas. We can make it by nightfall, but we might want to drive around a little once we get there, just to let it get good and dark before we go to ground."

"What if I have something I need to pick up?"

"Do you?"

"Well . . . no. To be honest, all I have are the clothes on my back. But I wondered what you'd say."

"Everything else takes a backseat to keepin' you alive. Once we get where we're goin', somebody can bring you anything you need."

She nodded. She seemed to be calming down. It probably helped that they were putting some distance between them and the border.

They couldn't go far enough to get completely out of reach of the cartel, though. Those evil bastards had connections all across the country.

Catalina probably hadn't thought about it yet, but she might have to spend the rest of her life looking over her shoulder for cartel gunmen, depending on the importance of the information she possessed.

"You have any idea how those fellas found you?"

She shook her head as she kept the pickup at a steady pace now, three or four miles above the speed limit.

"No. I thought I'd be safe in a church. Someone must have spotted me and called in a tip. I'm not sure how they knew it was me, though. I didn't think they have any pictures of me to spread around, just my name and description."

"It doesn't really matter," Bill said. "Those fellas were after you, that's for sure."

"Yes, I recognized two of them. They worked for the same men Marty worked for."

"Marty . . . ?"

"I told you, Martin Chavez. My friend. The one they killed while he was trying to get me safely across the border."

"I'm sorry for your loss," Bill said. "Chavez was the computer guy for the cartel?"

"One of them. He worked for the local branch, for a man named Pablo Estancia." Catalina's lip curled with disdain. "An animal, I should say. A pig."

"Yeah, I'll bet he's not a very nice fella. All this trouble, it's about your friend Marty's computer work?"

"And something called El Nuevo Sol."

"But you don't know what that is?"

"I don't have any idea," she said. She seemed to hesitate, then took one hand off the wheel and slid it into one of the pockets of the tight jeans she wore. When she brought it out she was holding something. She held it out toward Bill and went on, "But the explanation might be on this."

The thing she held was a flash drive, not even as big as one of Bill's fingers. But his instincts told him that whatever data was stored on it, there was a good chance the information was worth killing for.

His instincts warned him of something else, or maybe he just heard an engine being gunned somewhere behind them. Whatever prompted him to do it, he turned his head and looked back along the divided highway.

A black SUV was coming up fast behind them, and everything about it screamed trouble.

CHAPTER 11

Bill would have taken the flash drive from her for safekeeping, but before he could, she stuck it back in her pocket. As tight as those jeans were, he didn't figure he could dig it out without quite a bit of trouble, not to mention embarrassment. She might fight him for it, too, and he couldn't risk that while they were speeding along the highway with her at the wheel, weaving in and out of traffic.

"Somebody else is after us, aren't they?" she asked as she glanced at the rearview mirror.

"Looks like it," Bill admitted.

He pulled the Browning from its holster, dropped the double-stack magazine, and topped it off with shells he took from his pocket. There was still one in the chamber, so when he slid the magazine home, the gun contained fourteen rounds in all.

The Browning was a classic. As a rule the trigger pull was a little stiff, but he had worked his over until it was smooth as silk. And its high capacity in 9mm was the main reason he had carried it for years.

There were no rules in a gunfight. You never knew how many people you'd have trying to kill you or how many rounds you'd need to deal with them. So more, generally, was better. A simple but true concept.

"There's a crossover comin' up," Bill said, pointing it out to Catalina. Along this stretch, U.S. 90 was a divided highway but not a freeway with entrance and exit ramps. There were crossovers where major side roads came in.

"You want me to turn?" Catalina asked.

"Can you make it without hittin' your brakes until we're right on top of it?"

The disdainful snort she let out told him what she thought of that question.

Bill gestured toward the Colt on the seat and said, "Mind if I borrow your gun?"

"All right, but I don't have any extra ammunition for it," she said. "Just whatever's in it."

"That's all right. I've got ammo, once we're somewhere I can get to it." The crossover was coming up fast. "You always go around gunned up?"

"No, I took it off one of the men trying to kill me last night . . . after I killed him."

Before Bill had time to digest that, Catalina slammed her foot on the brake pedal, spun the steering wheel, and skidded into the turn at the crossover. For an instant Bill thought the truck was going to roll over, but its superior suspension did its job and kept the tires on the road.

"Brake!" Bill shouted.

Catalina hit the pedal again. The pickup's tires screeched as it slid to a stop in the crossover. Bill twisted around on the seat, reached up to throw the sunroof open, and stood up on the seat with guns in both hands.

In the eastbound lanes of the highway, the black SUV that had been pursuing them slowed violently in an effort to make the turn, too, but it had been going too fast and slid past the crossover.

As it did, Bill saw that the rear window was down and the barrels of two weapons protruded through it as the men inside tried to get a shot.

Bill opened up first. The Browning and the Colt both roared and bucked in his hands. Glass flew as bullets smashed the driver's window. What was left of the window was suddenly covered with crimson as slugs pulped the driver's skull.

The automatic weapons disappeared from the rear window. Bill knew that his slugs must have smashed the gunmen back across the seat.

With no one controlling it, the SUV went into a wild spin. One of the wheels dipped into a drainage ditch at the side of the road, and suddenly the vehicle was airborne, flipping over and over until it crashed on its top in the median between the eastbound and westbound lanes. The SUV rolled a couple of times before it came to a stop, still upside-down. Flames licked up from its undercarriage.

The silence that followed the crash was broken by the wail of sirens not far off. Citizens would have reported all the shooting going on as the chase stretched across Del Rio, and now the cops were closing in.

"Go," Bill told Catalina as he dropped back onto the seat. "Get off the highway onto the side roads. Keep turning every couple of blocks."

"I've run from the cops before, you know," she said as she drove out of the crossover.

"I'm not surprised, what with you stealin' cars when you were twelve."

"Well . . . I didn't actually steal any of them. I was just the lookout. But my friend who did boost them taught me how to hotwire an ignition."

"Some friend."

"You don't know," she snapped. "You weren't there."

"Yeah, I reckon that's true."

Bill reloaded the Browning, then checked the Colt's magazine. He was pretty sure he'd emptied it, and sure enough, he had.

Catalina made a right after going a couple of blocks, then a left after two more blocks. She kept up that pattern, working her way north and east of the highway, and after a while Bill couldn't hear the sirens anymore. He was confident they had given the slip to any law enforcement pursuit. That was good; he wouldn't have wanted to waste hours trying to get everything straightened out. Not to mention the very real danger that some of the cops might be in the cartel's pocket.

They found themselves on a county road outside of town that ran between seemingly endless cultivated fields. Unless somebody who worked for the cartel had the ability to hack into the feeds from Defense Department surveillance satellites or Border Patrol drones, they were fairly safe from detection out here, Bill thought. Of course, he couldn't rule out that possibility. Still, there were only so many things a man could worry about.

"Keep going east," he told Catalina. "After a few

more miles, we ought to run across a road that goes back to the highway. We'll take it."

"We might be able to take back roads all the way to San Antonio," she suggested. "You can call up the maps on your phone so we won't get lost."

Bill shook his head. "My phone won't do that. All I have is a cheap burner that can't be traced easily."

She gestured toward her purse that was lying on the seat beside them and said, "You can use mine."

"Son of a—" Bill grabbed the purse and dug out the phone. "These have GPS chips in 'em so they can be tracked."

A farm truck loaded with produce was coming toward them on the two-lane blacktop. Bill opened the sunroof again.

"What are you doing?" Catalina asked. As he stood up and stuck his head and shoulders through the opening, she exclaimed, "Hey, that's my phone!"

He threw the phone into the load of grapefruit that filled the back of the farm truck as the two vehicles met and passed each other.

Catalina glared at him furiously as he lowered himself onto the seat again.

"That was my phone!" she said again. "It had all my numbers in it!"

"Numbers of people you'll probably never be able to see again," Bill told her bluntly. "Chances are they weren't using it to track us, but if they are, they'll think we've doubled back."

"Oh." Catalina still didn't look happy about what he'd done, but evidently she understood the need for it. "I did that earlier today. Doubled back, I mean. I tried not to leave much of a trail, though."

"It's hard not to leave some sort of trail if somebody's determined enough to find you. Best we can hope for is to slow them down enough for us to make it somewhere safe."

Catalina sighed and said, "I'm not sure anywhere in the world is safe."

"Well, we'll do the best we can." Bill held out his hand. "You want to give me that flash drive?"

Catalina didn't reach for her pocket.

"That drive is my only bargaining chip," she said with a stubborn look on her face. "If I turn it over to you, you won't have any reason to keep me alive."

"Other than the fact that I'm not in the habit of lettin' no-good scum like the cartel murder innocent women."

"You should have figured out by now, Bill, that I'm not exactly what anybody would call innocent."

"Well . . . relatively speakin'," Bill said. "And I give you my word, I won't let anything happen to you if I can prevent it."

She thought it over and finally nodded.

"I guess you've already proved that I can trust you." She glanced over at him as she drove. "I'm sorry about trying to, you know, run out on you back there at the church. I guess I just lost my head."

"You've been through a lot," Bill told her. "It's understandable. When's the last time you slept?"

"I don't know . . . Yesterday sometime, I guess."

"It'll take us at least a couple of hours to get to San Antonio," he said. "Let me drive, and you can get some sleep."

She didn't have to think about that offer for very long before accepting it. As soon as there was a good place, she pulled the pickup off on the side of the road.

Bill reached for his door handle, but Catalina said, "You don't have to get out. You can just scoot over. There's room for me to slide past you."

Bill wasn't sure about that, but he was willing to give it a try. Catalina slid out from behind the wheel, turned, and put her hands on either side of his shoulders as he scooted into the middle of the pickup's bench seat. That put their faces only inches apart and caused her breasts to flatten against his chest. For a moment their thighs were tangled up with each other.

"I hope this isn't embarrassing you," she said.

"I've got boots older than you, darlin'," Bill said. "You're wastin' your time flirtin' with me."

They slid past each other. Bill settled behind the wheel as Catalina turned again and dropped into the passenger seat.

"I wasn't really trying to flirt with you," she said. "Just habit, I guess. You don't like women?"

"I like women just fine."

"But you're too old to be interested in them like that."

"The hell I am. If you'd wallered on me a little longer you probably would've figured that out for yourself."

That made her laugh. She said, "So you're not too old, I'm just . . . what? Too young? Too slutty?"

"Right now, señorita, you're a job I've got to do. That's all I'm thinkin' about."

"Fair enough." She took the flash drive out of her pocket and held it out to him. "Here."

"Much obliged," he told her as he took the drive

and slipped it into his shirt pocket. He fastened the snap holding the pocket flap closed.

Catalina stretched out her long legs as much as she could and leaned back against the seat. A vast sigh came from her as she closed her eyes.

Bill got the pickup rolling again and headed east toward San Antonio.

CHAPTER 12

San Antonio, Texas

He used the burner to call Clark before they got there and found out the address of the place where he needed to go. When he reached 1604, the big outer loop around San Antonio, he took it north to Interstate 10, then cut back toward town and exited on Fredericksburg Road.

As he drove past a Hooters, he glanced over at Catalina, who was still sleeping, and thought about how she would look in one of those little outfits the gals who worked there wore. It made for an intriguing mental image, and he didn't feel guilty for thinking about it. She was a full-grown woman, after all.

But despite her protests, there *was* a certain innocence about her. Sure, she had lived a rough life and probably had done a lot of things nobody would be proud of. Her sins were small ones, though, compared to the sort of things that went on in the world Bill had once inhabited.

And now, evidently, did again.

They hadn't run into any more trouble on the way to San Antonio. Catalina had slept the whole way, the drugged sleep of exhaustion. Bill knew the feeling; he had been there himself from time to time.

He remembered once in South America, in the Mato Grosso, with government troops chasing him from one direction and headhunters from another . . .

He shoved those thoughts away. That was the past. It was all right for a man to dwell on what had been when he didn't have anything in his future to look forward to. Bill wasn't at that point in his life yet.

He drove around northwest San Antonio until night had fallen. He expected Catalina to wake up every time they stopped at a red light, but she continued to sleep. Finally it was dark enough to head for the safe house. When he turned into the right block, he said, "Hey, you still alive over there? Catalina?"

She didn't respond. He took his right hand off the wheel and reached over to nudge her shoulder.

She came awake like a wild animal, instantly alert and ready to fight. Bill hadn't noticed that she'd slipped her hand into her purse before she went to sleep. Now it came out of the bag clutching something as she lunged at him.

His own reactions were still pretty good. His hand flashed up and his fingers closed around her wrist, stopping her movement when the tip of the dagger she held was still a few inches from his throat.

Another split second and the blade would have been in his jugular.

"Whoa there," Bill said, trying to sound cooler and calmer than he really felt. "Take it easy, Catalina, it's just me, Bill Elliott."

He didn't let go of her wrist until she said, "Oh, my God, I'm sorry, Bill. I should have warned you . . . Marty knew to always be careful when he woke me up."

"Are you sayin' you're like this every time somebody interrupts your nap?"

She sat back in the corner of the seat and put the dagger back in her bag. As she used her other hand to rub the wrist he had grabbed, she said, "You get used to people trying to hurt you, you know? And even though you know you're not in danger, when you're asleep you sort of go back to that . . ."

He nodded.

"I understand. And I reckon you *are* in danger, just not from me."

"I don't have the flash drive anymore. I can't hurt the cartel."

"They don't know that. And there's a good chance they don't know how much Marty told you. They want to get their hands on you so they can make you talk."

"And they wouldn't believe me if I told them I don't really know anything except that one phrase."

"Probably not," Bill agreed.

"They would torture me, and when they finally decided I was harmless, they would kill me."

"Yep."

She drew in a deep breath and blew it out in a sigh. "I thought I had known bad men in the past.

But these hombres, they are more than that. They are monsters."

"You're right about that," Bill said. He turned in at a driveway that ran beside a sprawling, Spanish-style house that looked like all the other houses in this affluent residential neighborhood. The driveway led to a two-car garage that was connected to the house by an enclosed breezeway. The house was probably sixty or seventy years old. It had the look of the postwar housing boom to it.

The garage door rose as the pickup approached it. Bill knew the truck had triggered a sensor of some sort. He drove into the darkened garage. The door rumbled down automatically behind them.

A light went on over the door leading to the breezeway. Bill drew the Browning and held it on the seat beside him as a man walked through the breezeway and stepped into the garage.

He was a medium-sized, balding man, with lean, alert features. The hair he had left was a nondescript brown. He wore khaki trousers and a polo shirt and looked like an insurance salesman who ought to be on a suburban golf course some-where, playing eighteen holes with his friends.

With a smile on his face, he said, "All clear, Bill."

Bill opened the pickup door and slid out.

"Clark," he said. "You didn't tell me you were gonna be here to meet me."

"I figured you'd find out soon enough." Clark looked past Bill into the front seat of the pickup. "I take it that's Miss Ramos?"

"Señorita Ramos, if you want to be accurate about it," Bill drawled. He put his gun away. He trusted Clark as much as he trusted most men, and more than any of the other spooks he had worked with. They had been in some tight spots together, and Clark had never let him down.

Clark stepped over to the open driver's door of the pickup and said, "Señorita Ramos, let me welcome you to San Antonio. Don't worry, you'll be safe here. We have our agents blanketing the whole neighborhood. This house belongs to an agency of the United States government, and we've used it to shelter people like you before."

"People like me," Catalina repeated. "You mean Mexican strippers and whores?"

"People with whom we have common enemies," Clark said, as unflappable as ever. "People who are in danger. People we want to help."

"People who have something you want," Catalina said.

Clark shrugged.

"Sometimes."

Catalina pointed at Bill and said, "He has it. I already gave it to him. Do you still want to help me?"

Before Clark could answer, Bill said, "Could we go inside to have this discussion? It's been a long day. When I got up this morning, I was still retired, and now I'm not anymore."

"That's up to you," Clark said. "You've done your job. You're free to go anytime you want, Bill."

"I'm a mite curious. I'd sort of like to know what this is all about and what makes El Nuevo Sol important enough to be worth killin' over."

"Well, then, let's go on inside, sit down, and have a talk," Clark suggested.

Bill looked at Catalina, who was still sitting in the

pickup. He nodded to let her know it was all right to get out. Once again he waited to see whether or not she was going to trust him.

After a moment she opened the door and stepped out of the truck.

Clark led the way into the house, where several men wearing bulletproof vests and carrying guns waited in the living room that had been turned into a command center. Another man monitored feeds from cameras concealed around the neighborhood. A man and two women worked at computer stations. All the activity looked a little out of place in the comfortably furnished house, which, although there was no visible evidence of it, was armored and secure enough to withstand anything short of a direct bomb hit.

"Would you like something to eat?" Clark asked. He gestured through an arched entrance into a genteel dining room where thick drapes were drawn over the windows.

"All I've had today is a bottle of water and a candy bar," Catalina said. "I'd love something to eat."

"We'll take care of that right away. Why don't you go ahead and sit down?"

"First, where's the ladies' room?"

Clark pointed out a door. Catalina vanished through it.

"She can't get out of there, can she?" Bill asked.

"What, after everything you've gone through, you think she might cut and run?"

"It's not likely," Bill said, "but I've already been around her enough to know she can do some unexpected things."

"Well, you don't have to worry. Unless she's got an industrial strength laser in her pocket, she's not going anywhere. And as tight as those jeans are, I don't think that's likely."

"Noticed that, did you? About the jeans, I mean?"

"I'm married," Clark said as he held up his left hand and wiggled the ring finger. "But I wasn't struck blind at the ceremony."

"I'm hungry, too. Reckon you can rustle up enough grub for me?"

"Why, sure, cowboy. But first . . ." Clark held out his hand. "The young lady said you have something for us?"

Bill took the flash drive from his shirt pocket and dropped it into Clark's palm.

"You can get those tech wizards of yours to work on it."

"You have any idea what they'll be looking for?"

"Not a damn clue, except that the phrase *El Nuevo Sol* seems to be important to everybody."

"That means 'the New Sun,' doesn't it?"

"Yep."

"Well, that makes no sense. There's only one sun. I mean, there are lots of suns in the universe, but you know what I'm talking about. Only one that means anything to us."

"Somebody else will have to figure it out," Bill said. "I'm just a hired gun hand."

"And a damn good one." Clark frowned. "I hear you shot up half of Del Rio. Seven men are dead back there. It's lucky for you they all had ties to the cartel and weren't innocent bystanders."

"I tried to be careful. Of course, with that much

lead flyin' around, there's only so much you can do . . ."

Catalina came back from the bathroom. She said, "I hope you can get me some clean clothes. I'd love to take a shower, but I don't want to put these things back on."

"We have everything you need," Clark assured her. "Now let's get you something to eat."

They sat down in the dining room to thick sandwiches and salads and big glasses of iced tea. There was nothing dainty about the way Catalina ate, which didn't surprise Bill. She was a big, athletic girl, so it made sense she would have a good appetite, especially after being on the run for so long and not being able to eat much.

Clark disappeared, and Bill figured he was supervising the effort to extract the intel from the flash drive. There was no telling how long that would take. It would all depend on how heavily encrypted the data was and how long it took to break through that encryption. Luckily, Clark had some of the best computer people in the world at his disposal, not just here on the ground in San Antonio but back in Virginia and in other places around the globe. This day and age, the way everything was connected, distances didn't mean much anymore.

"How long will I have to stay here?" Catalina asked while they were eating.

"Don't know," Bill said. "I guess that'll depend on what they find out."

"Will I be put in the, what do you call it, witness protection program?"

"That's not my call. Might be some diplomatic

problems if they did that. You're a Mexican national, right?"

"Yes."

"If your government finds out that we've got you, they're liable to demand that we give you back. You could be the cause of an international incident."

Catalina grimaced and said, "If you turn me over to the Mexican government, you might as well be turning me over to the cartel. There's not much difference in the two anymore."

"Well, that'll all get worked out," Bill said, knowing that in the end it might not work out to Catalina's satisfaction . . . or to anyone else's, including his. But like he had told her, he didn't make the decisions.

They had finished the meal but were still sitting at the dining room table when Clark came back into the room. Bill knew instantly that something was up. Clark never lost his calm demeanor, but he looked like he was about to now.

Bill got to his feet. So did Catalina. Bill said, "You found out something from that flash drive?"

"We did," Clark said. "There were a lot of emails on there, all in code, of course, but our people broke it. The cartel has teamed up with a Middle Eastern terror organization, Bill. They've set up a training camp in Mexico. Basic training for terrorists that the cartel will smuggle across the border posing as Mexican illegals."

"They've been doin' that for a while, haven't they?"

"Yeah, but from the sound of the emails, they're expanding the operation." Wearily, Clark scrubbed a hand over his face. "That's not the worst of it, though, at least not in the short run."

Almost wishing he didn't want to know, Bill asked, "What's the worst of it?"

"They've got a suitcase nuke, and they're planning to set it off in downtown San Antonio, right in front of the Alamo."

CHAPTER 13

San Antonio

The motel sat alongside the interstate, part of a long string of similar motels, car dealerships, and shopping centers. It was owned and operated by one of Tariq's countrymen who had immigrated to the United States more than twenty years earlier.

The man might have had a suspicion that Tariq was more than he seemed, but nothing of the sort was spoken. Tariq knew that the proprietor still had relatives back home and would have threatened them if he had to, but it wasn't necessary. The man did everything he could to be helpful. He had two rooms ready, one for Tariq . . .

The other for Alfredo Sanchez.

Tariq wasn't happy about the man coming along, but Sanchez had insisted. He wanted to make sure everything went according to plan, or so he said.

Of course, when the time came for the New Sun to rise, Sanchez would be far away, well out of the blast radius. Tariq knew and accepted that. He didn't expect Sanchez to sacrifice his own life. The man was a mercenary, not a true believer. Sanchez's only true allegiance was to his own profit and power.

And as such, not even his assistance in furthering the cause of Islam would keep him from going straight to hell when his time came.

The two rooms were next to each other, adjoining, in fact. Tariq parked the car in front of the door to his room. The device was in the trunk, and it would stay there, perfectly harmless with the detonator deactivated, until Tariq activated it and set it off at high noon the next day. He would park as close to the Alamo as he could, then walk to the plaza in front of the old building, stand for a moment watching the ebb and flow of the godless Americans around him, then take out his cell phone and punch in the fateful numbers.

That was all it would take to wipe downtown San Antonio off the map and resume the sacred task of punishing the Americans for their unholy ways.

Tariq knew about the Alamo. He had forced himself to watch the movie starring the imperialist infidel warmonger John Wayne. He knew the old building was a shrine of sorts . . . a shrine to evil and corruption. Tariq would go to his death gladly, knowing that it would be blasted to atoms, knowing as well that he would be striking a blow into the heart of the weak, crippled giant America had allowed itself to become.

"You're sure no one will bother the car?" Sanchez asked as they got out.

"Why would they?" Tariq said. "No one has any reason to suspect us."

"I'm worried about that damned whore," Sanchez said.

Tariq shrugged and said, "It is troubling that she got away, but how much could Chavez have told her? Even if he knew anything vital about our plan, why would he trust the information to an immoral woman like that?"

Sanchez snorted, which made a surge of anger go through Tariq.

"When it comes to women, not everyone is as concerned about their morals as you are, my friend. There's no way of knowing what Chavez might have let slip to her. I wish we could have gotten hold of her before we left. Estancia's men could have made her talk."

"And the man helping her," Tariq said with a frown, "he must be an American agent of some sort, considering the ease with which he dealt with the men you sent after them."

"He was lucky," Sanchez snapped. "They both were."

Tariq didn't say anything. He didn't believe luck had had much to do with Catalina Ramos's escape. The American intelligence community was involved, more than likely, and that did cause worry to nag at the back of his mind.

But before the Americans could figure out what was going on, it would be too late. Downtown San Antonio would be a glowing, smoking pit, obliterated by a new sun that rose at midday.

And Tariq would be in paradise, basking in his reward.

Four miles away

"A lot of this is reading between the lines and educated guesses made by our analysts," Clark said as he sat at the dining room table with Bill and Catalina. "We've known for quite some time that there are ties between terrorist groups like al-Qaeda and Hezbollah and the Mexican drug cartels. Drug money gets siphoned to the Middle East, and in return the cartels get weapons and other assistance they'd have a hard time getting their hands on otherwise."

"Like suitcase nukes," Bill said.

"Exactly. As far as we've been able to determine, the device came from Russia on the black market, brokered through a *Mafiya* with ties to the old KGB and Soviet army. The guy seems to have dropped off the face of the earth a while back, and my hunch is that once the terrorists had what they wanted, they disposed of him to cover their trail."

"Not very efficiently, if you've already figured that out," Bill commented.

Clark shrugged and said, "Our people are good at what they do. It doesn't take much for them to spot a pattern. A word here, another there . . . Anyway, one of the terrorists brought the device to Mexico on a ship that docked at Veracruz, then he drove it up to Ciudad Acuña and came across the border there. We have a possible vehicle identified and a partial plate number, and a car we think is the right one came across earlier today. Satellite footage shows it heading for San Antonio." He clasped his hands together on the table in front of him and sighed. "It's probably already in the city."

Catalina said, "Wait a minute. Are you saying there's a nuclear bomb here in San Antonio ready to go off?"

"You shouldn't even know about this, Señorita Ramos, but since you're already in the middle of it, I suppose we'll have to trust in your discretion—"

"And in the armed guards all over the place," she interrupted.

"That, too," Clark said. "And in answer to your question . . . yes, that appears to be the situation."

"Then why in God's name aren't you warning everybody and evacuating the city?"

Bill said, "That'd be the worst thing we could do. Chances are, the fella who brought the bomb here plans to trigger it while he's close enough that it'll get him, too. He figures he'll go out in a blaze of glory that'll send him straight to his version of heaven."

"So if he's already here," Clark said, "and he realizes that we're aware of the plan, he'll just go ahead and detonate the bomb wherever he is, whether it's downtown or not, rather than take a chance on us finding him and stopping him before he can make his grand gesture."

Catalina looked back and forth between Bill and Clark and then shook her head.

"That just sounds crazy to me. *Loco.*"

"That's because we're dealin' with a crazy man," Bill said. "He'd have to be loco to want to murder more than a million innocent people."

Clark said, "Except to his way of thinking, they're

not innocent. They're guilty of being Americans. That's enough of a reason for somebody like that."

"So if you can't evacuate the city, what can you do?" Catalina asked.

"Find him. Stop him before he gets a chance to set off the bomb."

"How will you do that?"

Bill said, "You mentioned something about the Alamo . . ."

"We think that's ground zero, according to the plan," Clark confirmed. "There was a mention of it in the emails, and nothing else makes sense. It's an important symbol, it's right in the middle of downtown, and there'll be a lot of people around it. That makes it a good target."

"Could be the Mexicans had something to do with that, too," Bill said. "They tried to take the Alamo back a few years ago, and that didn't work out too well for 'em."

Clark grimaced and said, "Don't remind me. That whole mess gave the country a black eye. And what did the administration do? Groveled and apologized for a bunch of things that weren't even our fault!"

"Better watch what you say," Bill warned. "With just one political party runnin' practically the whole shebang now in Washington, you got to toe the line."

"You know I've always tried to stay apart from politics, Bill. My job is to protect the country, period, no matter who's running it. I'll grant you, it's getting harder and harder to do that with the presidents we keep getting, but I suppose it's what the voters want . . ."

"Yeah, and they'll get what they asked for, one of these days, when everything comes crashin' down. But you're right, we've got a bigger problem right here and now, stoppin' that bomb."

Catalina said, "I still don't understand what the cartel has to gain from this."

"If the bomb goes off, it weakens and destabilizes the American government that much more. The economy's on life support already, and it might collapse completely from a terrorist attack of this magnitude. When the economy goes down, the government goes down. Then in the chaos that follows, Mexico can grab Texas and the rest of the southwest and a big chunk of California. Even if the country recovered, it would never be the same."

A solemn silence hung over the table following Clark's words. Finally, Bill cleared his throat and asked, "What about that terrorist training camp you mentioned?"

"Barranca de la Serpiente. Canyon of the Serpent, or Snake Canyon, to be informal about it. The name is really all we know at this point. We don't have a location on it yet. It's almost like a military base, a joint venture between the terrorists, the cartel, and corrupt elements of the Mexican army. They're putting together a paramilitary force the likes of which we haven't run into before. You were mixed up in something like that a while back, weren't you, Bill?"

"That was mostly the cartel's doin'," Bill said, remembering the bus full of teenagers that had been hijacked and taken across the border, where the prisoners were held for ransom. "There may have been some Middle Eastern advisors, but they weren't runnin' the show."

"Well, we'll have to do something about that camp pretty soon . . . assuming that we all live through the next twenty-four hours."

"How can you find the man with the bomb?" Catalina asked.

"Remember, we have a tentative identification of the car that's involved," Clark said. "Right now we have agents checking the footage from every traffic camera in the city, looking for it."

"How long will that take?" Bill wanted to know.

"A while," Clark admitted. "We're also running checks on every hotel and motel. The guy's got to have a place to stay."

"He could have a safe house like this one," Bill said.

"He could. But I think it's more likely he's staying at a motel owned by one of his countrymen. There are an awful lot of them in the hospitality business."

Bill chuckled and said, "Better be careful. You're gettin' into ethnic profilin' there."

Clark snorted in disgust.

"Well, pardon me for not thinking that some ninety-year-old grandma from Des Moines is really the one who wants to blow us to kingdom come, instead of the thirty-year-old Pakistani guy. I guess I'm gonna just have to be politically incorrect until we find that damn bomb."

"You're preachin' to the choir, old son. I've got just one more question."

"What's that?"

Bill nodded at Catalina and said, "What are we gonna do about Señorita Ramos?"

"I was wondering about that myself," Catalina said. "I mean . . . there's a bomb."

Clark nodded and said, "We'll get you out of town, of course. First thing in the morning, Bill and some other agents will take you to Dallas. You'll be well away from here before anything happens."

"Scratch that," Bill said. "I don't plan on leavin'. Might be something here I can do to help."

"Not your job," Clark said curtly. "I needed you to deliver Señorita Ramos and the intel she had to us, and you did that. You can go back to being retired again."

"I don't think so. Everything's changed now. We're all soldiers in this war, Clark . . . and I plan on bein' right here in the front lines."

CHAPTER 14

Tariq slept surprisingly well, considering that this would be his last night on earth. The next time he awoke it would not be from slumber, but rather from death, and he would be in paradise.

When he answered the knock on his door, he found Sanchez standing there wearing a worried frown.

"One of our contacts in the San Antonio Police Department reports that there are rumors about government agents accessing their traffic cameras," Sanchez said. "They must be searching for a particular car."

He half-turned and looked at the car parked in front of Tariq's room. It was a plain sedan with nothing to distinguish it and certainly no indication of the mass destruction that it carried in its trunk.

"The woman must have put them on our trail," Sanchez went on.

"You worry too much," Tariq said bluntly. "The woman could not have known anything about the vehicle we're using. The Americans fear that something is going to happen, but they have no idea what, when, or where. They're simply flailing around in futility, as they always do."

"You can't be sure of that. Perhaps we should postpone the operation long enough for them to slip back into complacency. There's no reason we can't wait a week, or even two . . ."

"No!" Tariq couldn't contain the anger that simmered inside him. "There is no need to wait. That just gives them more time to search for us. Destiny will not be delayed!"

"What you're doing is tempting fate," Sanchez insisted.

"It doesn't matter to you," Tariq said coldly. "You're not going to be here anyway, are you, Señor Sanchez?"

"It was never part of the arrangement that I had to die, too," Sanchez replied, his voice just as chilly as Tariq's had been. "That is *your* choice, amigo."

"It is what I am called to do."

"But you choose to answer."

"What would have me do? Forfeit my immortal soul?"

Sanchez didn't reply. Instead he said, "I'm leaving now."

"Fine. Go back and tell your masters that Tariq Maleef carried out his holy mission . . . after you finish licking their boots."

For a heartbeat Tariq thought Sanchez was going to attack him. He had wounded the man's Latin pride, after all. But Sanchez, like all infidels, really cared for nothing except himself. He wanted to be gone from here before that inferno of death erupted . . . and every passing second brought that glorious moment closer.

"Good luck to you," Sanchez said grudgingly.

"I need no luck. Allah watches over me."

Sanchez just grunted and turned away.

Tariq reached around his back to the handle of the knife tucked behind his belt. It would be easy enough to draw the weapon and plunge the blade into Sanchez's back. The man's decadent existence was an affront to Allah.

But as satisfying as killing Sanchez might be, it could upset the arrangement between the Mexican cartel and the organization to which Tariq belonged. He couldn't give in to his own petty personal urges when there was so much else at stake.

"*Vaya con Dios*," Sanchez muttered as he walked away. Tariq didn't know how the man intended to get out of town and didn't care; he supposed the cartel had people Sanchez could call on for transportation.

"Go with your own god," Tariq said quietly enough that Sanchez couldn't hear him. "Mine will soon be smiling with joy at the death and destruction I will bring down upon the Americans in his name."

Catalina's new clothes, a simple blouse and skirt and flat-heeled shoes, made her look a little like a suburban housewife, Bill thought. A spectacularly attractive suburban housewife. It was hard to imagine her fighting and shooting and stealing cars.

"I don't want to go," she told him as they stood in the kitchen of the safe house. "Well, that's not true, of course. I want to get as far away from that bomb as I can. But I want you to come with me. I'm not sure I trust any of these other people."

"You've known me less than twenty-four hours," Bill pointed out.

"But we have faced death together. That makes a difference."

She was right about that, Bill thought. The sort of intense danger they'd been in created a bond between people. Anybody who had been through a war knew that.

She went on, "I don't feel right about leaving you here."

"I wouldn't feel right about leaving Clark, either, not to mention all the other folks living here in San Antonio who're wakin' up this morning with no idea what's hangin' over their heads. I've got to do everything I can to save them."

"Even if it means losing your own life if you fail."

"Even if," Bill said. "But look at it this way . . . if we don't find the fella in time, I won't have to sit around worryin' about it."

She shook her head.

"That doesn't make me feel a bit better."

He gave in to an impulse and put his arms around her, drawing her against him. He felt the tense strength of her body, but after a moment she relaxed and rested her head against his chest.

"It's a little more than four hours until noon," Bill said quietly. "You'll be at least two hundred miles from here by then, and I won't have to worry about you while we're lookin' for . . . well, you know what we'll be lookin' for."

"Why would you worry about me?" she asked in

a voice thick with emotion. "You've known me less than twenty-four hours, remember?"

He chuckled and planted a kiss on the top of her head. She was tall, but he was taller.

"Go on and get out of here," he said as he let her go and stepped back.

"Bill . . ."

He gave her a stern look.

She nodded, summoned up a weak smile, and turned to go with the three agents waiting to take her away from San Antonio. Bill didn't know how the agents had decided who would go and who would stay to help with the search for the suicide bomber, but he supposed it didn't matter. Those who missed this battle would probably have another one to fight later on, because it seemed unlikely that the enemies who wanted to destroy this country would ever give up.

At least, not as long as certain elements of the country seemed hell-bent on trying to destroy it from within . . .

Catalina cast a last glance over her shoulder at Bill and then left the room. Clark must have been waiting for her to go, because he came into the kitchen less than a minute later.

"I didn't want to interfere with you saying goodbye to Señorita Ramos," he said as he poured himself a cup of coffee.

"You wouldn't have been interferin'. Hell, the girl's young enough to be my daughter. Damn near young enough to be my granddaughter."

"Yeah, but she's a mighty pretty one. I suppose if somebody could overlook her background—"

Bill said, "There are things in *my* background

that'd make a normal person turn pale and faint dead away. You ought to know. Some of 'em I did while I was workin' for you."

"That's a fair point," Clark said with a laugh. He took a sip of the coffee. "Have you had breakfast?"

"Not much of an appetite this morning."

"Yeah, me neither."

"Any leads on the car we're looking for?"

Clark shook his head and said, "No, but my people are still checking the traffic cam footage. The San Antonio PD and all the other departments in the surrounding cities have the description and the license plate partial. They think they're looking for a car used in a child abduction. We arranged for an Amber Alert to be put out a little while ago. That'll get the public involved without them knowing what they're really looking for." He took a deep breath. "The car's out there somewhere, Bill. We'll spot it and close in, grab up the guy before he knows what's going on."

"You'd better hope so. We don't know what sort of detonator he's using. If he has even a few seconds' warning, it might be enough for him to trigger the bomb."

"Of course, he might have it on a timer."

Bill shook his head and said, "I don't think so. You know how those fanatics are. He'll want to take a minute and stand there with his finger on the button so he can bask in the thought of how powerful he is."

"Yeah, you're probably right." Clark took another sip of coffee, then made a face and set the cup on the counter. "Coffee doesn't even taste good anymore."

"Tell you what I'll do," Bill said. "When this is all over, we'll go to one of those places down on the Riverwalk and have us a big ol' enchilada dinner and a few mugs of *cerveza*. How's that sound?"

Clark smiled and said, "You've got a deal, cowboy."

The morning seemed to go by in the blink of an eye. Almost before Bill knew it, the time was eleven o'clock.

An hour left, assuming the intel gathered from Martin Chavez's flash drive was accurate.

An hour before a new sun would burst into life in the heart of San Antonio and consume the historic downtown, along with hundreds of thousands of souls. And by the time all the damage was done, more than a million people might lose their lives.

An hour of his own life, maybe, because Bill knew where he would be when the time hit high noon.

Remember the Alamo.

If he died today, he would do so with a nearly clear conscience. There were things in his life he regretted: things he had done, things he *hadn't* done. He knew he had brought unnecessary pain into the lives of some people he had known, people he had been close to, people he had even loved. He had been stubborn, proud, and downright spiteful on occasion, just like everybody else in the world.

But he had done some good, too, and now he had to hope that balanced out the bad. Maybe, if he was lucky, more than balanced it out.

"I'm headed downtown," Clark announced a few minutes after eleven o'clock.

"I'll go with you," Bill said. He knew that they would be the last line of defense. If nobody else spotted the bomber in time, it would be up to them. "We can take my pickup."

"Sure, why not?"

Bill knew San Antonio fairly well. It didn't take him long to cut back over to the Interstate and turn southeast toward downtown. The skyscrapers were visible in the late morning sunlight, along with the Hemisfair Tower from the World's Fair that had been held there more than fifty years earlier.

They were still several miles from their destination, however, when they hit heavy traffic.

"Damn construction," Clark said. "Why now?"

"There's been road construction in San Antonio since General Santa Anna's brother-in-law was runnin' the place," Bill said. "We'll go around it."

"I've got agents all over downtown, but I wanted to be there myself."

"I'll get you there," Bill promised.

He was as good as his word, exiting the freeway and taking several shortcuts involving side roads. It was 11:45 when he steered the pickup into a parking lot on Crockett Street, around the corner from the Alamo.

His pulse was pounding pretty hard. There was nothing he could do about it. He knew Clark had to be feeling the same way. It was possible their lives could be measured in mere minutes now.

They got one of the few empty spots in the parking lot. Downtown was busy today. And why wouldn't it be? It was a beautiful early summer day, sunny but not overpoweringly hot. The Alamo and the Riverwalk and San Antonio's other attractions brought tourists not just from Texas but from all over the country. All over the world, actually, Bill thought as he and Clark went along the sidewalk and turned the corner into Alamo Plaza. He heard people speaking German and Japanese, as well as an assortment of accents from the various parts of the country. The plaza was full of comfortably dressed tourists taking pictures of each other, wandering along the Long Barracks where many of the Alamo's defenders had snatched a few minutes of sleep during the siege, and going into the old chapel itself.

The sight of the old stone building with its instantly recognizable pediment made Bill catch his breath. The Cradle of Texas Liberty, it was called, and even though Bill wasn't a Texan, there was something uniquely American about the place. It was here that men had stood up to tyranny and said "Enough!" Not once, but twice. And both times they had shed their blood and given their lives in defense of freedom. It was enough to make anybody proud.

And the idea that some fanatical son of a bitch whose beliefs were trapped in the Middle Ages was going to destroy it, along with the lives of so many innocent people . . . that just couldn't be allowed. They had to find him and stop him before he could carry out his evil.

"I wish I knew who we were looking for," Clark said as he scanned the crowd in the plaza. "Hell, it could be anybody—"

His phone rang.

Clark snatched it from his pocket.

"Go . . . What? My God. Send it to me. Now!"

He turned to Bill and went on, "We finally got a hit from one of the traffic cameras. But it was nearly real-time, just a few minutes ago and a few blocks from here. They're sending the image to my phone—"

The phone chimed, and Clark pushed a couple of buttons. He turned it so that Bill could see the screen.

"That's him," Clark said, and even an old hand like him couldn't keep his voice from trembling a little.

The image on the screen had caught a car pulling through an intersection. The driver was visible in the picture: a young man, either bald or more likely with a shaved head, a neatly trimmed beard on his chin. He could be Hispanic, but he could be Middle Eastern, too.

"The car matches, and so do the plates," Clark went on. "Now all we have to do is find him in the next—" He checked the time on the phone. "Five minutes."

"It won't take that long," Bill said as he looked at a group of people headed toward the chapel. "There he is now."

CHAPTER 15

The man wasn't actually with the group, but he was trailing along close enough behind them that a casual glance might mistake him for one of them. The chattering tourists were all fairly young, in their twenties and thirties, a mixture of Anglos and Hispanics, and the man Bill and Clark were looking for could certainly pass for Hispanic.

He wore jeans and an untucked, knit short-sleeved shirt, and there was nothing odd about that, either. Actually, he didn't look the least bit threatening, and for a second the wild thought went through Bill's head that they had made a mistake and there was no bomb, no plot to wipe downtown San Antonio off the face of the earth and kill a bunch of innocent people.

Then Bill's eyes narrowed as he spotted the slight bulge at the small of the man's back. He had some sort of weapon hidden there, most likely a gun or a knife. Again, not necessarily concrete evidence, since Texas was still a concealed-carry state despite the best efforts of the gun-grabbers in Washington to piss on the Constitution and disarm law-abiding citizens.

But they couldn't afford to take a chance. Bill and Clark started walking after him, not running or even hurrying too much, but closing in without any wasted effort. The guy was looking around, trying not to be obvious about it, but Bill could tell that he was nervous.

Anybody who was about to disappear forever in a flash of nuclear fire would be a little anxious, even the most dedicated, fanatical terrorist.

The man stopped short, and so did Bill and Clark. They stood in the shade of a tree that grew next to the sidewalk and looked like a couple of guys taking a walk on their lunch hour, Bill hoped. Bill even put his hands in his pockets and leaned a shoulder against the tree trunk.

The pose was a lot more casual than he felt.

"Turn and face me like we're talkin'," he said quietly to Clark. "I'll keep an eye on the mark."

"We could go ahead and jump him," Clark suggested tensely as he turned to face Bill.

"He might have activated some sort of dead man's trigger."

"He doesn't have anything in his hand."

Bill straightened and said, "He does now. He just took a cell phone out of his shirt pocket."

Clark started to turn again.

"That's it," he said, his voice hollow. "We've got to jump him."

"Hold on," Bill said. "He's turnin' around and holdin' the phone up . . . doesn't look like he's punchin' in a number . . . Good Lord. He's takin' a picture of himself standin' in front of the Alamo."

"So he can email it back to all his buddies in the sandbox and they can broadcast it all over the world when they claim credit for this," Clark said.

"Yeah, that's a good guess." Bill's pulse was so loud now inside his skull that he could hardly hear himself think. "He's sent it. Now he's turnin' back toward the Alamo."

"It's noon," Clark said. "We can't afford to wait any longer."

"If we're wrong about him, we're dead, and so are a lot of other people."

"We're all living on borrowed time now, anyway."

Clark was right about that. The guy had his back to them. Bill broke into a run toward him. They couldn't see the phone anymore, couldn't tell if he was still punching a number into it . . .

Some instinct must have warned the man. He jerked his head around to glance over his shoulder and saw the two grim-faced men running toward him. He twisted and groped for the weapon at the small of his back, which was actually a good thing because while he was doing that he couldn't push any more buttons on the phone.

And since the world hadn't come to an end for everybody in downtown San Antonio, that meant the detonator hadn't been triggered yet.

Bill launched himself into a flying tackle just as the man pulled a small-caliber revolver free and thrust it out in front of him. The gun sounded like three firecrackers going off one right after the other as the man jerked the trigger.

Bill didn't feel any of the bullets hit him during the second that he flew through the air. Then he smashed into the man and drove him backward. Both of them slammed into the sidewalk.

Screams and shouts filled the air in the wake of the gunfire. Panic erupted in the plaza as people tried to get as far away from the shooter as they could.

Bill had landed on top of his quarry, hoping to knock the breath out of the man and stun him. The man was still conscious, though, and alert enough to slash at Bill's head with the pistol. Bill ducked the blow and brought up his knee, driving it into the man's stomach.

He had hoped to jostle the phone loose, too, but that effort had also failed. The man writhed on the ground and brought the elbow of his gun arm around to jab it under Bill's chin and lever him partially off.

That gave the man the opportunity to squirm away. He rolled onto his side and desperately thumbed another number into the phone.

Bill lunged and brought the side of his hand down on the man's wrist. This time the blow did the trick. The phone slipped out of his fingers and went skittering away on the sidewalk.

Clark was waiting for it. He scooped up the phone, being careful to get his fingers underneath it rather than grabbing it and taking the chance that one of his fingers might push just the wrong button . . .

Seeing that Clark had the phone, Bill hammered a fist into the terrorist's face. The man still held the gun, but when he tried to bring it to bear, Bill caught his wrist and twisted hard enough to make bones grind together. The man cried out in pain and dropped the gun.

Bill hit him again and again, smashing the man's face into a crimson ruin. All the tension and danger of the past twenty-four hours exploded out of Bill in the savage blows. All the outrage he felt that somebody would want to commit such an atrocity drove his arm up and down like a piston. He didn't stop until a couple of Clark's agents grabbed him and pulled him off. They dragged him a few yards away on the sidewalk while more agents swarmed over the senseless terrorist.

"Wild Bill," Clark said. He was breathing heavily, too. "Some things sure haven't changed."

Bill willed his rampaging pulse to slow down. When he trusted himself to speak, he asked, "Where's the phone?"

"We slabbed it just like it was. I had an agent standing by with the box."

Bill nodded. Under the circumstances, the safest thing to do was to not touch any of the buttons on the phone's keypad. Slabbing it meant putting it in a specially constructed container with enough layers of electronic baffling to keep any signal from getting out. As long as the phone was in the box, it was incapable of sending a signal to a detonator.

By now the panic-stricken crowd had cleared out of the plaza, meaning the only ones left in front of the Alamo were federal agents and the prisoner.

But wailing sirens filled the air and Bill knew the San Antonio cops would be arriving at any moment in response to the emergency calls about a gunman in Alamo Plaza.

"You ready to deal with the cops?" Bill asked.

"I don't have to deal with them, they have to deal with me," Clark said with a touch of the smug arrogance that all federal bureaucrats felt, even the good guys like him. "But under the circumstances, I don't mind."

"Yeah, nothin' blowed up real good," Bill said. "That means it's a mighty pretty day."

CHAPTER 16

Even with the power of the federal government behind them, dealing with the local authorities was a long, drawn-out, frustrating process. Bill lost track of how many times he and Clark had to tell their story.

But the most important thing was finding the bomb, and that didn't really take long because they knew what kind of car they were looking for. Once they located it a block and a half from the Alamo, the specialists moved in with all their high-tech equipment. The device might have all sorts of fail-safes built into it, redundant systems designed to set it off if anyone tampered with it.

It was a hell of a job, but downtown San Antonio was evacuated for two miles around the Alamo.

It was nightfall by the time the bomb was dealt with safely. It had been removed from the car and transported to a secure location at Fort Sam Houston, the sprawling military base on San Antonio's north side. Once that was done, a task force comprised of the Department of Homeland Security, the National Security Administration, the Central Intelligence Agency, and the San Antonio Police Department began allowing citizens to return to downtown.

It was nearly ten o'clock before Bill found himself sitting in one of the little cafés below street level beside the San Antonio River, which, like the Los Angeles River, had been converted from a natural stream into a concrete-lined, man-made one.

Unlike the L.A. River, though, this one was a tourist attraction. The famous Riverwalk, which stretched for a dozen blocks, was lined with everything from snack bars to gourmet restaurants, pricey art galleries and antique shops to deliberately tacky souvenir stands.

Bill sat on the patio of an open-air Mexican restaurant, a mug of beer on the wrought-iron table in front of him as he waited for Clark, who had promised to be along as soon as he finished talking to his bosses back in Virginia.

The tourists had flocked back to the Riverwalk tonight, which sort of surprised him. He thought they might be cowering in their hotel rooms, brooding over how close they had come to dying.

The authorities had managed to shut down a lot of the story before it ever got out, though. People knew there had been an attempt at a terrorist attack on the Alamo, but they weren't aware of the sheer magnitude of what had almost happened.

That was the way it needed to be, Bill thought. Letting them know the truth wouldn't serve any real purpose. People were better off not knowing just how many metaphorical bullets they had dodged over the years . . .

Luckily, the real bullets fired by the prisoner hadn't struck anyone in the plaza. The only injuries resulting from the incident were the accidental bumps and bruises and a few broken bones that befell people as they tried to flee.

An air of desperate gaiety hung in the air. Folks might not know the truth, but they knew that *something* bad had almost happened, and tonight they were celebrating the fact that they were still alive and could continue their vacations. Knowing there had been a near miss of some sort just made them more eager to seize the moment and enjoy themselves.

With that going on, nobody paid much attention to the lean, craggy-faced, graying man who sat nursing a beer. Bill had made an effort not to let the media know that he had played any part in the drama. Tonight he was just another tourist.

He saw Clark coming toward him. His old friend looked tired. Clark heaved a sigh of relief as he reached the table and sank into one of the empty chairs.

"I was startin' to worry you weren't gonna make it for that enchilada dinner I promised you," Bill said.

Clark glanced around, then keeping his voice pitched low enough he wouldn't be overheard easily, he said, "I had to talk to the White House."

"His own self?"

"Yeah." Clark grimaced. "He wanted to make sure we hadn't done anything to offend any foreign governments. Then he asked if we had any foreign nationals in custody, because if we did, the State Department would have to be involved."

Bill made an effort not to let the disgust he felt show on his face.

"What did you tell him?"

"I said I'd look into the matter immediately and get back to him as soon as possible." Clark looked around, caught the eye of the attractive blond woman working behind the bar at the edge of the patio, and pointed first at Bill's beer, then at himself. The woman smiled and nodded.

"So you're on a fact-findin' mission now?" Bill drawled.

"Something like that. Have you eaten here before?"

"No, but the food's supposed to be mighty good."

"We'll find out."

When their server brought over a beer for Clark and a fresh one for Bill, they ordered their dinners, then sat back to wait.

"This fella that may or may not be in custody," Bill said. "Has he done any talkin' yet?"

"No, not a word. But we have a tentative ID on him. We think he's a Pakistani named Tariq Maleef. Comes from money, educated in Saudi Arabia and England. There are indications that he's part of a loose-knit organization of terrorist groups. Those medieval bastards all hate each other, but they're willing to work together because they hate us worse." Clark took a sip of his beer. "We think Maleef's organization is behind Barranca de la Serpiente."

"Snake Canyon," Bill said. "The little terrorist university they set up."

"Yeah. In fact, there's a good chance that's where this whole New Sun plot was hatched. It's not just a training camp. It's a . . . think tank, I guess you'd call it. A seminar for bloodthirsty thugs who want to kill us."

"Sounds like a place that ought to be put out of business before something even worse comes from there."

Clark leaned back in his chair and nodded slowly.

"I've been thinking the exact same thing," he said, "and I think I know just the man for the job."

Bill sat up straighter and frowned.

"I hope you don't mean what I think you—"

He stopped short as he spotted a woman coming along the Riverwalk toward their table. He wasn't the only one watching her. Nearly every male eye was on her, and so were a good number of the female eyes.

"Catalina," Bill breathed.

Clark twisted in his chair to look back at her. He grinned as he said, "Yeah, I told the agents with her that this was where they'd find us. They're close by, keeping an eye on her."

"I thought she was in Dallas."

"As soon as she heard that everything worked out all right down here, she made her minders turn around and bring her back." Clark chuckled. "From all reports, she's a very forceful young woman. Used to getting her own way."

"Yeah, she's all of that," Bill agreed. "Pretty good car thief, too."

Clark raised his eyebrows.

Bill ignored that and got to his feet to meet her. Catalina ran the last few yards and threw herself into his arms. There was nothing romantic about it; at least Bill didn't think so. It was just the grateful embrace of two friends, two comrades in arms who had thought they might never see each other again.

Catalina stepped back, rested her hands on his shoulders, and said, "It's all over, Bill?"

"Sure," he answered without hesitation, but even as he said it, he knew that might not be true. He remembered what Clark had said about Barranca de la Serpiente and knew there was still work to be done.

But not tonight. Tonight was for being grateful that they were still alive and that the nation hadn't been wrenched even further off its moorings.

"Hope you're hungry," Bill said with a grin. "You got here just in time for a late supper."

Tariq had been praying almost nonstop since he was captured, praying for Allah to deliver him from the hands of the American infidel dogs. He couldn't believe he had come so close to achieving his glorious destiny, only to have it snatched away from him.

Two more seconds and paradise would have been his.

Instead he was stuck now in this dreary cell, aching from the beating the old infidel had given him, locked away on the American military base behind layers of steel, concrete, and barbed wire. He was sure that he would be spirited away to some even more secret prison, possibly out of the country, where he would be tortured and humiliated by the blasphemers.

The little room contained only a bunk and a toilet. The light fixture was set into the ceiling where it was impossible for anyone to get at it. One wall was concrete, the other three impenetrable steel, as was the door, which had a small window set in it, the shatterproof glass laced with wire inside, and a slot where food could be passed into the cell.

The hour was late, but Tariq had spent a long time being interrogated. He hadn't told them anything, of course, not even his name. The only words he had spoken had been to call on Allah for help.

The slot in the door opened, the panel that formed it rising from some sort of electronic signal. A tray of food appeared. Finger food, small sandwiches and pieces of fruit, because he wouldn't be trusted with utensils of any sort.

Tariq wanted to refuse the food, but his stomach rebelled. He hadn't eaten that morning, and by now he should have been dead for almost twelve hours. As much as he might have liked to, he couldn't ignore the prodding of the flesh.

He stood up, took the flimsy cardboard tray, and returned to his bunk to eat. As he chewed a bite of one of the sandwiches, he paused suddenly as he came across something small and hard inside it. His tongue explored the object. It was a capsule of some sort, he decided.

He immediately thought that someone had smuggled it in to him so that he could take his own life. But that would accomplish nothing. While Tariq had no objection to hurrying his own passage to paradise, he wanted his death to *mean* something.

With the next bite he took, he slipped the capsule out of his mouth into his hand. He was sure that a camera was hidden somewhere in the cell to observe his every move. He kept the capsule concealed so that the watchers would remain unaware of its existence. It might come in handy later on.

Sometime during the night, the light went out so that he could sleep. When it did, he stood up from the bunk, went to the door, and used the faint light that came through the tiny window to examine the capsule. He twisted the two halves, breaking them apart.

The capsule didn't contain powder or a liquid. Instead, hidden inside it was a small piece of paper rolled into a very tight cylinder. Tariq unrolled it, and a smile appeared on his face as he read the words printed on the paper in English, the only language he had in common with the man who had sent the message.

When he had committed the words to memory, he rolled the paper up again, inserted it into the capsule, and swallowed it without hesitation. He knew now that it contained not death but the promise of life.

Life . . . and vengeance on the Americans who had ruined everything.

The message had read: *Be ready. We will get you out. Sanchez.*

BOOK TWO
THE TEAM

CHAPTER 17

New York City, four years before the New Sun

"You sure they'll be there?" Bailey asked.

"Yeah, yeah, no doubt about it," T.J. replied. "My information is solid, man."

Bailey curled his hand around the grips of the heavy revolver stuck in the waistband of his trousers.

"Better be," he said. "If we're gonna do this, I don't want anything to go wrong."

"Nothin' gonna go wrong," T.J. insisted. He bounced up and down on his toes, too full of nervous energy to be still as they stood in the shadows watching the warehouse across the street, not far from the docks.

Knowing T.J., he was probably full of something else, too, thought Bailey. A little chemical courage. T.J. could handle it, though. He had used all the time they were together in the sandbox and hadn't let the unit down once. Not once. He and Bailey were the only survivors, true, but the others getting wiped out in an ambush hadn't been T.J.'s fault, not by any stretch of the imagination.

If anybody was to blame for that "incident," it was Bailey. He'd been on point when they were clearing the houses in a village. He was the one who'd let the insurgents flank them on both sides and catch them in a crossfire . . .

Bailey shoved that thought out of his mind. He'd been brooding about it for years now, and that hadn't changed a damn thing. Dead was still dead. Those guys weren't ever coming back. So he had to look out for himself, and when T.J. had come to him, first time they'd seen each other in a good six months, with the idea of ripping off the guys in the warehouse, Bailey hadn't had to think about it for very long before he said yes.

"You can make more in one night than you could make in a year working at that club, man. And it ain't like these are good guys we'd be rippin' off. They're assholes, man. Drug-dealin' assholes."

"So if we steal the drugs and sell them, what does that make us?" Bailey had wanted to know.

A cocky grin had spread from one side of T.J.'s face to the other.

"Robin Hood, man. That makes us Robin Hood."

"Stealing from the rich and giving to the . . . We're not exactly poor, T.J."

"Speak for yourself, man. You can't be rakin' it in, workin' the door at some club. And I know I'm not makin' much bartending in this joint."

They were sitting in a booth in the little bar where T.J. worked. It was late, and they were alone. The bar was closed, and so was the club where Bailey worked.

They were quite a contrast, sitting across the table from each other. The ponderous-looking white guy, so big the other grunts in the squad had nicknamed him The Incredible Hulk, and the frenetic little black guy. But Bailey and T.J. were best buds and had been since the day they'd met, which oddly enough was half a world away, even though they had both grown up in New York City—T.J. in Manhattan, Bailey across the river in Brooklyn. New York was a big place, though, so it wasn't surprising they had never run into each other.

"We're liable to get ourselves killed," Bailey had objected when T.J. laid out the plan. "The buyer and the seller will each have a crew of hardasses with him. The two of us won't be any match for them."

"But we'll have the element of surprise on our side," T.J. had argued. "Plus we'll have some of these."

He reached into his backpack, which lay on the seat beside him, and took out something that he placed on the table between them. Bailey's eyes grew wide as he looked at the object. A pleasant haze from the alcohol he'd consumed this evening had enveloped his brain until now, but it burned off like fog in the morning sun at the sight of the thing on the table.

"What the hell? That's a grenade!"

"That's right. Ordnance, man. We can blow their asses off if we have to."

Bailey shook his head and said, "We'll blow our own asses off, more than likely. Where the hell did you get that?"

"I got my sources," T.J. said serenely. "Look, it's simple. We go in and show them these babies, and they turn the money over to us. Actually, I've been thinkin' about it, and I think we should leave the coke there. It'd be easier to trace than the money will be."

"You think? Couple mooks like us turn up with a fortune in coke, that'll draw attention we don't want." Bailey pondered and then slowly nodded. "But the cash is a different story, especially if we're careful and don't make a big splash with it. We'll have to hold it back, though, T.J., and just spend a little at a time. Think you can do that?"

"Sure, no worries."

Bailey didn't really believe that. T.J. and the concept of impulse control were total strangers. He might intend to lay low for a while with his share of the loot. He might even believe that he could do it successfully.

But Bailey knew better. The cravings would hit T.J. and he'd have to do something to satisfy them, and once he was flying, there was no telling what he might do or say.

Maybe Bailey could sit on him, though, until the heat died down. If the take from ripping off that drug deal was as much as T.J. claimed, it might be worth running the risk.

"All right," Bailey had said, that night in the bar. "Let's do it."

That was how he came to find himself standing in the shadows with a couple of grenades in his pocket on a hot, muggy night. The water was close enough that the air stunk . . . or maybe that was just his own sweat and worry he smelled.

"Ooh," T.J. said beside him. "Here they come."

A big, expensive car slid to a stop in front of

the warehouse. According to the intel T.J. had overheard in the bar, that would be the Ukrainians with the money. The Arabs with the drugs were already inside the building, waiting for the cash just like Bailey and T.J. were.

Bailey leaned toward his friend and said in a low, urgent voice, "Maybe we should hit them out here, leave the Arabs out of it entirely. They're just something else than can go wrong."

"Out in the open? No, man, we can handle it better inside. Those camel humpers, they'll stay out of it once we tell 'em we ain't after their coke. They'll still have their merchandise, and they can always sell it to somebody else."

The plan still seemed a little sketchy to Bailey, but what the hell. A man had to run a few risks to get ahead. He wouldn't ever do it working the door at some club, letting in a bunch of rich kids who had more money than sense.

Two big men got out of the car, one from the passenger seat in front, the other from the seat behind the driver. The driver stayed where he was for the moment, and so did the other man in the backseat. The two big guys looked around but didn't seem to see anything threatening. Not surprising, since there was nothing to see in this neighborhood at this time of night. All the buildings were dark.

One of the men nodded to the second guy in the backseat. He got out carrying a briefcase. Bailey's eyes fastened on the case. According to T.J., there would be 1.2 million dollars in there.

The driver emerged from the car as well and reached back into it to retrieve a pump shotgun with a pistol grip. He walked beside the money man toward the door that led into the warehouse's office area. The other two men fell in behind them.

The door opened before they got there. All four of the men disappeared inside.

"Time to go to work," T.J. said, still bobbing on his toes.

Bailey reached up and pulled the rubberized ski mask over his head. On a night like this the thing was hot and stifling, and for a second he felt a surge of claustrophobic panic. He shrugged into the cheap Windbreaker he had brought with him and worked tight-fitting gloves onto his hands. The only skin visible was around his eyes, and he had worked lampblack into it earlier.

The goal was that nobody would be able to tell if he and T.J. were white, black, brown, yellow, or whatever. If somebody started looking for a big white guy and a little black guy, there was a chance the trail would lead back to them sooner or later, and they didn't want that.

Bailey tried to take a deep breath, but the ski mask made that difficult. He said, "Screw it, let's go."

A few days earlier, after they had decided to pull the job, T.J. had asked him, "Whatchu gonna do with your share, man?"

It was a question Bailey hadn't really considered. When you got a bunch of money, you had that money. That was as far as his thinking had gone. Bailey had forced himself to ponder the matter for a moment, then said, "Go to the mountains, maybe."

"The mountains? Why? Most guys, if they rich, they wanna go sit on a beach somewhere."

"I've been where it's hot and sandy, remember?"

Bailey had said. "Didn't care much for it. But I've never really seen any mountains."

"All that snow? I dunno, man. I'm not much for the cold."

"What do you think the weather's like here all winter? At least if you're some place up high where there's a lot of snow, it'd be . . . I don't know . . . cleaner somehow."

"Maybe so, man, maybe so. You gonna be rich enough you can do whatever you want, that's for sure. One point two mil, baby, that's what we gonna split."

Those snowcapped mountains Bailey imagined might as well have been a million miles away from this squalid New York street. He put all thoughts of them out of his head to concentrate on the job at hand.

T.J. had scouted the place ahead of time, once he knew where the deal would go down, and had found a way in, a window in an alley that had been boarded up. He had pulled all the nails except a couple in each board, so Bailey with his great strength had no trouble wrenching them loose. He had to do it carefully, though, and not make too much noise that might alert the men inside. The window was so narrow that his shoulders barely fit, but he made it.

Once they were in, T.J. led the way, finding a path through a maze of hallways the same way his instincts had led him through streets like rabbit warrens in those dusty towns on the other side of the globe. He had an instinct for such things that made him valuable despite his drug habit and his jumpy nature.

If it had been T.J. on point that day instead of him, maybe the rest of the squad would still be alive, Bailey had thought more than once.

They reached the open area of the warehouse. The huge, high-ceilinged room was like a cavern. It was empty except for a folding card table that somebody had set up.

The two crews stood facing each other across that card table. Two briefcases sat open on the table. The glare from a bare lightbulb overhead shone down on clear plastic packets of white powder in one case and tightly banded bricks of money in the other.

In the shadows, T.J. licked his lips and whispered, "Maybe we'll take just a little bit of the coke, okay?"

"No, just the money," Bailey said.

"Okay, okay," T.J. muttered.

The boss of each crew stood slightly ahead of his companions. The two men talked in heavily accented English, the Arab promising that the cocaine was high quality goods, the Ukrainian saying that it had better be.

Bailey took one of the grenades from his pocket and pulled the pin. As long as he held on to the arming lever, nothing would happen. He slipped the pin in his pocket so he could replace it once they were out of here . . . assuming, of course, that he didn't have to use the grenade. Then he drew his revolver.

Beside him, T.J. had armed one of his grenades and drawn his own gun, a Glock 9mm that he had gotten hold of somewhere. T.J. was a champion scrounger and always had been.

But Bailey suddenly found himself wondering

about the grenades. T.J. swore they were the real thing, but you couldn't exactly test that out, could you? What if they wound up tossing the grenades at the feet of those ruthless killers, and the damn things just thudded to the floor and lay there, harmless?

In that case, he and T.J. would wind up very dead, very quick, Bailey thought.

But he couldn't back out now. He didn't want to, and anyway, it was too late, because T.J. had just stepped out into the open, waved the Glock, brandished the grenade where the men couldn't miss it, and yelled, "Don't move or we'll blow you all to hell!"

CHAPTER 18

Bailey stepped out behind him, moving to the right and waving his own grenade in the air so they couldn't miss it. He pointed his revolver at the Arabs while T.J. covered the Ukrainians. The man with the shotgun started to raise it, but T.J. waggled the Glock at him and said, "Uh-uh, man, don't do it. This baby'll turn you into hamburger if I toss it over there."

Bailey felt himself trembling a little inside as he looked over the barrel of his gun at the Arabs. T.J. hadn't been sure where they were from—he thought maybe they were Syrians—but it didn't really matter to Bailey. The swarthy faces, the beard stubble, the mustaches . . . after his time in the sandbox, they all looked the same to him.

They all looked like the enemy, and he had to control the impulse to start blowing them away.

"All we want's the cash," T.J. went on. "You babies pick up your coke and back on outta here, do you another deal some other day, *capisce*?"

The head Arab was the only clean-shaven one of

the bunch. He said, "You men are very foolish to be interfering with our business."

The bald-headed boss of the Ukrainian crew said, "You think we let you walk out of here with our money?"

"I don't think you got any choice, man, long as me and my partner got these grenades."

T.J. could have at least tried to disguise his voice, thought Bailey. He didn't plan to speak at all unless he had to. There were plenty of guys in New York City who were as big as he was—well, maybe not plenty, but some, for sure—so that was all he was going to let them know about him.

All the gunmen had started to reach under their coats for their weapons at the first sign of trouble, but the sight of the grenades had stopped them from completing their draws. Bailey didn't know how long that would keep them frozen, so he wanted to get this over with. He was glad when T.J. went on, "Close the case with the money, put it on the floor, and slide it over here."

"Go to hell," the boss Ukrainian said, adding some colorful and anatomically improbable suggestions. He finished by saying, "You can't throw those grenades at us. You'll blow yourselves up, too!"

"Not when you're over there and we're over here," T.J. said. "Anyway, it's a chance we're willin' to take. Are you?"

The Arab said, "Leave us out of it," and reached for the briefcase full of coke.

"Don't touch that!" the Ukrainian snapped. "Our deal was concluded." He glanced toward Bailey and T.J. "The cocaine is ours now, as per our agreement. So if anyone is to lose the money, it is you."

"Lies!" the Arab responded. "The deal was not finished. That is still our cocaine!"

Bailey saw T.J. glance over at him uneasily. This argument was something they hadn't anticipated. When you're ripping off crazy foreign gangsters, any complication is a bad one, Bailey realized.

T.J. said, "Look, you guys can hash that out after we've got the cash and gone." He giggled. "Hash it out. Only that's coke, not hash!"

The two groups ignored him. They were glaring at each other now. The Ukrainian pointed at the case with the coke in it and said, "Those are my drugs."

"No, those are *my* drugs," the Arab insisted.

T.J. said, "Hey! We're the ones with the grenades!"

Both leaders lunged for the coke at the same time. As they did, the men with them clawed guns from under their coats and started shooting at each other. Flames flickered from the muzzles of machine pistols as lead spewed from them. The shotgun boomed.

T.J. yelled, "No!" and ran forward, probably intent on grabbing the briefcase full of money from the middle of the firefight. Bailey made a grab for him with the hand holding the grenade but missed.

The grenade slipped from his fingers and fell to the floor, bouncing once and then rolling. The arming lever had spun away as soon as Bailey let go of it. Bailey's eyes bugged out as his brain automatically started counting down the seconds.

He sure as hell wasn't going to throw himself on the grenade to protect this warehouse full of scumbags. Instead he took a fast step forward and kicked the damn thing, sending it scooting past T.J. as it slid straight toward the table over which the

Ukrainians and the Arabs were blazing away at each other.

The grenade detonated just as it went under the table.

Bailey had already thrown himself flat on the floor when the explosion rocked the building. With his head down, he couldn't see anything, but the image in his mind's eye of what had to be happening was pretty clear.

The blast blew the table into a million pieces. A cloud of smoke mixed with cocaine billowed toward the ceiling. Deadly shrapnel sprayed through the air and shredded the flesh of the men standing nearby. Tiny pieces of money swirled around and floated back to the floor like snowflakes.

Bailey was untouched. With his ears ringing from the explosion, he lifted his head and looked around. The single high-intensity bulb fastened to one of the rafters overhead still burned, casting its harsh light over the scene. Bailey saw huddled lumps of bloody flesh and torn clothing lying on the floor near the site of the explosion. He looked for T.J. . . .

A moan made him turn his head. T.J. lay to one side where the force of the blast had thrown him. He was still alive. He had been farther away from the grenade, so it hadn't killed him—yet—but he had caught some shrapnel. Bailey saw blood on T.J.'s Windbreaker.

As Bailey tried to gather his wits, T.J. rolled onto his side and started struggling to his feet. Bailey knew they had to get out of here. The explosion would draw the cops, and they didn't want to be here for that.

The coke and the cash were gone, destroyed in the blast, but at least maybe they could escape with their lives, Bailey thought as he got his hands and knees under him and tried to lever himself up off the floor.

A thought struck him. Where the hell was T.J.'s grenade?

Still on all fours, Bailey looked around wildly, thinking that T.J. must have dropped the grenade when he was knocked down. It might go off at any second.

Then Bailey spotted the ugly thing lying on the floor a few feet away. His heart slammed against his chest and then tried to crawl up his throat. The terror that gripped him was stronger even than anything he had experienced during the war.

But as he stared at the grenade, he realized that the pin was still in it.

T.J. had never pulled it.

Either T.J. had forgotten to pull the pin, or he had been running a bluff he'd neglected to tell Bailey about. Anything was possible where he was concerned. But the important thing was that the grenade wasn't going to explode. Bailey's muscles were limp with relief, and that kept him from getting up for a moment longer.

T.J. staggered toward the blackened crater in the floor where the table had been.

"T.J.," Bailey croaked. "What are—"

"Might be some money left," T.J. mumbled without looking back. Even injured, he wanted the payoff. "Might find some—"

One of the lumps on the floor moved then.

Something lifted and pointed toward T.J., and Bailey didn't even have time to shout a warning when he recognized it as the shotgun carried by the Ukrainian driver. Somehow, the man wasn't dead yet.

Flame gouted from the weapon's muzzle. The buckshot caught T.J. in the chest and flung him backward. He hit the floor right after the shotgun, which had been torn from the wounded man's hands by its recoil.

Bailey scrambled over to T.J. on hands and knees. He sat down and pulled the limp body into his lap. T.J.'s head lolled loosely on his neck. His chest was a bloody mess where the shotgun's blast had struck him, not to mention the shrapnel wounds scattered around his body.

He might have survived the shrapnel if Bailey had been able to get some medical attention for him. The buckshot had killed him, though. His eyes were wide open, staring sightlessly. They were all Bailey could see of his face because of the ski mask. Sobbing, Bailey took hold of the mask and peeled it off.

"T.J., I'm sorry, I'm sorry, buddy, I should have stopped him, oh, God, I'm so sorry . . ."

The words poured out of Bailey in a river of sorrow. He cradled T.J.'s bloody form against his chest and rocked back and forth. They had been through so much together, and now suddenly, shockingly, it was over. It couldn't be, it couldn't be.

Bailey wasn't thinking about the cops anymore. There was no room in his brain for that. Instead it was filled with grief, and then slowly, anger began to filter in and replace some of that sadness. He reached up and pulled his own ski mask off, gulping down deep lungfuls of air between sobs. After a few minutes, he eased T.J.'s body to the floor and staggered to his feet.

The revolver he had dropped lay close by. He scooped it up and walked toward the Ukrainian who had wielded the shotgun. The stubborn son of a bitch *still* wasn't dead, although he was so close now he was too weak to lift the weapon or even reach for it. All he could do was lie there, his body a wreck where the explosion had torn into it, his face a bloody mask with grotesquely staring eyes.

Bailey stood over the man and pointed the revolver at his face. He couldn't tell if the Ukrainian actually saw him or not. It didn't matter.

Bailey pulled the trigger.

Then he pulled it again and again until the hammer clicked on an empty chamber. The Ukrainian's head looked like a pumpkin somebody had dropped from the top of a ten-story building.

Bailey lowered the empty gun and let it slip from his fingers. It thudded to the floor beside his feet. He turned away from the gory mess, not really thinking about anything, just allowing the primitive instincts inside him to move his muscles.

The door into the warehouse office crashed open. Heavy footsteps pounded on the cement floor. Uniformed shapes flitted in front of Bailey's eyes. Dimly, he heard a lot of strident, shouting voices telling him to get down on the ground.

He fell to his knees, but not because anybody ordered him to. He was just too tired to stay on his feet anymore. Something hit him in the back and knocked him forward onto his face. The rough concrete scraped his face. He didn't care.

He just didn't give a damn about anything anymore.

CHAPTER 19

Georgia, three years before the New Sun

Wade Stillman burrowed his head down in the pillow, hoping he could get it deep enough to shut out the sound, that awful, endless, screeching yap that haunted his waking hours and lately his nightmares, too.

No luck. He could still hear Lucy Kammen talking to him.

"Don't forget the rent's due day after tomorrow, Wade. And if we don't pay the electric company, they're gonna shut off our power, honey. I can't handle that, so you better see if you can get an advance at work, okay? I'd ask my sister, but I've already borrowed so much from Trish . . . Oh, hey, I know, sweetie. You can ask your daddy for a loan. Why don't you go over there and do that today before you go to work, okay? I'm sure he wouldn't mind helpin' us out a little."

Wade raised his head and blinked bleary eyes. Lucy was standing on the other side of the room in front of the mirror on the old dressing table. She had her blouse on but hadn't pulled on her pants yet, so that meant he had a good view of the round curves of her panty-clad butt.

He moaned and dropped his head back into the pillow so that he couldn't see her anymore. When he looked at her and his brain got addled by how sexy she was, her words actually seemed to make sense, and he didn't want that. He couldn't handle that.

"Did you hear what I said, honey? About goin' to see your daddy?"

Wade wondered if he could push his face into the pillow's soft, enfolding darkness hard enough to suffocate himself. It might be worth a try, rather than facing another day.

"Sweetie?"

He knew she wasn't going to stop until he answered her. He lifted his head again and said, "My daddy don't have any money, Lucy. You know that."

"Oh, he's got a little put away. You told me he did."

"That's to pay for the rest home when he gets old. He's been puttin' a little aside for that for years."

Lucy picked up a brush and started stroking it firmly through the thick auburn hair that tumbled around her shoulders. The motion tensed her muscles and made her butt look even better.

"He's still a long way from needin' a rest home," she said. "He can spare a little now. Just enough to keep our power on. You know, if you were to go down to the electric company and talk to them, you might could pay them part of what we owe, and that'd be enough to keep 'em from turnin' off the power. What do you think about that?"

"I think you should come back over here to the bed," Wade said.

"Oh, hell, no, honey, there's no time for that, no matter how good it sounds. I got to get to work." She set the brush aside, reached for her pants, and drew them up her sleek legs. "If I'm late for the lunch rush, Solomon will kill me, you know that." She stepped into her shoes and blew him a kiss. "Don't forget what we talked about."

Two minutes after she was gone, while he was still lying in bed, Wade said aloud, "Wha . . . what was it I wasn't supposed to forget?"

He rolled over and went back to sleep. Chances were, it wasn't important anyway.

When he woke up, he realized he had overslept and had to hurry to make it to work on time. Avery Calhoun, the manager of the sporting goods department at the MegaMart, always tried to cut Wade as much slack as he could—"Once a Marine, always a Marine," Avery liked to say, and if he wanted to use that as an excuse to do favors for Wade, that was just fine—but there was only so much he could do. If Wade was late too many times, he'd wind up getting fired, and although the MegaMart job wasn't the best one in the world, it was probably the best one Wade could get in his hometown. He wasn't exactly what anybody would call highly skilled.

Except at killing people. He had gotten damn good at that while he was in the Marines.

So he took what he could get, which in his case was working in the MegaMart selling fishing poles and deer rifles and hunting and fishing licenses.

And putting up with Avery's boring stories about 'Nam. All for not much more than minimum wage and no freaking benefits, although he'd been promised that he'd move up to that after he'd been there for a while. Wade wasn't convinced the day would ever come, though.

He took a quick shower and was out of the house he and Lucy rented. A quick stop at a drive-thru window fortified him with a cup of lousy coffee and a greasy breakfast sandwich.

A look of relief came over Avery Calhoun's face as Wade walked into the sporting goods department. Avery was tall and mostly bald, with glasses and a little belly that hung over his belt. The days of him being in good enough shape for the Marines had vanished into the mists of time.

Avery said, "I'm glad to see you, Wade. I was about to get a little worried."

"Yeah, I know I cut it a little close. But I'm here, and I ain't late."

"No, you're not," Avery agreed. "And that's good, because we've got a truck coming in any time now."

That meant they would spend the afternoon unloading merchandise and storing it in the stockroom. That wasn't Wade's favorite thing in the world, but it beat waiting on customers.

"You look a little tired," Avery went on. "Are you getting enough sleep these days?"

"Yeah, I guess." Wade felt a flash of annoyance. He liked Avery, he really did, but the guy could be too much of a mother hen. "Sometimes I dream a little too much."

Avery nodded knowingly and said, "I understand. It took me years to get to where I didn't dream almost every night about some things that happened in country."

There he went again, the wise old Vietnam vet. Truth was, Wade hardly ever dreamed about what had happened in Iraq. Most of his nightmares involved Lucy nagging him. Once he had even dreamed that she was trying to beat him to death with a shovel. He had no idea why she'd been using a shovel instead of some more conventional weapon, like a baseball bat, but there it was, for whatever it was worth.

The first couple of hours on the job went okay. They weren't too busy and were able to get half of the truck's cargo unloaded. Then Avery answered the phone behind the counter and held the receiver out toward Wade.

"Lucy," he said in a quiet voice.

Wade frowned. He wasn't supposed to get personal calls at work any more than she was, and she knew that. So this might actually be an emergency of some sort.

He took the phone from Avery, who was keeping his expression carefully noncommittal, and said into it, "What's up?"

"Did you go by the electric company and talk to them?"

The tense tone of her voice as she asked the question told him that she already knew the answer. He winced, knowing that was one of the things he had forgotten. He wouldn't have had time, anyway, since he'd slept so late.

"Sorry, I didn't get a chance—"

"You didn't talk to your daddy, either, did you?"

"No, but how—"

"How did I know? Because they just called my cell phone. The account's in my name, you know."

How could he not know that? She was the only one who had any semblance of good credit.

She went on, "They called to tell me they were there at the house right then to shut off the power unless I could bring them the money for that over-due bill. And of course I had to tell them to go ahead and shut it off because I didn't have the money, and anyway I couldn't leave work. Which means that I'll have to go home to a house without electricity and it'll cost even more in the long run to get it turned back on!"

"Now, honey, take it easy," Wade said. "I'll get it all straightened out—"

Again she interrupted him, saying, "If you trip on something in the dark when you get home, it'll be all your crap that I've thrown out on the front lawn!"

"Look, I'm sorry, I just didn't—"

"No," she broke in coldly. "You never do."

The phone clicked in his ear.

Wade looked at it for a second, then replaced it on the base. He sighed and said, "Well, hell."

"Don't worry, she'll cool off and it'll all blow over," Avery said. "If I had a nickel for every time my wife got mad at me . . ."

He was the wise old married man as well as the wise old vet, Wade thought. He said, "Lucy and I ain't married."

"Well, I know that, but still, it's pretty much the same—"

A loud, angry voice somewhere nearby overrode what Avery was saying. Both men turned to look and saw a large man in blue jeans, a T-shirt, and a feed store cap berating a small boy who hung his head in misery and shame. A pale, narrow-faced woman who was obviously the boy's mother stood nearby, fidgeting nervously.

Wade didn't have a clue what the trouble was about. The kid must have done something to annoy his dad, and the guy was the type who didn't mind lacing into him in public and humiliating him. He probably knocked the boy around at home. The woman, too. In fact, Wade thought he saw a bruise on the woman's face that she had tried to cover with makeup.

Wade stepped out from behind the counter.

Avery said, "Now, wait—" but Wade ignored him. He went up to the man in the cap and said, "Excuse me, sir."

The man jerked his head toward Wade and snapped, "Yeah?"

"You're causin' a little bit of a disturbance here—"

"You see that?" The man pointed at a basket half-full of merchandise. "I'm buyin' all that crap, which makes me a customer, which means you treat me with respect and keep your damn nose outta my business."

Wade smiled. He knew the man looked at him and didn't see much to impress him, just a slender, sandy-haired guy, medium height, young. Just somebody else he could run roughshod over the same way he bullied everybody else he ran into, including his own family.

"Didn't mean any disrespect," Wade drawled softly. "Just wanted you to quit bein' such an asshole in front of your wife and kid."

"You just . . . What the hell did you say? I'm gonna get you fired, you little—"

"Go ahead," Wade said. "Then I won't have to deal with worthless sons o' bitches like you anymore."

The man's face was almost as red as a sunset by now. The muscles in his shoulders bunched. He might as well have been wearing a sign explaining what he was about to do.

Avery came up behind Wade and said, "Please, sir, there's no need for a scene—"

The man threw a punch, telegraphing it so blatantly Wade felt like he had a week to get out of the way. Instinct made Wade weave to the side as the fist came at him. The blow went harmlessly past his ear.

Unfortunately, Avery ran right into it. Blood spurted from his nose as the customer's fist landed on it. Avery grunted in pain and went over backward.

Wade saw his friend lying on the floor bleeding, and that was the last straw. Moving almost too fast for the eye to follow, he hit the big man four times, right, left, right, left, driving him back into a display of fishing poles. As the guy rebounded from that, Wade caught his arm and broke it with a simple, efficient twist. The man started to howl in pain, but Wade kicked his legs out from under him and dropped on top of him, jabbing his knees into the man's belly and hitting him in the face again and again . . .

In the end, it took Avery, Carl from Paint, and Lucas from Automotive to pull him off. By that time the cops were there, and they fastened his hands in plastic restraints behind his back and marched him out of the store to put him in the backseat of a cruiser.

Wade laughed the whole way. So much for those benefits he'd been hoping to get one of these days. Getting locked up did have one benefit, though.

He wouldn't have to listen to Lucy bitch anymore.

CHAPTER 20

Somewhere in Africa, three years before the New Sun

Dixon settled in on the hilltop and rested his cheek against the smooth wooden stock of the sniper rifle. The weapon was more than thirty years old, but it still shot straight and true. Dixon knew it, liked it, trusted it. The rifle had done the job for him more times than he could remember.

The job was killing, of course, and few in the world were better at it than Henry Dixon.

When he'd first gotten into this line of work, after a couple of tours of duty, he had let his hair grow out into an impressive Afro, a throwback to the seventies. That hadn't lasted long because he realized it made him noticeable, and he didn't want people to notice him. He wanted to ease into a place, do his work, and ease out again with nothing to show he'd ever been there except for a body . . . or two or three.

So he'd shaved off his mustache, cropped his hair close to his head, and he still wore it that way all these years later. It was mostly gray now.

Six hundred yards away, the rebel leader who called himself Dugo stepped out of his tent into the early morning sunlight and stretched. He was a tall, lean man who wore boots and a pair of khaki trousers. His torso was bare.

Through the scope, Dixon watched Dugo yawn, then turn toward the prisoner who was tied to a thick post set in the ground, tied so securely that he couldn't slide down and sit. From the looks of the dried blood that covered his dark skin, the rebels had tortured him for hours the day before, until they had grown tired of their sport. Obviously the man hadn't told them what they wanted to know, or they would have gone ahead and killed him and been done with it.

Now it would start all over again. Eventually, no matter how strong he was, the man would break and reveal all the secrets of Colonel Mfunda's lakefront hideaway. Once they knew that, Dugo and his men could start planning their mission to assassinate Mfunda.

The colonel wasn't aware of the threat that hung over him, of course. He would have been outraged to think that any of his people wanted him dead, even that malcontent Dugo. Why, he was their beloved leader, wasn't he? They idolized him, and why shouldn't they? He had taken his small, mineral-rich country and dragged it kicking and screaming into the twenty-first century. All it had taken to accomplish that was almost wiping out several of the tribes that had stubbornly and foolishly opposed his benevolent, well-intentioned rule.

Luckily for Mfunda, he had some advisors around him who weren't as blinded to the truth, and they watched out for him by hiring men like Dixon. The colonel had no idea how many times they had saved his life.

From time to time, Dixon had wondered why Mfunda didn't just go ahead and declare himself a general. Or president. Or even king. He was the absolute ruler of this country and could call himself whatever he wanted. But he had been a colonel in the army when he'd led the coup and seized power, and Dixon supposed that was good enough for the man. Titles didn't really mean anything, anyway.

He shifted the rifle slightly and centered the sights on the back of Dugo's head. A squeeze of the trigger would put an end to the man's dreams of rebellion.

But someone else would just come along to take his place, and Dugo was a known quantity, after all. And the colonel's advisors weren't Dixon's only employers. He also worked for men who operated out of fancy drawing rooms in Washington and basements in Virginia. They liked the tension between Mfunda and Dugo and wanted it to continue. If Mfunda got too secure, too complacent, he might decide to kick all the foreign interests out of his country, and nobody wanted that. Better for him to keep on worrying a little, and as long as Dugo was around, he would.

So Dixon shifted the rifle's sights back to the prisoner, one of Mfunda's security officers who had been kidnapped by the rebels a couple of days earlier.

The rest of the camp was coming alive now. Women emerged from some of the tents and stirred up cooking fires. Men went into the trees to empty their bladders. It was all very primitive, except for a truck parked to one side that had a satellite dish mounted on it. Even here, people had to have the Internet.

Dixon had gotten into position while it was still dark. He could have carried out his mission as soon as it was light enough for him to draw a bead on his target. But his employers had asked him to wait and kill the man right in front of Dugo. They wanted to send a message to the rebel leader, a message making it perfectly clear that they could reach out and have him killed whenever they wanted to.

It struck Dixon as melodramatic nonsense, but he did what he was paid to do.

He drew in a couple of deep breaths and blew them out. His body was absolutely still. His mind was serene.

He stroked the trigger.

Six hundred yards away, the bullet passed close enough by Dugo's ear to make him feel the heat of it, then the prisoner's head exploded.

It was merciful, really. Soon he would have been screaming his lungs out in agony as the torture started again.

Through the scope, Dixon saw Dugo stagger back from the corpse. He twisted around, his face splattered with blood and brains. His mouth opened grotesquely wide as he shouted at his men. At this distance, Dixon heard the yelling, but only faintly. The words meant nothing to him.

He crawled backward down the far side of the hill until he couldn't be seen from the camp and then stood up. His jeep was parked on a trail about a quarter-mile away. He trotted toward it, his eyes scanning his surroundings for trouble as he moved. While he was at his best making long, carefully planned and aimed shots, he could handle impromptu fighting, too. He was a good shot with the rifle under any circumstances.

The trees and the undergrowth thickened as he approached the trail. Dixon slid through them without making much noise. Sometimes he thought of himself as a ghost, moving unseen and unheard through life, lacking in substance except for his trigger finger.

Dugo's men would have to take a roundabout route to reach the spot where Dixon had left his jeep. It would take them half an hour, at least, and by then Dixon would be long gone. By noon he would be on an airplane headed to Paris, where he intended to spend at least a week relaxing.

He stepped out of the brush onto the trail and froze.

A truck was parked on the trail behind the jeep. It was military issue, a deuce-and-a-half, but Dixon instantly knew from the ragtag clothing worn by the eight or nine men around it that they weren't regular soldiers. They were members of Dugo's rebel force who had stolen the truck somewhere.

There was no reason for them to be here. Dixon had scouted the trail and knew it was little used. No other vehicle had come along it for days, if not longer.

So what had brought these men here today?

Dixon could think of only one answer.

Bad luck. Sheer bad luck.

And it was worse luck that one of them had a walkie-talkie with him. As they all stood there around the two vehicles in the trail, staring at him as if frozen, a burst of static came from the walkie-talkie, followed by squawking that Dixon recognized as Dugo's voice. The rebel leader was furious as he ordered his men to start searching for the sniper who had just killed their prisoner.

Dixon didn't give the man with the walkie-talkie a chance to reply. He whipped the rifle to his shoulder and shot the man through the head. The walkie-talkie flew out of the man's hand and went high in the air as the heavy bullet cored through his brain and knocked him down.

Dixon worked the rifle's bolt and shifted his aim with blinding speed. He fired again, this time drilling a man who was trying to raise a machine gun. The slug took the man in the chest and spun him around.

With two men down, the others panicked and scrambled for cover. Dixon dropped another one, hitting the running man between the shoulder blades. Then he leaped toward the jeep in the hope that he could start the engine and get out of here before the rebels gathered their wits.

All he needed was a small lead. He had been the hunter most of his life, but on occasion he had been the hunted, too.

It might have worked, but he hadn't counted on the fact that one of the rebels had walked on down the trail to see what was up ahead and now was behind him. The man came running back and opened fire with the machine gun he carried. Dixon had no warning before the slugs laced into the back of his legs and spilled him off his feet. He yelled in pain.

But he kept his wits about him and rolled over to spot the gunner running toward him. The man skidded to a stop and tried to open fire again, but Dixon shot him first. Blood sprayed into the air from the rebel's bullet-torn throat, forming a parabola as the impact flipped him backward.

Dixon knew he was bleeding out from the multiple wounds in his legs. He had only moments to live, and that reduced everything to the starkest, most primitive terms. He wanted to take as many of the bastards with him as he could, so he rolled onto his belly again and started firing as the rebels charged him.

Through the red haze that was slowly dropping over his vision, he saw one man fall, then another, and then the red began turning to black and he knew he was slipping away . . .

Then the oddest thing happened. A great wind began to beat at him, and a deafening noise descended on him. Just before he lost consciousness, he realized that the two things were connected and figured out where they came from.

The beating of a helicopter's rotors.

When Dixon came to, he had to lick his lips a couple of times before he could rasp, "Am I . . . dead?"

"Not yet, old buddy-roo," a familiar voice said. "Somebody got the bright idea of keeping an eye on you to make sure you got out all right after you finished the job. When we saw that firefight break out, we swooped down to get you. You *did* finish the job, didn't you?"

"Y-yes. Am I going to . . . going to die?" he asked as he felt the helicopter bank in the air.

"I'm just a civil servant, not a doctor. But we're gonna get some help for you just as quick as we can, so you hang on, okay?" The man paused, then asked, "You still with me, Dixon? You stay with me, you hear?"

"I'm . . . here," Dixon said as the man's face swam into view above him. It was a bland, white man's face, the face of someone who ought to be selling insurance instead of treading the murky back roads of international espionage. "Do you think they can . . . save my legs?"

"Sure they can. You're gonna be good as new, buddy."

"For a spy . . . you always were . . . a terrible liar, Clark."

CHAPTER 21

London, two years before the New Sun

Megan Sinclair leaned closer to the young man and whispered in his ear, "Your suite? Half an hour?"

His eyes were big with anticipation. He swallowed and said, "Oh, my, yes, please."

"You're sure you can get away from your minders by then?" Megan asked.

"They'll do whatever I tell them to. They work for me, you know."

Actually, they don't, Megan thought. They work for this young man's father. So it was possible the bodyguards might pretend to go along with his orders while still keeping an eye on him without his being aware of it.

She'd just have to keep an eye out herself.

She gave him a sultry smile and did the quick little up-and-down trick with her eyebrows that she knew excited men, then moved away from him to mingle with the crowd in the big hotel ball-room. She sipped from the flute of champagne in her hand, and when she'd finished it she snagged another from a passing waiter in a red jacket.

It hadn't been easy to get an invitation to this exclusive, black-tie charity event, but a few weeks of effort had managed it. Megan had a lot of contacts and had worked them for all they were worth. Even at that, she probably wouldn't have been able to swing it if any important members of the royal family had been attending. There was nobility in the room, but more of the garden-variety type.

She wasn't interested in noblemen. The young man she had targeted with her attention was the son of an industrialist and financier who had risen from nothing, the offspring of Moroccan immigrants, to become one of the richest men in England. He had established a trust fund worth five million dollars for his son, who had a reputation for being what earlier generations would have called a playboy and a wastrel.

Megan liked that word, wastrel. She supposed that was because she was an old-fashioned romantic at heart.

And what could be more romantic than stealing from the filthy rich?

From the corner of her eye, she watched as Peter Mahmoud spoke to his bodyguards and then left the room. The two burly men followed him. Megan knew they would accompany him up to his suite, but once he was safely inside maybe they would seize the opportunity for a little downtime.

She would believe that when she actually saw it, though.

When she judged that she had killed enough

time, she started to leave the party herself. She was well aware of the heads that turned and the eyes that watched her go. The long waves of her hair were like dark honey, and the classic little black dress she wore showed off the sleek lines of her body to their full advantage. More than one man had told her that her eyes were deep green pools in which they would happily drown. She looked like a successful attorney, or a business executive on her way straight to the top of the corporate ladder.

A few of the male guests spoke to her on her way out of the ballroom and tried to convince her to stay, but Megan turned them aside with a smile and a gently humorous comment or two. She'd had plenty of experience at deflecting passes, since she had spent several years surrounded almost entirely by men.

The ballroom was on the third floor of the hotel. She timed it so that she was able to get in an elevator by herself and start down. But she stopped it at the second floor, got out, walked quickly past some meeting rooms, and slipped through a door that opened onto the fire stairs.

The stairwell was deserted, as she had expected it to be. She went up nine flights to the tenth floor, which was also the top floor. It was divided into two suites, one being used by Peter Mahmoud, the other empty tonight since it cost a small fortune to book it.

Peter had a large fortune.

Megan eased the stairwell door open a crack and peered through it. The door opened onto a short corridor. The elevator was at one end of it, two doors at the other end. The door to Peter's suite was to the left.

No one was waiting outside it. Maybe the bodyguards really had left.

Megan couldn't see behind her to the elevator, though, and she couldn't open the door far enough to look in that direction without being seen. So she eased it closed again, walked back down to the ninth floor, and went out into the corridor there. She was in superb condition, so all the going up and down stairs hadn't winded her.

She summoned the elevator, then rode it up one flight to the tenth floor. When the door slid open, she stepped out with an air of unconcern, as if she had just come from the party in the ballroom down on three.

As she started toward the doors to the suites, a British-accented voice said behind her, "Hold on there a moment, miss."

Megan put a smile on her face as she turned and said sweetly, "Yes?" She let a trace of her native New Orleans creep into her voice. Most men couldn't resist a beautiful woman with a Southern accent.

This one looked like he didn't give a damn where she was from. Big, shaven-headed, broken-nosed, clearly not comfortable in the tuxedo he wore. He glared at her and said, "You're not on the list of approved visitors on this floor, miss."

"How do you know?" she asked coyly. "Do you have it memorized?"

"As a matter of fact, yeah. It's only got two people on it. Wasn't much of a chore."

His voice held a trace of dry wit, and to Megan's

surprise, she found herself liking this guy. Even more surprising, she was attracted to him.

Not that she didn't have the usual appetites. Very healthy ones, in fact. But she'd always been able to switch them off when she was working.

Well, it was nothing to worry about. No matter what she was feeling, she wasn't going to let it distract her from the job at hand.

She frowned slightly as she took a step toward him.

"Isn't this the ninth floor?" she asked.

"Tenth. And I suspect you know that."

She tried the coy smile again and said, "You caught me. But doesn't it make a difference that Mr. Mahmoud invited me up here?"

"Which Mr. Mahmoud?"

"Peter."

The bodyguard shook his head stoically. "I work for the lad's father. He and Peter are the only ones allowed up here. You'll have to go back down to the party." For the first time, he smiled. The expression didn't make him any less ugly, but it made a throb go through Megan anyway. He went on, "Nice try, though. But you know the boy's only twenty, don't you? He doesn't come into his trust fund until next year."

"Close enough," Megan said.

And in fact, she was. Her hand came up and drove the hypodermic needle into the side of his neck. The syringe was small enough that she had been able to conceal it in her palm, but the drug inside it packed plenty of punch, which she delivered with a push of her thumb against the plunger.

The guard made a grab for her in the second he had before he passed out. Megan darted back, kicked her shoes off, and bent sideways at the waist as she drove her right heel into his midsection. That doubled him over, and the drug took care of the rest. He hit the floor, out cold.

Too bad, Megan thought as she shook her head. He didn't seem like a bad guy . . . and he would probably lose his job when this was all over.

She slipped back into her shoes, tucked the empty syringe away in her handbag, and bent to take hold of the unconscious man's coat collar. She had spotted the little alcove with a tiny round table and a chair where he had been sitting to keep an eye on the elevator. He was a load, but she was stronger than her slender frame seemed to indicate. She dragged him in there, took the gun from the shoulder holster under his tux, dropped the magazine, and ejected the round that was in the chamber. The magazine and the extra bullet went in her bag, too.

Then she straightened her dress, took a deep breath, and sauntered toward the door to Peter Mahmoud's suite.

He looked surprised when he swung the door open in response to her knock.

"You came!" he said, then quickly went on, "I mean, I didn't really expect to see you up here. I didn't think Keegan would let you get by him."

"Who's Keegan?" Megan asked, all sincere innocence.

"The minder who stayed to watch over me." Peter leaned to the side to look past her along the short corridor. "Huh. I don't see him."

"Maybe he stepped out for a smoke." Megan smiled and rested a hand on Peter's chest. He had taken off his coat and tie but still wore the tuxedo pants, cummerbund, and white shirt. "No matter where he got off to, let's not waste the opportunity."

"I should say not." He stepped aside to let her into the suite. "Please. I have some champagne . . ."

"I've already had quite a bit, but some more would be lovely," Megan said. "You don't mind if I'm a little drunk, do you? I promise not to get *too* crazy."

"Don't make promises you can't keep," he told her.

Her tolerance for banter like this was pretty small. As soon as the door was closed behind her, she moved into his arms, wrapped her arms around his neck, and pressed her body against his. Again Peter seemed surprised, but obviously he didn't mind her boldness. He brought his mouth down on hers.

He wasn't the greatest kisser in the world, Megan thought. But he was young yet and certainly had plenty of enthusiasm. He would improve with practice, and he would get plenty of practice because he was young, handsome, and rich. He still had years to look forward to in which an abundance of beautiful girls would throw themselves at him. She hoped he was smart enough to appreciate just how lucky he was.

In the meantime, she had work to do. She was going to make him slightly less rich. He wouldn't miss it, but it would be a fortune to her.

She jabbed a needle like the one she had used on Keegan into his neck.

Peter jerked back, his eyes widening in shock and pain.

"What . . . what did you—"

He threw a wild punch at her. She blocked it

easily and took him to the floor, which was so thickly carpeted in this fancy suite that it was almost like knocking him onto a mattress. He tried to struggle as she pinned him down, but the drug was already taking hold and he weakened rapidly.

The shot didn't knock him out like the one she had given Keegan. It just made him too groggy and feeble to put up a fight. And it had an effect on his brain, too, removing all the safeguards that might have been there otherwise. Megan figured she could have seduced him into telling her what she wanted to know, but this way was so much quicker.

"Tell me the code for your trust fund drawing account," she said.

She wouldn't be able to touch the bulk of the fund, but Peter's father made sure he had plenty for day-to-day expenses, which in Peter's case could be astronomical compared to a normal person's. Megan's contact at the bank had assured her that the balance in the account never dropped below half a million pounds and might be twice as much as that.

Peter said groggily, "Wha . . . wha' you do—"

Megan slapped him hard enough to make his head jerk to the side.

"The code," she repeated. "Now."

He started slurring numbers. She struggled to understand him and commit the string of figures to memory. When he was finished, she stood up and went to the laptop that she had already spotted sitting open on an antique writing table.

It took her only a moment to get into the bank's database. Her hacking skills were excellent. She had a natural talent for it, and her years in Special

Forces had only increased her abilities. She had been driven to succeed, in no small part because there were so few women in the unit. Ninety-five percent of male soldiers couldn't make it; the odds against women were even higher. They had to be even better.

She typed in the code Peter had given her.

ACCESS DENIED.

Megan took a deep breath. Maybe she had hit a wrong key somewhere in there. It was a long number, after all. She went through it again, slower this time.

An account screen popped up. She sighed in relief. Her glitch had cost her a moment or two, but that was all. Quickly, she initiated the transfer and watched in satisfaction as the money in Peter's account began draining into her Cayman Islands account.

Out of curiosity, she looked to see what the balance was in his trust fund. Her eyes grew big with amazement. She had known he was rich, or soon would be, but that number was just . . . astounding. And that was just a trust fund. Peter's father, Hasan Mahmoud, was many, many times richer.

Maybe she had made a mistake. Maybe she should have played a long game and gotten Peter to marry her.

Even better, Hasan was a widower. He might have enjoyed having a gorgeous young American wife . . .

The transfer finished, ending that line of speculation in Megan's mind. Time to get out of here.

She had just stood up from the writing table

when the door to the suite burst open and Keegan charged in like a bull.

That was crazy. He should have been out cold for at least another half-hour. His metabolism had to be incredible for him to start throwing off the drug's effects this soon.

But he wasn't at the top of his game, that was for sure. He swung a wild punch at her that she easily avoided. She chopped at the side of his neck, but she might as well have been hitting a block of wood for all the effect it had.

As he lunged at her again, she bent low and swept his legs out from under him. He hit the floor with a crash. She started to dart past him.

He caught her ankle and dragged her down. She cried, "Oh!" and kicked at his face. That didn't make him let go. His fingers were locked around her ankle like bands of iron.

She was afraid she was going to have to hurt him to get away. She was reaching for the little knife she carried in her bag when more men rushed into the suite from the hallway. They had guns, and they leveled the weapons at her as they shouted for her to surrender.

She looked at Keegan, who was staring along the sleek lines of her legs as he clung to her ankle. He had to have triggered some sort of alarm when he came to. She said, "You damn fool, look what you've done."

"It's a . . . soddin' shame . . . innit?" he forced out.

Then he lost consciousness again, his forehead thudding against the floor, but too late to keep her from being captured.

CHAPTER 22

Indianapolis, two years before the New Sun

Braden Cole watched from his van, parked up the block from the motel. It was one of the budget places, and Cole thought that if it were him planning to cheat on his wife, he would have taken his girlfriend to a better rendezvous than this. He would have been ashamed to ask a woman to sneak around in such a low-class fashion.

Of course, he thought as he pushed his glasses up, he wasn't married and never had been. His relationships with women had all been of the commercial variety, and not just the obvious sort. So he didn't really know what he would do under the same circumstances, now, did he? He told himself that he shouldn't be judgmental about his targets.

After all, it was enough that he killed them. He didn't have to look down on them, too.

It was hard not to get a little judgmental, though, when you dealt with the dregs of humanity for the most part. Adulterers, embezzlers, blackmailers, abusers . . . You had to have done *something* pretty bad for somebody to want you dead badly enough to pay a total stranger to do the job. Now and then a client hired Cole's services strictly for reasons of profit, but usually there was a personal angle to it as well.

Well, without all the pissed-off people in the world, he wouldn't have a job, would he?

The door of the unit he was watching opened. The woman came out first. Her name was Holly McAleer. She was blond, thirty-five, reasonably attractive. She worked at the same federal office building as the man who followed her out of the motel room, Allan Dubbert, who was as bland and unappealing as his name. In Cole's opinion, Dubbert was batting out of his league as far as Holly was concerned.

But there was no accounting for the taste of a woman looking for an affair, was there?

Even though there were layers of cut-outs and intermediaries between him and the client, Cole felt relatively certain that Margaret Dubbert was the one who had hired him to a) make sure her husband really was cheating on her, and b) kill the son of a bitch and the slut who was sleeping with him. Although it was possible that Holly McAleer's husband Todd was the client.

Either way, somebody was both suspicious and vindictive, and it hadn't taken Cole long to determine that the suspicions had merit. At one point in his life he had been a licensed private investigator, and a skilled one, at that. He could have stayed in that line of work, but branching out had proven to be so much more lucrative.

Dubbert and Holly went to his car. It would have

complicated things if she had brought her car, too, but as was their habit, they had left it in the vast parking lot of the office building four miles away. They really were careless, as if they believed that nobody would ever catch them.

They paused outside the car. Holly leaned in for a kiss, which Dubbert gave her with one arm around her. Then he opened her door—chivalrous bastard, wasn't he, thought Cole—and went around to get behind the wheel.

Cole hadn't done anything so crude as to rig the detonator to the ignition switch. That took the control out of his hands. He liked to choose the precise moment himself. He waited until Dubbert turned to Holly and smiled and she smiled back at him and he opened his mouth to say something . . .

That was when Cole pushed the button.

The blast that engulfed the car in a fireball shook the ground. Cole felt it a block away in the van. He smiled faintly as he set the remote on the seat beside him and started the engine. Most people wouldn't drive away from the scene of an explosion like that one. They would want to see what had happened. Somebody might notice him leaving and get suspicious, but it didn't really matter. The van was completely nondescript, the license plates were smeared with mud so as to be unreadable, and anyway, it was stolen and he would dump it in the airport's long-term parking lot later tonight. Nor did he have to worry about fingerprints, since his had been surgically altered so as to not be on file anywhere in the world.

He drove away at a leisurely pace as the bombed car burned furiously in the night behind him. Like any other law-abiding citizen, he even stopped at a red light a couple of blocks away and didn't go on until the light turned green again.

He had just started across the intersection when a pickup with a drunk driver at the wheel ran the light, rammed into the passenger door of Cole's van, and knocked the vehicle on its side. Cole was so shocked by the unexpectedness of it all that for a long moment after the grinding crash all he could do was lie there, not even thinking about trying to get out.

Then he smelled smoke and heard the crackle of flames and knew that he had to climb up the now-vertical seat and squirm through the crumpled, shattered window before the fire hit the gas tank. He reached for the seat belt release.

Jammed.

No matter how hard he tried, it wouldn't come loose.

He had a knife in his pocket. He could cut the seat belt with it. Trying to stay calm as he worked his fingers into his pocket, he searched for the knife.

He couldn't find it. How could it have slipped out while he was being thrown around? It should be there.

But it wasn't, and the seat belt release still wouldn't work, and Braden Cole started to laugh as he listened to the fire burning around him. If that didn't beat all. The detonator remote was still somewhere in the van, more than likely, and other things he wouldn't want the cops to find, but none of that mattered anymore.

Nothing mattered except the sheer irony that made Cole laugh.

Then the windshield, which had somehow survived the impact, shattered only a few feet away, spraying him with glass, and hands reached through, groping for him.

Help had arrived.

Maybe he wouldn't die here after all.

South Dakota, two years before the New Sun

Jackie Thornton pushed the curtain aside a little, just enough to glance out across the front yard of his ex-wife's house. He stepped quickly to the side and let the curtain drop. He was sure the police had a SWAT team out there with snipers covering all the windows. He didn't want to give them time to line up a shot at him. If he was being honest with himself, he would have had to admit that he didn't much care if he lived or died, but he didn't want to go out until he was good and ready.

And he wouldn't be ready until Maggie Louise Redmond had paid for her sins.

Maggie Louise Thornton, he amended. She had taken his name when she married him, and it was hers for life, no matter whether she'd divorced him or not. It sure didn't matter that she had married that fella Greg Redmond. *He* was the one sinning, sleeping with another man's wife the way he was.

Well, he wouldn't do it anymore, because he was lying on the floor under the arched entrance from the living room into the dining room, staring sightlessly at the ceiling. The blood had stopped leaking from the red-rimmed hole in his forehead where Jackie had shot him. There really hadn't been much blood, probably because Redmond had died so fast.

A quiet moan came from Maggie. She was regaining consciousness. Jackie hadn't meant to hit her so hard, and he felt bad about that. He'd just been trying to get her attention. He wanted her to die, but he didn't necessarily want her to suffer.

"What . . . what have you . . ." The words trailed off into a gasp. "Oh, my God! Greg!"

Jackie looked over his shoulder and saw her crawling toward the corpse.

"Might as well save your breath," he told her. "He's dead, like he deserves to be for takin' another man's woman."

She ignored him—that was no surprise; when they'd been married she had ignored him most of the time—and threw herself on her husband's body as sobs shook her. Jackie just shook his head. She oughtn't be carrying on so. Redmond had had it coming.

The phone rang.

Jackie looked at it. It was a cordless phone, sitting with its base on a little table next to Redmond's chair where he watched TV. The shrill rings got on Jackie's nerves in a hurry, and it didn't seem like the damn thing was going to stop ringing, so with a sigh he went over to it and picked it up with the hand that wasn't holding a gun.

"Yeah?"

"Is that you, Jackie Thornton?"

Jackie recognized the voice. It belonged to Caleb McBurney, the chief of police of this small town that sat on the vast plains. McBurney had arrested him more than once for this, that, and the other. The charges usually involved drunk and disorderly, disturbing the peace, and bodily assault. McBurney had hauled him in on armed robbery charges, too, when Jackie learned the painful lesson that if you live in a town of less than a thousand people and everybody knows everybody else, it's probably not a good idea to hold up the local grocery store.

But that was all in the past. They had thought he was just a cheap crook, but now they knew better. Now he was a killer. A mad-dog killer.

He liked the sound of that.

Those thoughts flashed through his mind as he said into the phone, "What is it you want, Chief McBurney?"

"You know what I want, Jackie. I want you to come out of there with your hands empty and in the air where we can see 'em. Once you've done that, then we can talk about whatever's happened in there and see if we can straighten this mess out."

"Ain't nothin' to straighten out, Chief," Jackie said. "Greg Redmond's dead. I shot him, the damn homewrecker."

"Ohhhh, hell," McBurney said with a long, weary sigh. "Blast it, Jackie, why'd you have to go and do that?"

"I told you. He stole my wife. Man's got a right to defend what's his, don't he?"

"Greg Redmond didn't even live here when Maggie Louise left you, Jackie! She didn't meet him until later, and you know it. He didn't have anything to do with your marriage breaking up."

"Well, that's not the way I see it," Jackie said calmly.

"Maggie Louise left you because you couldn't

stay out of trouble," McBurney went on as if he hadn't heard what Jackie said. "She didn't want to stay married to a man who couldn't hold a job, couldn't stay out of jail, and spent most of his time hanging around with a couple of crazy, meth-cooking skinheads!"

"Now, don't you be talkin' bad about the Franklin brothers, Chief. Those boys have been good friends to me."

"Good friends, hell! I know about how they've got you delivering that junk all over the county. Damn it, Jackie—!" The chief's voice softened slightly as he went on, "I knew your mama and daddy. I knew you when you were in school, playing ball. We all hoped you'd go to college, and when you went in the Army instead, we thought that might do you some good, but you can't . . . you just can't seem to settle down!"

Jackie sighed again and said, "I tried, Chief. I surely did. But there's just somethin' wild in me, I guess. There's only one way this is gonna end."

"Jackie, don't—"

He set the phone down without disconnecting the call, then turned and pointed the gun at Maggie Louise, who was watching him with a look of sheer terror on her face.

"You should've been faithful to me," he said.

She screamed.

Jackie heard glass break somewhere to his left, then a thud and a soft pop. Suddenly the room was full of blinding, choking smoke. Tear gas! The bastards had shot tear gas through the window.

He started pulling the trigger, but he couldn't see where he was aiming anymore. He just shot blindly, hoping that one of the shots would connect with Maggie Louise. It didn't matter if he emptied the gun. He'd still wave it at the officers when they broke into the house, and that would be enough. He'd never leave here alive. Suicide by cop, some called it. As good a way as any to go out. He didn't want to hurt anybody who didn't have it coming.

He heard the crash as they used a battering ram on the door and broke it open. He turned toward the sound as the gun's hammer clicked on an empty chamber.

"I'll kill you all!" he bellowed, even though he had no intention of killing anybody else. "I'll—"

Something hit him in the back of the knees and knocked his legs out from under him. His face bounced on the carpet as he landed on it. A weight landed on his back, and fists rained down on his head.

"You crazy son of a bitch!" Maggie Louise screamed as she battered him. "You crazy son of a bitch!"

"Don't shoot!" a man yelled. "Hold your fire!"

No! They were supposed to kill him. This was all going wrong, Jackie thought as the weight went away and somebody grabbed his hands and jerked them behind his back. He felt handcuffs go around his wrists and snap into place.

He couldn't see anything because his eyes were stinging so bad from the tear gas, and he could barely talk because it made him cough and choke so much. But as he was hauled to his feet he managed to say, "No, no . . . this ain't right . . . this ain't the way it was supposed to be!"

There was no getting around it. He had screwed up again.

CHAPTER 23

*A federal detention facility, somewhere in the U.S.,
six months before the New Sun*

With the sun shining brightly, the exercise yard looked warm, but actually there was a bone-numbing cold in the air, the sort of cold you get on the high plains when the sky clears and the wind dies down and the bottom seems to fall out of the thermometer.

The three guards huddling in their parkas would have rather been somewhere else. Anywhere as long as it was warm and maybe there was a cup of hot coffee.

Their orders said they had to be out here, though, because Madigan was.

And Ellis "Bronco" Madigan didn't seem to feel the cold. In fact, he was stripped to the waist as he worked out with the weights set up in one corner of the yard, revealing his massively muscled, heavily tattooed torso. Those muscles worked smoothly and easily as he lifted more weight than a human being should have been able to lift.

Of course, there had been a considerable amount of debate over the years as to whether or not Bronco Madigan really was human.

Some people seemed to think that he had been created in some mad scientist's lab.

Others were more of the opinion that he wasn't a creature of science but rather a demon from some dark hell.

Either way, he looked the part.

The only hair on his head was a neatly trimmed goatee and his eyebrows. His scalp was as bald and gleaming as a skull. Tattooed across his shoulder blades was a winged dragon with the head of a laughing Satan. On his arms were pentagrams and other sinister, eldritch symbols. On his bulging right pectoral muscle was a swastika. An inverted cross decorated the left pectoral. He was every normal person's nightmare.

One of the guards clapped his gloved hands together for warmth. While he was doing that his gaze strayed across the yard, and he said to his companions, "Oh, crap. Here comes the other one."

Calvin Watson hadn't taken off his shirt, but he wasn't wearing a coat, either. His breath fogged and plumed around his head like a wreath of smoke. He was a couple of inches shorter than Madigan's six-five, but his shoulders were maybe an inch wider than the taller man's. His black skin was tattooed as heavily as Madigan's white skin was, only with urban gang symbols. He wasn't bald, but his hair was cropped extremely close.

Watson couldn't move very fast because he wore leg irons. His wrists were shackled together, too. Even with those precautions being taken, sharp-shooters up on the wall had a bead on him, just as other guards kept their rifles trained on Madigan anytime he was out in the open. Nobody wanted to take any chances with either of these two men.

Between them they had killed at least forty people.

The exact number of their victims was unclear, but Madigan had been convicted on twenty-two counts of murder, Watson on eighteen. They were both suspected of being involved in numerous other crimes, including homicides, but there hadn't been enough evidence to bring charges against them in those cases, usually because the bodies were never found or because witnesses mysteriously disap-peared before they could testify for the grand jury.

But the murders were enough to put these two away for life, especially combined with multiple charges of attempted murder, rape, extortion, con-spiracy, drug trafficking, arson, kidnapping, and assorted other felonies.

The only reason they hadn't gotten the death penalty was because the feds had intervened in their cases and persuaded the judges that Madigan and Watson would be more valuable alive. They were important figures in the criminal underworlds of the Midwest and the West Coast, and if they could be persuaded to talk, they might lead to people even higher up the chain . . .

So far Madigan and Watson hadn't said anything to federal interrogators except for the occasional anatomically impossible suggestion.

They had been talking to each other, though,

here in the federal pen. Talking trash. Like now, when Madigan set the barbell he'd been using back on its stand and said, "What are you doing here, you—"

He finished the question with an obscenely modified ethnic slur.

Watson grinned at him and said, "That's hate speech. That's against the rules. You might hurt my feelings."

"Why don't you go—" More invective spewed out of Madigan's mouth, followed by, "This is my time to work out, and you know it."

"They had to rearrange my busy schedule," Watson said mockingly. "Got a meeting with my new lawyer in a little while."

"How many lawyers does that make?"

Watson's shoulders rose and fell in a shrug.

"I've lost count. For some reason they don't like me. Important thing is, I get my hour outside now."

Madigan glared at the guards who had brought Watson out here into the yard.

"Can he do that?" Madigan asked.

"The warden says he can," one of the guards replied.

Madigan described the warden in unflattering terms, then said, "He's just scared of some chicken-shit lawsuit. Doesn't want the ACLU on his back screaming about discrimination."

"Got to be fair," Watson said. "Now get your ass outta here, white boy."

One of Madigan's guards said, "Come on, Bronco. Maybe we can bring you back later, get you a little extra time today."

Madigan nodded. He still wore his leg irons, but

his shackles had been removed so that he could work with the weights. Now he stuck his arms out so the shackles could be fastened around his wrists again.

At least, that's what it looked like he was doing at first. But as Watson took another step toward the weights, Madigan suddenly whirled and lunged at the huge black man.

Madigan's attack was so swift that Watson didn't have time to brace himself. The impact as Madigan slammed into him drove him backward. With his legs in irons like they were, Watson couldn't catch his balance. He crashed to the ground with Madigan on top of him.

One of the guards yelled, "Don't shoot, don't shoot!" into a walkie-talkie, letting the sharpshooters on the wall know to hold their fire. A couple of others yanked short clubs from holsters on their belts, underneath the parkas, and rushed forward to bludgeon Madigan on his bare back as he tried to get his hands around Watson's throat.

The blows seemed to have no effect on Madigan. He ignored them as he continued grappling with Watson. He tried to drive his knee into Watson's groin, but Watson twisted from side to side, blocking Madigan's efforts with his thighs.

He hammered a punch against Madigan's left ear. Madigan might not have felt it when the guards hit him, but Watson's fist had so much power behind it that it couldn't be ignored. The blow slewed Madigan's head to the side and unbalanced him enough that Watson was able to heave him off.

Watson rolled away and came to his feet just ahead of Madigan. With incredible agility, Watson let himself fall backward and kicked Madigan in the face with both feet while Madigan was still on one knee. That left both men stretched out on the ground. Madigan was stunned, though, and Watson wasn't. The black man scrambled up and dived at Madigan. He looped his arms over Madigan's shaven head and tightened the shackles against his throat.

"Now you're gonna die, you damn skinhead," Watson growled in Madigan's ear.

Madigan's face started turning purple as Watson cut off his air. Bucking and heaving, Madigan fought to get loose, but to no avail. His knees scrabbled around on the asphalt yard, but he couldn't get enough purchase to throw Watson off him. His hands were free, but he couldn't pry the chain away from his throat, no matter how hard he tried.

The guards had all backed off, and now the one with the walkie-talkie gave the order to fire. Shots sounded from the top of the wall, but they weren't the high-pitched cracks of regular rifles. Watson stiffened as the needles of the tranquilizer rounds pierced his shirt and stabbed through skin into muscle. The drugs they pumped into him spread rapidly through his body along with the blood driven by his wildly pounding heart. The adrenaline coursing through him just made the knockout rounds take effect that much quicker.

Watson went limp as he passed out.

Finally, Madigan was able to pull his head out of the other convict's deadly grip. He rolled Watson off him and surged to his knees, gasping for breath. As soon as he got enough air in his lungs, he let out of a bellow of rage, clubbed his hands together, and raised his arms, obviously intending to batter Watson's face until the man was dead.

Madigan paused before the blow could fall and lowered his head to stare stupidly at the hypodermic rounds protruding from his chest where they had just struck him. After a moment he snarled, ripped the needles loose, and threw them to the side.

"Good Lord!" one of the guards gasped. "There's enough of the stuff in him to knock out a horse."

Madigan seemed to forget about Watson. He lumbered to his feet and swung around toward the guards. As he did, two more rounds fired from the wall struck him in the back. He staggered a little as he took a step, then weaved wildly as he tried to take another. He flung his arms out to the side in an attempt to balance himself on his tree trunk-like legs.

It was no use. The drugs finally caught up to him, and his eyes rolled up in their sockets. He toppled forward, again like a tree—one that had been cut down at the base. The ground didn't actually shake when he landed on it . . . but he was so big it seemed like it should have.

The guards were sweating now despite the cold.

"Just think," one of them said. "They're both in here for life. That means we're never gonna get rid of those monsters!"

CHAPTER 24

Bakersfield, California, six months before the New Sun

"Don't you ever sweat?" the member of the crew in the front passenger seat asked Nick Hatcher.

"Why would I sweat?" Nick asked from behind the wheel of the getaway van. "The weather's nice and cool today."

One of the men in the backseat laughed.

"Nick doesn't get rattled. That's why he's the best wheelman in the business."

"Maybe not *the* best," Nick said, not taking his eyes off the traffic around them. "Oh, who am I trying to kid? I am the best."

"See?" Chadbourne said. He had put this crew together and was the nominal leader. "That's how you stay alive in this business, by surrounding yourself with good people."

"I think you mean talented people," Nick said. "We're bank robbers. We can't actually be considered *good*."

Chadbourne laughed and said, "We can debate philosophy later. There's the bank, just up the block."

Nick knew perfectly well where the bank was. He had scouted it half a dozen times in the past two weeks, since the crew had gathered in Bakersfield in response to Chadbourne's summons. He knew every building, every foot of sidewalk, every pothole in the pavement for blocks around. Preparation was the key to success . . . and often to survival.

The other man in the front seat was named Harris. He was short and stocky, with curly black hair and a neatly trimmed beard. In the backseat with Chadbourne was Galloway, tall and lanky with blond hair that tended to fall across his forehead. Chadbourne was the oldest of the bunch, close to fifty, square-faced, mostly bald. Since he'd first gone away to juvie at fourteen, he had spent almost exactly as much time behind bars as he had out. That didn't mean he wasn't good at what he did, though. It was just that he pulled so many jobs, the law of averages kept catching up to him.

Nick was the youngest member of the crew, but he had been at the game long enough that he was considered an old pro, anyway. He had never been caught, never done time. Although it wasn't evident when he was behind the wheel, he was tall and well-built, with the body of a tight end. His brown hair tended to stick straight up, which was why he kept it cut fairly short.

The bank's parking lot sat to the right of the building. Nick hung a bogus handicapped parking placard from the rearview mirror as he pulled in. All four handicapped spaces, the closest ones to the bank's front door, were empty at the moment. He parked in the one all the way to the left. A wide sidewalk was between him and the street.

He would have been able to get out quicker if he'd backed in, but a van backing up like that at a bank might draw too many curious glances. Pulling straight in like he had made everything look normal, which was exactly what they wanted.

Chadbourne put on a baseball cap and tugged down the brim a little. He picked up a cane and opened the door beside him. People resented an able-bodied person taking up a handicapped space, which meant they were more likely to notice something like that. If somebody got out moving stiffly and using a cane, though, that was all it took to alleviate suspicion. Even if the other people who got out of the vehicle—in this case, Harris and Galloway—didn't seem to be handicapped, it didn't matter. Chadbourne's slow-moving, slightly awkward gait was enough to justify parking there.

Harris wore a baseball cap, too. Galloway was in a hoodie with the hood pulled up. The air was cool enough today to warrant that. Some crews rushed in wearing ski masks or helmets and body armor, so that things got tense and potentially violent right away. Chadbourne and his men strolled into a bank, unobtrusively keeping their heads turned just at the right moments to make sure the cameras didn't get a good enough shot of them to be identified in court. Only after they were inside and had sized up everything would the guns come out.

Nick drummed his fingers on the steering wheel as he watched the three of them disappear into the bank. He wasn't really nervous; the drumming was just an idle habit, something to pass the time. His gaze shifted back and forth between the bank's front door and the traffic passing by on the street.

He spotted a Bakersfield police car coming toward the bank. No reason to think it would turn in. There hadn't been time even for a silent alarm to go out, and Chadbourne was good at keeping such things from happening in the first place.

But the cop car turned into the bank parking lot, anyway. Two officers were in it, a man and a woman. The woman was driving. She parked half a dozen spaces away from the van, but nobody was parked between the two vehicles so Nick got a good look at her. She was pretty, with a lightly freckled face and red hair pulled into a short ponytail that hung at the back of her neck.

She looked over at Nick and smiled.

He returned the smile. What else was he going to do? Cop or no cop, she was a pretty girl, and any man would have smiled at her if she smiled at him first.

Barely moving his lips, Nick said, "Cops in the parking lot."

The Bluetooth phone in his ear was connected to an identical one in Chadbourne's ear. Nick knew that somebody could be looking right at Chadbourne and never see a hint on the man's face of the warning he had just received. The guy was that in control of himself.

The redhead's partner got out of the car. She stayed behind the wheel and kept the engine running. Her partner probably just wanted to dash into the bank to cash a check or make a loan payment or something. Whatever errand had brought him here, why couldn't he have taken care of it online like a normal person?

No, thought Nick, some people still liked to actually *go* to the bank, and obviously this jackhole was one of them.

"One coming in," Nick told Chadbourne.

The cop disappeared into the bank.

This didn't have to be a disaster. It was possible Chadbourne, Harris, and Galloway hadn't made their move yet. They might still be pretending to be customers, in which case they would just wait for the cop to conclude his business and leave.

And if they *had* shown their guns, the heads-up Nick had provided them should have given them enough time to get ready and get the drop on the officer. They could disarm him, put him on the floor with the others . . .

Shots blasted inside the bank.

"Damn," Nick said softly, under his breath.

The numbers started counting down in his brain. Chadbourne and the others knew they had thirty seconds to get back out here. That was as long as he was obligated to wait. Once the count hit zero, he was gone, baby. That was the way it had to be.

The female cop got out of the car in a hurry as soon as she heard the shots. She was talking into the radio on her shoulder as she drew her weapon and trotted toward the front door. She was using a two-handed grip and advancing rapidly but cautiously, just as they had taught her at the academy.

She was only halfway to the door, though, when she stopped short and turned to look at the van. Her gaze came straight through the windshield and into Nick's eyes, and just like that he understood.

She knew.

She had figured out he was the wheelman, and instinct told her to take him down, but an even stronger instinct commanded her to get inside and help her partner. He might be hurt, maybe even dead.

The internal debate she had lasted only a second, but that was long enough for the door of the bank to fly open and for Galloway to charge out. Chadbourne and Harris were right behind him. Harris had an arm around Chadbourne, and the older man was limping and stumbling for real now. He was hit.

The female cop whirled toward them and yelled for them to stop. Galloway didn't slow down. He fired on the run, flame spouting from the muzzle of his revolver as he blazed away. Nick breathed hard through his nose as he saw the cop's body jerk under the impact of the bullets. She probably had a vest in the car, but she hadn't taken the time to put it on. A rookie mistake.

But even though she was hit, she stayed on her feet and returned fire. Blood sprayed in the air as one of her bullets hit Galloway in the left cheekbone and blew away a big chunk of his face. He went down.

Harris brought up his gun in his free hand and triggered a shot. It missed because blood loss had caught up to the cop and dropped her to her knees. The slug went past the van and whined off the concrete of the parking lot somewhere behind Nick.

The cop swayed back and forth but fired again. She was either really good or phenomenally lucky, because her bullet shattered Harris's left shoulder and knocked him away from Chadbourne, who fell to the sidewalk without Harris's support.

The cop slumped to the side then, done with this battle. Probably done, period. Grimacing, Harris scrambled to his feet and loped past her toward the van. Nick leaned over and had the door open by the time Harris got there.

The count had reached zero almost half a minute earlier, but Nick hadn't been able to abandon his partners in the middle of a gunfight like that. It would have been different if they'd never even made it out of the bank. He would have been in the wind by now.

As it was, he had to grab Harris's jacket and practically haul the wounded man into the front seat. With the door still swinging open, Nick threw the transmission into reverse and gunned back out of the parking space. He whipped the wheel around so violently that the van's rear corner clipped another vehicle parked in the lot. Then the entrance was in front of him and he squirted through it onto the street.

Lights were flashing in both directions.

"Close that door!" Nick yelled at Harris. The cops might not have a description of the van yet, but they would notice a vehicle speeding away from the vicinity of the attempted bank robbery with its passenger door flopping back and forth.

Harris reached for the door and fumbled with it, but he got it closed after a couple of seconds. Nick breathed a little easier.

A monumental snafu like this had been bound to happen sooner or later, he told himself. But things would be all right. Even if Chadbourne and Galloway survived their wounds, they wouldn't give up their partners. Harris needed medical attention, but he looked like he would pull through. Nick made a left, taking them off the street that ran by the bank. A few more turns, and they would be out of the woods.

Flashing lights appeared in the rearview mirror.

Nick bit back a curse. Somehow the cops must have gotten a description of the van. The redhead, maybe? Nick had thought she was either unconscious or dead, but she could have revived and put the description out on the radio.

Whatever the source of the bad luck, it was here and he just had to deal with it. He whipped the van into an alley.

More bad luck. The far end of the alley was blocked by a truck parked behind a store to make a delivery.

Nick slammed on the brakes, threw the van into reverse again. As he came out of the alley, a cop car screeched out of nowhere and plowed into the van's left rear. The collision slewed the boxy vehicle around. Nick hit the gas. It still ran, although the left rear wheel was making an ugly thumping sound.

Cop cars skidded up ahead, turning sideways to block the road. More behind, Nick saw in the mirrors.

Looked like his streak of not going to jail was finished. He took his foot off the gas.

"What are you slowin' down for?" Harris yelled. "We gotta get out of here!"

"There's nowhere to go," Nick told him. "We're boxed in."

"You're supposed to be the best wheelman in the world! You said so yourself! Now get us away from those cops!"

"We can't get away. It's over, Harris."

"The hell it is!" He reached under his shirt,

pulled out a hideaway gun, a little .32. He twisted in the seat to reach across his body and jab the barrel into Nick's side. "Drive, you son of a bitch!"

Nick could see only one way this was going to end—in a shootout with the cops that would probably leave both him and Harris dead, because with two of their own down the boys in blue weren't going to be in the mood for anything else—so he did what Harris told him. He drove.

He turned the wheel and drove right into a parked car.

The van was old enough that it didn't have a passenger side airbag, only one for the driver. It exploded out into Nick's face and cushioned the impact for him, but Harris was thrown into the windshield hard enough that it shattered and shredded his flesh as he wound up hanging halfway out of it, unconscious.

Nick kept his hands empty and in plain sight as cops surrounded the van, dragged him out, and threw him roughly to the pavement.

He wanted to ask if that cute female cop had made it, but he didn't figure that would be a very good idea.

CHAPTER 25

Langley, Virginia, one month after the New Sun

The windowless room Bill Elliott was in didn't exist. Langley was famous for being where the headquarters of the Central Intelligence Agency was located. That wasn't where Bill was. Any connection between the CIA and the outfit that leased this building was carefully hidden. Every yokel in the country knew about The Company. The people who knew about Bill's former and once again current employers numbered in the dozens.

Three men and a woman came into the room where Bill sat at a long, gleaming, marble-topped conference table. One of the men was Clark. He grinned at Bill and said, "Good to see you again, old buddy-roo. Looks like you've been busy since San Antonio."

Clark pointed at the thick file folder resting on the table under Bill's hand.

"You told me to look for who I wanted," Bill said. "I've been lookin'."

As the newcomers sat down around the end of

the table, he slid the file toward them. Then he reached over to an open laptop computer and hit a few keys. A big screen on the wall lit up.

"The information I'm about to go over is in that file," Bill said, "but it'll be quicker if I just tell you about it and let you study the stuff in more detail later. These are the candidates I've picked."

"Wait a minute," the woman said. "You were supposed to come up with a pool of potential candidates, Mr. Elliott, and we would pick the team."

"No offense, ma'am, but if you want me to lead this team, I'm gonna decide who's on it."

The woman frowned and looked over at Clark, who shrugged and said, "I told you he's got a mind of his own. But I trust his judgment."

"Very well," the woman said coldly. "We'll listen . . . but no guarantees."

"Fair enough," Bill said, "since I don't have any guarantees that these folks will go along with what we want. The odds are gonna be stacked pretty heavy against 'em, after all."

"Just get on with it," one of the other men said. "I have to get back to the White House so I can brief the president. He's been very clear that none of this can ever come back on him."

"We know," Clark said. "Can't have the president doing anything that might offend other countries . . . even countries that hate us and are trying to destroy us."

The other man flushed angrily.

"Can't we leave politics out of this?" he asked. "We have to put the good of the country first."

"Since when did your party ever put—" Clark stopped short, shook his head, and went on, "Forget it. It's a waste of breath arguing with you. Just tell the guy in the Oval Office that nothing we do will come back to bite him on the butt."

"You mean the president," the other man snapped.

"I mean the guy sitting in an office that he bought, just like the two bozos before him."

The third man started to get to his feet, saying, "If you're going to waste my time with your bickering—"

"Sit down, General," Bill drawled, even though the man was in civilian clothing.

"You're not supposed to know who I am, Mr. Elliott."

"I'll bear that in mind," Bill said dryly. "For now—and I say this with all due respect—all of you just shut the hell up and listen."

For a moment he thought at least two of them were going to storm out, but then they settled back in their chairs. Clark said, "Go on, Bill."

Bill tapped a key on the computer and an image appeared on the big screen on the wall. It showed a big man in combat gear with a sandy wasteland behind him.

"John Bailey," Bill said. "Did two tours in Iraq. Highly decorated. Then his squad was ambushed and wiped out except for Bailey and another soldier. Bailey was wounded. Got shipped home, and after he'd rehabbed, he waited out his enlistment and didn't re-up. Went back to New York City, where he was from. Had the same trouble fitting in that a lot of vets did, drifted from job to job, finally started workin' as a bouncer and doorman at a nightclub. But his friend from the squad, the other survivor of the ambush, was in New York, too, and he was a pretty scummy character. He got Bailey mixed up in a plan to rip off a drug deal. The job went bad, things blew up—literally—and a lot of people died, including Bailey's friend. Bailey wound up goin' down on murder, armed robbery, and weapons charges. He's been behind bars the past four years and has been nothin' but trouble there, too. He beat two other convicts to death after they attacked him for refusin' to join their gang. Doesn't seem to want anything to do with anybody. They've got him away from general population and plan to keep him that way, because they know if he goes back into gen-pop, sooner or later he'll kill somebody else."

"Why do you want him?" the woman asked.

"Because I met him while I was over there in the sandbox doin' a little job for somebody who can just remain nameless. His squad helped get me where I needed to be. Bailey may have screwed the pooch when he got back stateside, but in combat he was damn good. A born warrior who can follow orders *and* take the initiative when he needs to."

The man from the White House said, "You know all this from being around him for, what, a day or two?"

"A day or two when folks are tryin' to kill you nearly the whole time can tell you a lot about a man," Bill said flatly.

"I don't have any problem with Bailey," Clark said. "Can we move on?"

None of the other three raised an objection.

Bill tapped keys and changed the image on the screen. This one was a police mug shot of a mild-looking, sandy-haired young man.

"Wade Stillman," Bill said. "Georgia boy. Also a

decorated vet. He fit in better once he got back, or at least he seemed to. Until one day he snapped while he was at his job—workin' at a MegaMart, by the way—and nearly beat a customer to death. The way I understand it, the guy probably had it comin', but Stillman wound up in prison anyway."

"Let me guess," the general said. "He's killed men in prison, too."

"Nope," Bill replied with a shake of his head. "From all reports, he's been a model prisoner. Keeps his head down and stays out of trouble. Works in the prison library, even."

"Then why do you want him?" the woman asked. "Do you know him personally?"

"Never met the young man. But I put out the word to some old acquaintances, and Stillman's commanding officer was one of 'em. He said I won't find a better fightin' man once he's riled up. Only possible problem is that Stillman's pretty laid back and it's hard to make him lose his temper. That shouldn't be a problem where we'll be goin', though, since everybody there will want to kill us."

"So you want Bailey as your second-in-command and Stillman behind him, because of their military experience?" Clark asked.

"I don't know if it'll be that cut-and-dried, but basically, yeah."

"Well, that sounds doable. Who else do you have for us?"

The next image that came up on the screen was that of an attractive young woman with a nice smile and long, honey-colored hair.

"This is Megan Sinclair. Used to be in Special Forces."

"Special Forces!" the general repeated in surprise. "That little girl? You're crazy, Elliott."

Bill controlled the flash of anger he felt. He said, "You can look her up if you want, General. She worked mostly in the command center with computers, but she did some fieldwork, too, and handled herself well. Until she took her skills and dropped off the grid. She surfaced in London a couple of years later when she was arrested for trying to rip off the son of a British billionaire. Turns out that after she deserted, she became a professional thief, mostly in Europe. Interpol wanted her, and so did several countries. But after untanglin' a lot of red tape, we got her back, since the first crime she committed was desertin' the Army. She's still in military lockup, and once she gets out of there, she's lookin' at bein' extradited back to England. In fact, it looks like she might spend the rest of her life goin' from one country's prison to the next, unless we step in and offer her a way out."

"Do you know her personally, Bill?" Clark asked.

"As a matter of fact, I do." Bill paused. "Her father's an old compadre of mine. The girl went off the rails, no doubt about that, but I don't want to see her spendin' the rest of her life behind bars."

The woman said, "Do you really think someone like her can be of assistance on a job like this, Mr. Elliott? I have to say, she looks harmless."

"Looks can be deceiving."

"It's your show," Clark said. "Who else do you have for us?"

Bill tugged on his earlobe, grimaced slightly, and said, "Here's where it starts to get tricky. Bailey, Stillman, and Sinclair all have military backgrounds. I know I can work with them. The rest of this bunch . . . well, they're lowlifes. Criminals. There's no gettin' around that. But some of 'em have skills we can use, and some of 'em are just plain badasses. And where we're goin', the badder the better."

"They're all convicts?" the woman asked.

"Yes, ma'am. All of 'em serving life sentences without parole."

"Then working for us is really their only chance to have a normal life again. Surely they're smart enough to see that."

"Maybe," Bill said. "As a rule, criminals aren't the sharpest knives in the drawer, if you know what I mean. And if they *are* smart, they're liable to see that their odds of comin' out of this alive are pretty damn slim. But when you don't have anything to lose . . ."

The others didn't say anything, so Bill took that as a sign to continue. He tapped computer keys again.

"Braden Cole," he said as the image of a man in his forties appeared on the screen. Cole was pale, with a brush of dark hair that made the skin of his fox-like face seem even more washed out. So did the dark-framed glasses he wore. "Freelance killer. A hit man, as they say in books and movies. There's no tellin' how many jobs like that he's carried out."

The woman said, "And you want an animal like that working for us?"

"Cole can kill in lots of different ways," Bill said, "but his method of choice is with explosives. He's a demolitions man, and he's mighty good at it. That's a handy skill to have."

"I suppose. Can you work with him?"

"We'll find out." Bill changed the screen. "This fella's name is Nick Hatcher. Another professional thief, but unlike Megan, he didn't work alone. He was part of a crew that robbed banks all over the West and Southwest. Wheelman for the gang. Supposed to be a great driver. That's exactly what you need if you have to get out of a place in a hurry."

"Was he sent away for bank robbery?" Clark asked.

"Murder," Bill said. "His last job, two cops were killed. Hatcher didn't do any of the shooting, but since he was involved in the commission of a felony, legally he was just as responsible as the ones who did. And since he was the only member of the gang who survived, the legal system came down on him just as hard as it could."

"He doesn't look like a criminal," the woman said as she frowned at the image of a handsome, brown-haired young man. "He looks like he should be dating that Sinclair girl."

"I don't think they'll have time for that."

Bill changed the image again. This time, two pictures came up, side by side. He was watching from the corner of his eye, and the woman and the man from the White House both visibly recoiled. Not much, and they controlled the reaction instantly, but Bill caught it anyway.

"Now those two look like criminals," the man from the White House muttered.

"That's because they are," Bill said. "The white guy is Ellis 'Bronco' Madigan. Ran a gang of bikers and skinheads that was tied in with organized crime all over the Midwest. He was convicted of twenty-two counts of murder and the cops are convinced his list is even longer than that. The black guy is Calvin Watson. His deal is similar to Madigan's: he was in charge of an extensive gang with ties to organized crime, convicted of multiple murders but probably not as many as he's actually guilty of. In a perfect world, they'd have both been executed by now, but the feds are keepin' them alive to try to get information out of them. They're in the same federal facility, where they've been tryin' to kill each other ever since they met. Talk about hate at first sight."

"Why haven't they been separated?" the woman wanted to know.

"You'd have to ask somebody else about that, ma'am. I suspect the feds are keepin' 'em together to keep the pressure on them to talk. It's not workin', though. Madigan and Watson have never said a useful word since they went into the system."

"Why do you want a couple of animals like that on your team?" the general asked.

"Remember what I said about badasses? Those two are some of the baddest you'll find."

"You can't work with them," the woman declared. "If they're the sort of men you say they are, they'll never cooperate with you. They'll have no reason to."

Bill said, "They'll have a reason, all right. New

identities, new lives. Because you see, whatever happens on this mission, Madigan and Watson are going to die . . . the same as all the others."

"What in the world do you mean by that?" the man from the White House asked.

Clark said, "Officially, they'll be dead."

"You mean like witness protection."

"Witsec is different. What we'll be offering goes beyond that. The new identities we give them will be as impenetrable as we can possibly make them, and we won't have to keep them around to testify or anything like that, either. The federal government will be through with them. They can go off and live their lives however they please."

The woman's lips pursed in disapproval. She said, "In other words, you'll be turning a pair of monsters loose on society."

"Oh, there'll be some safeguards in place," Clark assured her. "Madigan and Watson won't know it, but we'll be keeping an eye on them. If they try to go back to their old lives, we'll deal with the problem then."

The general said, "If they try to kill each other, how can you expect them to function on the same team?"

"By dangling that carrot," Clark said.

Bill added, "You might not think it to look at them, but Madigan and Watson aren't stupid. They wouldn't have lived this long if they were. They'll cooperate as long as it's in their own best interest."

"If they get a chance, they'll double-cross you," the general warned.

"More than likely," Bill agreed. "I don't intend to give 'em that chance."

"All right, let's say we agree to those two," the woman said. "Is that all?"

"Couple more." Bill changed the image to that of a man in his thirties with big, scared eyes. "This is Jackie Thornton. Small-time criminal from South Dakota who wound up on death row because he murdered his ex-wife's new husband and tried to kill her. He's about as much of an all-around loser as you could find."

"Then why in the world do you want him? At least those other two are big and tough."

"Jackie's got something they don't." Bill tapped a key on the computer, and the screen went dark. "What's he look like?"

"What do you mean?" Clark asked.

"Describe Jackie Thornton to me."

The four of them glanced at each other. Clark said, "His hair . . ." and then stopped.

The general said, "He's got . . ."

A frown creased his forehead as he tried to think of what to say next. The woman and the man from the White House didn't even attempt it.

"That's right," Bill said. "You all looked at him, but you can't describe him. You probably couldn't even pick him out of a lineup. Jackie Thornton's just about the most forgettable son of a gun you'd ever want to meet."

"That's not fair," the woman protested. "His picture was up there less than a minute."

"But if I'd shown you the pictures of Madigan and Watson for the same amount of time, you'd remember what *they* looked like, I'll bet."

"Well, probably. But they're so big and . . . and

brutal-looking. That other man . . . why, he looked more like a scared rabbit."

"Exactly. So if I need to send a man into a situation where nobody's gonna pay any attention to him, Thornton's the man for the job."

"You said he killed a man. He's a vicious criminal, too."

"He's a sad sack who worked himself up into a killin' state," Bill said. "I talked to the chief of police in the little town where Thornton's from. He told me that Thornton never hurt anybody until his wife left him and that pushed him over the edge. Even that took a couple of years to fester before it came out. Thornton held up a grocery store at gunpoint one time, but it came out later that the gun he used was unloaded. He said he just intended to scare people with it and wanted to make sure he didn't hurt anybody by accident. He's not really dangerous."

"So despite being a murderer, he's not much of a badass," Clark said.

"That's right. But with Madigan, Watson, Bailey, and Stillman, we got plenty of badasses. We got a demolitions man in Cole, we got an intelligence team in Sinclair and Thornton, and we got a transportation guy in Hatcher."

"What else do you need?" the woman asked.

"A shooter," Bill said. "And that one's non-negotiable. I have this man on my team, or I don't go."

"Well, show us his picture," the man from the White House said with a tone of impatience creeping into his voice.

"I'll do better than that," Bill said. "I'll introduce him to you."

As Bill got up and went over to a door at the side of the room, Clark said with a worried frown, "Bill, you really shouldn't have brought anybody here—"

"It's all right," Bill told him. "This fella's been here before."

He opened the door. A middle-aged black man with close-cropped hair walked slowly into the room. He gave Clark a faint smile and nodded, then said, "Good to see you again, Clark."

"Henry," Clark said. "I thought you were retired."

"And I thought *I* was retired," Bill said, "but here I am, puttin' a team together again."

Clark glanced down at the legs of Henry Dixon's slacks and said, "But I thought . . ."

His voice trailed off as if he didn't know what else to say.

"You thought right," Dixon told him. "They're prosthetics, both of them. I spent more than a year in a wheelchair after that mess you pulled me out of in Africa, but then I decided I'd had enough of it. I asked Bill for help, and he convinced his boss to pay for it."

Clark looked at Bill and said, "I thought I was your boss, but I never heard anything about this."

"You're my associate," Bill drawled. "As far as the government's concerned I'm a freelancer, remember? The boss Henry's talkin' about is Hiram Stackhouse."

The man from the White House made a face at the mention of Stackhouse's name.

"That man's a damn menace. Always questioning the administration—"

"And we all know how questionin' the administration these days gets you on a list of suspected terrorists and traitors," Bill said. "This country used to elect a president, not a damn king." He snorted. "But that was before the news media became just another arm of the government."

"You're distorting everything—"

"Gentlemen," Dixon broke in, and his deep, powerful voice made everyone else in the room look at him. "If our enemies succeed, we won't have to worry about elections anymore. And they already have a strong foothold for their goals in Mexico. We can't allow any more plots like the New Sun to come out of there."

Clark shook his head and said to Bill, "Boy, you just told him everything, didn't you?"

"What can I say? I trust the man. He's saved my life a few times in the past. Yours, too, as I recall."

Clark shrugged and said, "Yeah, well . . ."

"Let me understand this," the woman said. "This man has no legs."

Dixon smiled faintly again as he told her, "I have artificial legs, ma'am. State of the art. I can't get around as fast as the Six Million Dollar Man, but I do all right."

"And once he's where he needs to be, there's not a better long-range shot in the world," Bill said. "Anybody who's about to waltz into hell needs an angel lookin' over his shoulder." He nodded toward Dixon. "Henry's my angel."

"A tarnished angel, to be sure," Dixon said with a chuckle.

"Good enough for me."

Clark looked like he was counting in his head. He confirmed that by saying, "You're going to take on a whole training camp full of Mexican drug smugglers and Arab terrorists with eight men and one woman? Those are pretty stiff odds, Bill."

"You're forgettin' that I'm goin' along. There'll be ten of us."

"Oh, well, that makes all the difference in the world," Clark said. "Ten against three or four hundred is much better than nine against three or four hundred."

"You said you didn't want an international incident—"

"Absolutely not," the man from the White House interrupted. "We can't have that. It would make us look bad in the eyes of the rest of the world."

"And every day that givin' a rat's ass what the rest of the world thinks of us takes precedence is a day that a little more of what this country used to be just ups and dies," Bill said.

The man from the White House sneered and said, "This isn't the twentieth century anymore. It's all about globalism now."

"I'm an American, by God. Globalism can pucker up and kiss my—"

Dixon put a hand on Bill's shoulder and said, "An argument for another day, perhaps."

"You're right, Henry." Bill looked at the others in the room. "Right now, we've got to decide whether we're doin' this or not."

The general cleared his throat.

"I say it's a go, and I'm willing to go along with

your choices for your team, Mr. Elliott. I think some of them are pretty risky, but no war was ever won without running some risks."

The woman sighed and said, "I'm willing to sign off on it, too, although not without some serious reservations that I want noted."

"That's going to be hard to do," Clark told her, "since this meeting never took place and none of us are even here right now."

"Well, the five of you heard what I said," the woman snapped. "Just remember it, that's all."

"Then consider it duly noted, ma'am," Bill said. He looked at the man from the White House. "How about you?"

"I can't speak for the president—"

"Sure you can. Good Lord, we all know the man's an empty suit and he's takin' his marchin' orders from somebody else."

The man ignored that and said, "I have some definite concerns, but . . . I suppose this threat is too big to be ignored. I'll advise the president that we should turn a blind eye to your activities."

That sort of tacit, cover-our-own-asses response was the best they could hope for from this administration, Bill knew, so he nodded.

"I guess it's settled, then. We go in and knock out the camp at Barranca de la Serpiente, whatever it takes."

"And no one outside of this room, other than the members of your team, ever know about it, is that understood, Mr. Elliott?" the woman cautioned.

"Yes, ma'am," Bill said.

He could have told her that she didn't need to

worry about the team ever revealing anything. The odds of any of them coming back were almost too small to be reckoned. Two words described this job better than any others.

Suicide mission.

BOOK THREE
THE MISSION

CHAPTER 26

Somewhere in West Texas

The staging area was part of what had once been an Air Force base until it was closed down years earlier when a previous administration had decided that it couldn't afford to both defend the country *and* buy reelection votes by giving away millions of free cell phones like prizes in cereal boxes.

After that the neighboring city had bought part of the property and tried to turn it into an industrial park, only to have that effort fail. Since then the old base had sat moldering in the elements, used only for occasional training by reserve units in the area.

As far as all but a few people knew, that was what was going on now. Just some routine training. That accounted for the occasional truck going out to the old base, or helicopters landing and taking off every now and then.

Bill Elliott met the first of those helicopters. He was standing on the tarmac as the bird touched down. A couple of armed guards climbed out first, followed by a tall, heavily muscled man with a rugged face and hair clipped close to his head. His hands were cuffed in front of him, but his legs were free so he could walk unhindered. Two more guards disembarked from the chopper behind him, and the whole group walked toward Bill.

After nodding to the guards, Bill addressed the prisoner, saying, "Hello, Specialist Bailey. It's been a while."

John Bailey frowned at Bill and asked, "Do I know you, sir?"

"Think back," Bill told him. "About a dozen years ago, in a place where it was hot and sandy."

"Good Lord," Bailey breathed. "You're that spook."

"Private contractor," Bill corrected with a smile.

"I never did know what it was you were up to."

"You weren't supposed to. You got me where I was goin', and that was your only job, Bailey."

"No offense, sir, but in your line of work I'd have thought you'd be dead a long time ago."

"I'm stubborn about stayin' alive. The same seems to hold true for you. You've survived some bad times."

An unreadable hardness settled over Bailey's blunt face as he said, "My problems are my own fault, sir."

"Most of 'em, more than likely. But we're gonna talk about it." Bill turned and motioned for the guards to follow him. "Bring the prisoner."

A few minutes later, the two of them were seated across from each other at a table in one of the buildings. Bill said to the guards, "You can leave us alone."

"Our orders are to remain with the prisoner, sir," one of the men said.

"Well, I'm countermandin' those orders, son. I'm going to talk to Specialist Bailey in private."

Bailey said, "You shouldn't use my rank. I've been a civilian for a long time."

"Man goes through what you went through over there, he's never completely a civilian again," Bill said.

Bailey's massive shoulders rose and fell in acknowledgment of that point.

The guard who had objected said, "You don't want to be left alone with this animal, sir."

"The prisoner has no reason to harm me," Bill snapped, "and I still want to speak with him in private."

The guards looked at each other, and finally the spokesman shrugged.

"We'll be right outside if you need us."

"I won't," Bill said flatly.

With obvious reluctance, the guards filed out. When they were gone, Bailey asked, "What's this about?"

"I had you brought here so I could offer you a job, son," Bill said.

Bailey frowned.

"I'm serving a life sentence in prison," he pointed out. "I'm not exactly in the market for a job."

"Maybe the job's in the market for a man like you. And as far as prison goes . . . maybe we can do something about that."

Bailey's eyes narrowed. He asked, "Are you promising what I think you're promising?"

"I'm not promisin' anything except the chance

to risk your life for the good of your country, and a chance to do yourself some good at the same time."

"Or at least a chance to get myself killed, eh?"

Bill chuckled and said, "You were always pretty smart, Bailey."

"I don't know about that." Bailey leaned back in his chair. "The smartest thing to do might be to tell you to go to hell and let them take me back to prison."

"But you're not gonna do that, are you?"

For the first time since his arrival, John Bailey smiled faintly.

"No, sir, I'm not. Why don't you go ahead and tell me more about this job you've got for me?"

Wade Stillman came in the next day. The security around him wasn't as heavy. He hadn't killed anyone, after all . . . at least not as a civilian. Bill and Bailey met the helicopter together and escorted Wade into the same room where they'd had their discussion the day before.

Wade was as suspicious as Bailey had been, although he tried to cover it with a cocky attitude. Bill began by saying, "I understand you used to work in a MegaMart."

"Doesn't everybody?"

"I've done some work for Hiram Stackhouse myself."

"Stackhouse," Wade repeated. "You mean the guy who owns the whole shootin' match?"

"That's the one."

Wade's eyes narrowed as he said, "Something

tells me you didn't wear a vest when you were workin' for him."

"No, I didn't," Bill admitted. "And if you agree to work for me, you won't be wearin' a vest, either . . . unless it's made out of Kevlar."

From the corner of his eye Bill saw that John Bailey was struggling not to smile at that one. Bailey succeeded in keeping his rugged face expressionless.

"There's something mighty fishy about this whole business," Wade said. "All the secrecy . . . Is this some sort of spy deal?"

"Not really. But we have to keep the details under wraps until you agree to work with us."

"You can't even tell me what the job is?"

"No, just that it's dangerous. It's strictly volunteer, too. If you're not interested, you can leave and go back where you came from."

"Prison," Wade said heavily.

"But if you agree, there's one thing I can promise you . . . you won't be goin' back to prison."

"Because I might be dead?"

Bill inclined his head slightly and said, "Or you might not be."

Wade thought it over, but not for long. He nodded and said, "I don't care what it is, you've got a deal, mister. Just tell me who I've got to kill . . . or who's gonna kill me."

"Do I know you, sir?" Megan Sinclair asked as she looked across the table. Bill was seated on the other side, with Bailey and Wade behind him in white T-shirts, camo trousers, and boots, flanking him, both standing stiff and straight and not betraying any emotion.

"We've never met," Bill said, "but I know your father."

Megan grimaced.

"I haven't had any contact with the colonel for a good number of years. I believe he's of the opinion that he no longer has a daughter."

"You might be surprised about that," Bill told her. "Could be he still loves you so much it hurts him to know . . ."

"To know that his little girl has become a deserter and a criminal?" Megan shrugged. "You might be right about that. I don't know and I don't care."

Bill could tell she was lying about part of that statement. She cared, all right. She just wasn't about to let herself show it. She might not even allow herself to acknowledge it, even deep in her heart. But she still cared.

Megan wore a white prison jumpsuit, and even though it was far from flattering, she was still attractive. Bill had seen both Bailey and Wade checking her out, although they tried to be unobtrusive about it. It was easy to understand how she'd been able to get close to unwary male victims all over Europe and help herself to diamonds, art treasures, bank accounts, and assorted other loot.

"You've gotten yourself into a heap of trouble," Bill told her, "but we'd like to help you out."

"As a favor to my father?" Megan sounded like she couldn't believe that.

"No, because your country needs you."

She laughed softly and shook her head.

"I fell for that line once," she said. "Not again."

"It's more true now than it ever was. There are threats—major threats—that most folks never know about. We need somebody to stop one of those threats, and most people will never know about that, either."

"If you really know my father, you probably know I was in Special Forces," Megan said. "I know all about the sort of threats that are out there. Somebody else can deal with them. I did my part."

"I'm not disputin' that. But we still need you."

"Black ops? Counterintelligence?"

"Some of that, but more like kickin' butt and takin' names," Bill said. "The sort of thing you never really got to do that much of when you were in the service."

"That's because they had me stuck in front of a computer in some command center all the time," Megan snapped.

"I'll be honest with you, we need your computer skills, too. But you won't be stuck in a room somewhere. There'll be plenty of excitement, if that's what you're lookin' for." Bill paused, then added, "Considerin' how you've made your livin' the past few years, I'd say excitement's pretty important to you."

She glared at him and said, "You think you've got me all figured out, don't you?"

"No, ma'am. But I'd like to try."

"Save it. You're old enough to be my dad. Maybe my granddad."

"Didn't mean it like that," Bill said.

She considered for a moment, then waved a hand at Bailey and Wade and asked, "Are these two part of the deal?"

"They're on the team," Bill admitted.

"Well, that *might* make it interesting enough to take a chance." She clasped her hands together on the table. "Why don't you tell me more about it?"

"Can't do that until you give me your word that you're in. If you're not willing to do that, you'll have to go back where you came from."

"You'd take my word for something that important?" Megan asked, sounding surprised.

"Like I told you, I know how you were raised."

Another moment of silence went by while she looked like she was pondering the offer, then she said, "All right, I'm in. But it had better be as exciting as you promised it would be."

"That," Bill said, "is one thing I don't think you have to worry about."

CHAPTER 27

John Bailey and Megan Sinclair were known quantities to Bill, at least to a certain extent, and Wade Stillman was the sort of man Bill knew and understood.

The rest of the team was a different story.

Nick Hatcher arrived first. He was even taller than Bill and definitely affable looking, not the sort who would be tabbed by most people as a professional bank robber. He was friendly, too, smiling and offering to shake hands, although Bill didn't take him up on that.

"I have no idea why I'm here," Nick said as he sat down across the table from Bill. "I figured I was just being transferred to another facility, but that's not the case, is it?"

"This isn't a prison," Bill admitted. "But it is a secure location."

"I'll say. I think I would have stood a better chance of breaking out where I was . . . not that I intended to try and break out. I'm not looking for trouble."

"And yet you robbed . . . how many banks was it?"

"Eighteen, I think. Or maybe nineteen. I don't remember for sure. I just drove, though. I never actually set foot in any of the banks."

"You drove for people who murdered cops," Bill said, not bothering to keep the harsh anger out of his voice. "That makes you a murderer, too."

Nick met his gaze squarely and said, "In the eyes of the law, sure."

"You don't feel any remorse?"

"I feel plenty of remorse." Bill saw how Nick's hands clenched into fists for a second as the prisoner went on, "I saw that female cop get hit and go down. I didn't want that to happen. I'm sorry it happened. But I didn't pull the trigger, and I didn't tell Harris to shoot her, either. Nobody got hurt in any of our other jobs." He paused. "It was like everybody's luck was up that day."

"But you're still alive."

"My partners aren't."

"Still, you're luckier than them, or either of those police officers."

"I've already said I was sorry. I'm doing the time. I don't know what else I can do."

"Something to make up a little for what happened, maybe."

That made Nick's eyes narrow with suspicion. He said, "Ah, now we get down to it. There's something shady going on here. This place is off the books. There's no official record of me being here, is there?"

"As far as the prison's concerned, you're sittin' in your cell right now, Hatcher."

Nick laughed.

"So you can do whatever you want to me and nobody will care. Is that it?"

Bill didn't answer that question. Instead he asked one of his own.

"How'd you wind up drivin' getaway cars?"

"I fell in with bad company at an early age," Nick replied with a smirk that made Bill want to go across the table and slap it off his face.

The comment also made Bill think of Catalina Ramos, who he hadn't seen since a few days after the nearly catastrophic incident in front of the Alamo. Clark had promised to help her get set up with a new identity and a new life. Catalina had nothing waiting for her in Mexico, so the best thing would be for her to start over in Texas, or somewhere else if that was what she preferred.

Bill had thought a time or two about asking Clark how Catalina was doing, but he hadn't done it. She had played her part—as far as Bill was concerned, she had saved hundreds of thousands of lives, maybe more, because they couldn't have stopped Tariq Maleef from carrying out his deadly plan without her help—and now she deserved to be left alone.

"What did you do when you were a kid, start stealin' cars?" Bill asked Hatcher.

"As a matter of fact . . . no. I had a friend who got into building hot rods and racing. I talked him into letting me drive some of his cars. I didn't have any interest in working on the blasted things, but the first time I got behind the wheel, I knew I'd found what I was born to do."

"Why didn't you stay with it? Some of those NASCAR drivers make more money than God.

More than you'd get bein' a bank robber, and you don't get shot at, either."

"Well, as it turns out, I was born to do something else. I, ah, enjoyed betting on the races, too."

"Ohhhh," Bill said in understanding. "Gamblin' problem, eh?"

"Not at all. I could gamble just fine. It was more of a paying-off-the-bets-I-lost problem."

Nick grinned as he said it, and Bill realized to his surprise that he found himself almost liking the young man. Nick had an easygoing charm that made people forget he was a professional criminal.

Bill wasn't going to forget two dead cops, though, so he concentrated on that and said, "Can you use a gun?"

"I told you, I didn't shoot anybody—"

"That's not what I asked. Can you handle a gun?"

Nick shrugged and said, "I've done some shooting. Just practice, you understand. I never carried a gun on a job. Didn't want to be tempted to use it."

"We've got a good range here. We can try you out, see how you do."

"Wait a minute," Nick frowned. "You're talking about giving a felon, a convicted murderer, a gun?"

"Just to practice with," Bill said. "For now."

Another grin spread slowly across Nick's face as he said, "You need a wheelman."

"I didn't say—"

"You've got some sort of job coming up, and you need a driver. But it's dangerous, so you want to know if I can use a gun, too. I know you're not a crook, so that means you work for the government."

"All too often that's the same thing."

"No, this is some top-secret military deal," Nick guessed, demonstrating that he could be intuitive. "Or maybe some sort of spy outfit. And you want to recruit me to help."

"What if we do?" Bill asked.

"Then it's going to cost you."

"How much?"

"My freedom, to start with. After that . . . well, we'll have to negotiate."

"How about this for negotiation?" Bill snapped. "You help us, or you go back to a six-by-eight cell for the rest of your natural-born life?"

"I think we can work something out," Nick said. "I think you'll find that I'm a pretty good shot, too."

"You'll need to be," Bill said, "or else that cell's liable to start looking mighty pretty to you."

Bill felt an entirely different impulse when he met Braden Cole. Just like when he spotted a venomous snake, he had an urge to grab a hoe and chop the damn thing's head off.

Cole sat on the other side of the table with a tiny smile on his face. He was a physically unimpressive specimen, but there was an air of menace about him anyway, no matter how mild-mannered his appearance.

He pushed his glasses up where they had slid down his nose and didn't say anything. After Cole had sat there placidly and silently for several minutes, Bill asked, "Don't you want to know why you're here?"

"I assume you'll tell me when you're good and

ready," Cole said. "Until then I don't see any point in worrying about it."

"You're a pretty cool customer, aren't you?"

"I'm not given to emotionalism."

"Yeah, havin' emotions might be a drawback when your line of work is killin' people."

"I was only an instrument. A tool, if you will. A way for other people to get what they wanted."

"So you do have to rationalize murder to yourself," Bill said. "Must be a heart in there somewhere after all."

"Think whatever you want," Cole said, still smiling.

Bill thought about it for a moment, then said, "I want to hire you."

He saw a flicker of surprise in Cole's eyes. So it was possible to get through the man's ice-cold façade after all.

"Hire me to do what?"

"What you do best, of course. Blow stuff up and kill people."

Cole tipped his head slightly to the side, reached up with his cuffed hands, and used a fingertip to scratch inside his ear. Then he asked, "Who is it you want me to kill?"

"I'm not sure yet. There may be quite a few folks the world would be better off without. We'll sort of have to wait and see when the time comes."

Cole shook his head.

"I don't work that way. I need a specific target and sufficient time to plan. And I decide how much time is enough. That's the only way I'll take a job."

"How about this?" Bill suggested. "We'll pay you a bonus."

"What sort of bonus?"

Bill reached in his pocket, drew out a small revolver, and set it on the table in front of him.

"I won't do the world a favor and blow your sorry brains out."

Again there was a flicker of something in Cole's eyes. Fear was too strong a word to describe it. Uncertainty, maybe. For a second Cole wasn't sure that Bill wouldn't do exactly what he had threatened.

But then Cole's natural arrogance—the arrogance of a true sociopath—asserted itself, and he said, "You won't do that."

Bailey and Stillman were in the room, as they had been for the other meetings. They had remained standing and hadn't said anything. Now Bailey drew a Colt .45 1911A1 that was holstered on his hip and pointed it at Cole.

"I will," he said.

This time Cole did look afraid.

"Stop and think about it, Cole," Bill drawled. "Besides the four of us in this room, only a handful of people know that you're here, and they occupy a high enough level that they don't give a damn about what happens to somebody like you. You had a hood over your head when you were flown in here, but if you'd been able to look out of that chopper, you'd have seen miles and miles of nothin'. We could bury a thousand varmints like you out here, and nobody would ever know the difference. And even if they did, they wouldn't care."

"You're not murderers," Cole insisted. "You work for the government."

"We had a president once who said it was fine and dandy to kill American citizens just on his say-so.

I'm not claimin' he was right or wrong, but hey, with an example like that . . ."

Cole pushed his glasses up again. They seemed to be slipping more now, an indication that while he wasn't openly sweating, his skin was damper than it had been.

"I asked you before, what is it you want?"

"You're good with demolitions. I need a man like that."

"You want something blown up, but you don't know what it is yet?"

"You're gettin' the idea," Bill said. "We won't know for sure until we get where we're goin'."

"You're talking about a covert mission into another country. You're recruiting people like me who won't be missed so the government will have maximum deniability if anything goes wrong."

The man might be an inhuman monster, thought Bill, but that didn't mean he was dumb.

"Let's say you're right. Let's say there's a threat to your country that needs to be neutralized."

"I wouldn't advise you to play to my patriotism," Cole said. "I don't have any."

"You go along with us, we're prepared to make it possible for you to start over with a new identity and a new life. All you have to do is agree to go along and follow orders."

"I'm not a fool, Mister . . . what is your name, anyway?"

"You can call me Bill."

"I'm not a fool, Bill," Cole said. "You're not going to just let me walk free if I help you with this mission, whatever it is."

"That's the deal."

Cole shook his head.

"No. The only reason you'd make such an offer is that you don't expect me to ever be able to take you up on it. You don't expect me to come back alive."

"Does that make a difference?"

Cole didn't answer right away, and when he spoke again he still didn't give Bill a direct answer. Instead he said, "Do you know what the worst part is about being locked up?"

"Why don't you tell me?"

"It's feeling useless. I have a very specific set of skills, and I very well may be the best in the world at what I do." Cole spread his hands. "But sitting in a cell, I can't accomplish anything. You may not believe this, but I have a very strong work ethic, Bill."

"So . . . do we put you to work?"

"I'll take the job . . . but if I do survive to collect that new life, I want a bonus. I want one million dollars."

"Done," Bill said.

CHAPTER 28

Knowing Jackie Thornton's history, how cold-bloodedly Thornton had shot another man in the head just because the unlucky fella had married Thornton's ex-wife, Bill expected to react to him with as much dislike as he had to Braden Cole.

Instead, Bill looked at the slightly built man who shuffled into the room and sat down at the table without meeting anyone's eyes, and had to stop himself from feeling sorry for Thornton. In the meeting with Clark and the other government officials, he had described Thornton as a sad sack. Not many people these days would understand that World War II–era reference, but it was a perfect description of Jackie Thornton anyway.

Bill reminded himself that Thornton had also tried to kill his ex-wife, and it was only sheer happenstance that he hadn't succeeded. He had fired a lot of rounds in that living room, and one of them easily could have found Maggie Louise Redmond.

Thornton kept his head down, staring at the

table. After another moment went by, Bill said, "Hello, Jackie. You don't know me. My name's Bill."

Thornton nodded, just an almost imperceptible movement of his head, and didn't say anything.

"You know why you're here?" Bill went on.

"No, sir," Thornton replied in a voice that was little more than a whisper. "The warden said I was being sent down to Texas. That's all I know." He paused. "Is this some sort of maximum-security prison? If it is, that's not necessary. I've never tried to get away, and I never will."

"Why is that?"

For the first time, Thornton glanced up. He had a surprised look in his eyes.

"Why . . . I did wrong. I killed an innocent man. Greg Redmond didn't deserve what I done to him. I've got to pay for my crime."

"He married your wife," Bill said, wondering what it would take to get a rise out of Thornton. "Wrecked your happy home."

"No, sir, I done that. Maggie Louise leaving me was all my fault, because I was a weak, sinful man and run with bad companions. Made bad choices. That's all on me."

"Well, it's good that you take responsibility for your actions. How'd you like a chance to make up a little for what you've done?"

"When I saw this place, I got to thinking maybe it was something like that. You want to try some new drug on me, don't you? Or maybe perform some sort of experiment? I don't care, sir. You just do whatever you want to me, and if I don't make it, well, I'm fine with that."

Bill heard a little noise behind him and glanced

over his shoulder to see that Wade Stillman was having a hard time not breaking out in laughter. Even the normally taciturn John Bailey had a smile tugging at the corners of his mouth.

"That's not exactly what we had in mind, Jackie," Bill said. "We need volunteers, but it's not for some sort of . . . experiment."

"Oh." Bill thought Thornton sounded vaguely disappointed, as if he had convinced himself they were going to turn him into a zombie or a cyborg or some such fanciful notion. "Well, then, what would I be volunteering for?"

"A dangerous mission. There's a better than even chance you wouldn't be comin' back. But it's for the good of the country."

Unlike Braden Cole, Thornton must have had some patriotism in his personality. He perked up at that and said, "You know, for a while I thought about joining the Army. I wanted to do something to help. Probably would've been a lot better off all around if I had."

"Likely you're right about that. So you're interested in signin' on with us?"

"What would I have to do? I mean, I'm not that good at fighting. Never have been." Thornton nodded toward Bailey and Wade. "I wouldn't be any match for fellas like these."

"Then it's a good thing you'll all be on the same side," Bill said. "Don't worry, if you want to be part of this, we'll teach you everything you need to know."

"Well, then, I guess . . . I guess I could give it a try."

Bill frowned and asked, "Don't you want to know what you'll get in return?"

"You said it was a chance to do some good. I'm not expecting anything else in return."

Either Thornton was a consummate actor and was pulling the wool over all their eyes, Bill thought, or else he was exactly what he seemed to be, a none-too-bright small town boy who had screwed up his life and gotten into deep trouble.

Either way he might be useful. Bill nodded and said, "All right, consider yourself part of the team, Jackie."

"Really?" There was a note of pride in his voice as he added, "I don't reckon I've been on a team since I played ball in high school. I always liked that—" He stopped short, then said, "But I don't reckon we'll be playing football, will we?"

"Nope," Bill said. "It's a lot more dangerous game than that."

Bill, John Bailey, and Wade Stillman met that evening in Bill's quarters. They were all staying in what had been base housing for the Air Force officers, back when the base was active. Bill got beers from the refrigerator and carried them into the spartanly furnished living room. He handed sweat-dripping bottles to the other two men.

In the several days they had been here, Bailey and Stillman had settled into old, comfortable roles. Both men had been noncoms in the Army, and that was essentially their function in this operation, too, backing up Bill as their commander.

That didn't come as easy to Bill. He hadn't always been a lone wolf, but he had spent more time operating on his own than he had as part of a group, let alone in charge. That wasn't to say that he couldn't take command when he needed to. He could and would. When it came time to strike at Barranca de la Serpiente, he would be in charge, no doubt about that.

Bill sat down to talk about the members of the team that had been assembled so far, but before he could launch into the discussion, the walkie-talkie clipped to his belt chirped. He unhooked it, held it to his mouth, and said, "Elliott."

The voice of one of the guards said, "We've got a chopper headed this way, sir. Looks like it intends to land."

Bill frowned in surprise and asked, "Any identification on it?"

"It's one of ours, sir. They have the right call sign."

"We expectin' anybody tonight?" Bill asked Bailey and Stillman.

Both men shook their heads. Bailey said, "The last two members of the team aren't supposed to get here until tomorrow."

"You were gonna brief us on 'em tonight," Wade added.

Bill's brain raced. Not many people knew the old base was being used again, and even fewer knew what they were doing out here. He didn't see how the unexpected arrival of the helicopter could be any sort of threat, but there was no point in taking a chance.

"We're on our way," he said into the walkie-talkie. "Have a couple of guards meet us at the helipad."

He and Bailey and Stillman were all armed as

well. He figured they could handle any problems that came up.

The chopper wasn't trying to sneak onto the base. Its running lights were on as it descended. Bill could see it clearly as he and the other two men walked toward the landing area.

A couple of uniformed guards carrying carbines met them there. The men waited together as the helicopter settled down on its skids. It was a smaller corporate-style chopper rather than the big Hueys used to bring in equipment and supplies.

As the rotors slowed to a stop, the door opened and a familiar figure climbed out into the glow from the helipad lights. Bill walked toward the man and called, "You could've let us know you were comin', Clark."

"I didn't know I was coming out here until a little while ago," Clark said as he came up to Bill and shook hands with his old friend and colleague. "I'm afraid I've got some bad news."

"I had a hunch that's what you'd be sayin' as soon as I saw you."

Clark nodded toward the building where the team was quartered.

"Let's go inside. I'll tell you all about it. And if you've got a drink you can offer me . . ."

"I reckon we can manage that, if you're all right with beer."

"Right now I'll take one . . . or six."

Bill grinned and said, "Come on."

Before they left the helipad, Clark turned to one of the guards and said, "Take care of the package I left on the chopper, will you?"

"Of course, sir," the man said. "What do you want me to do with it?"

Clark frowned in thought for a moment, then replied, "Bring it to Mr. Elliott's quarters in fifteen minutes."

The guard nodded in understanding.

"You're bein' mighty mysterious," Bill said as they walked toward the building with Bailey and Stillman. "What's in this package of yours?"

"You'll see. We need to talk about something else first, though, so you'll understand why I brought it here."

Bill wasn't the sort to get nervous, but he didn't like what he was hearing from Clark. Something was going on that might have an effect on the mission.

Once the four men were back in Bill's quarters, he got another beer from the refrigerator and tossed the bottle easily to Clark, who caught it and twisted off the cap. He took a long swallow and then sat down in an armchair. Bill resumed his usual seat in a recliner, and the two younger men sat on the sofa.

Clark didn't wait for Bill to ask him again what had prompted this visit to the old air base. Nor did he sugarcoat the news he had to deliver. He said bluntly, "Tariq Maleef has escaped."

Bill drew in a sharp breath through his nose. "Escaped," he repeated.

"Well . . . more like he was rescued. A force of what we think were cartel soldiers hit the convoy that was transporting him from the facility where he'd been housed to the airport so he could be taken to another facility outside the country."

That statement came as no surprise to Bill. Ever

since the procedure of housing terrorist enemies at Guantanamo had come about in the days following the 9/11 attack, other high-security facilities had been established for the same purpose in a number of other places, only their existence had been maintained as a strict secret. These days, Gitmo served as more of a decoy than anything else.

"You've been movin' him around quite a bit, haven't you?"

"That's right," Clark said with a nod. "For the very reason that we didn't want the cartel to get wind of where he was and try to break him out." Clark paused, then added, "We also figured it was a good idea if certain people in Washington couldn't get their hands on him."

Bill sighed in understanding.

"It's a damn shame when you have to keep your own government from tryin' to sabotage everything you do to protect the country," he said.

"Yeah, but that's the way it is ever since that crowd took over and rigged things so they're always in power. We just have to deal with it and do what we can."

"Until it all comes down like the proverbial house of cards," Bill said grimly.

"Yeah, but we're gonna postpone that day for as long as we can. And part of that is keeping the country safe from threats like Maleef and his south-of-the-border buddies."

"Excuse me, sir," John Bailey said. "When the cartel rescued Maleef . . . did we lose any men?"

"Twelve," Clark said flatly. "Everybody who was with the convoy."

"Damn," Wade Stillman breathed.

"You got any details we need to know, other than the fact that Maleef's in the wind again?" Bill asked.

Clark shook his head.

"No, that's it. We've kept what happened shielded from the media, thank goodness. If they ever find out the truth about the New Sun and how close we came . . . well, it wouldn't be good, and they sure don't need to know that Maleef is on the loose again and able to get up to more mischief."

Bill grunted.

"Mischief. That's a good word for almost nukin' downtown San Antonio."

He didn't have to watch what he said. Bailey and Stillman had been thoroughly briefed about their current situation and the things that had led up to it, as had Megan Sinclair. The other members of the team were still in the dark about the details. They would be carrying out their parts in the mission on a strictly need-to-know basis.

"There is one good thing we think might come out of this," Clark said. "We figure there's a good chance Maleef will head for Barranca de la Serpiente. If we can pick up his trail, maybe he'll lead us right to the place."

The intelligence they had gathered so far had given them a rough location for the terrorist training camp in the mountains of northern Mexico, but the Sierra Madre was a big area and they couldn't just wander around looking for their destination. Clark was right: if they could pin down the location, it would be a big help.

A quiet knock sounded on the door. Bill stood up and said, "That'll be that package you told the guard to bring here."

"That's right," Clark said. He got to his feet as well. He started toward the door, but Bill waved him back.

"I'll get it."

"It might not be what you expect," Clark said.

"How big could it be?" Bill asked as he opened the door.

Then he stood there, stiff with surprise, as Catalina Ramos smiled at him and said, "Hello, Bill. Aren't you going to ask me in?"

CHAPTER 29

Bill had long since learned to roll with the punches, mental as well as physical. His surprised reaction lasted only a second before he controlled it. He stepped back, returned Catalina's smile, and waved a hand for her to come in.

"Didn't expect to ever see you again, young lady," he said. He glanced at Clark. "I thought you had her stashed somewhere safe."

"We did," Clark said. "She insisted on coming to see you."

Bill knew that wasn't the whole story. Clark never did anything without a good reason that would further his own agenda. Bill just had to figure out what that was . . . assuming Clark didn't just come out and tell him.

Bill glanced at Bailey and Stillman and saw that they were eyeing Catalina appreciatively. There was a lot to appreciate. She wore camo trousers and a white T-shirt, like they did, only the outfit looked a lot better on her. It also emphasized how athletic she was. She looked like she was ready to kick ass.

As that thought went through Bill's brain, he felt a tingle of alarm. He muttered, "Oh, hell no."

"What was that?" Catalina asked as she came into the room. "Aren't you going to offer an old friend a beer?"

"We didn't spend all that much time together," Bill said. "I don't know if you could call us old friends."

Wade Stillman said, "Shouldn't you introduce us to the lady, Bill?"

He glared briefly at the young ex-soldier and said, "You fellas are smart enough to have figured it out already. This is Señorita Catalina Ramos. She's the one who helped me keep San Antonio from bein' blown off the map."

Bailey nodded gravely and said, "It's a pleasure, ma'am."

"It sure is," Stillman added.

Bill sighed, shook his head, and said, "I'll get that beer. And then you're gonna tell us what you're really up to, Clark."

"Me?" Clark said in mock innocence. "I just came to deliver the bad news about Maleef."

"Uh-huh." Bill's skepticism was obvious.

He brought another beer from the kitchen, gave it to Catalina, and nodded her into the chair where he had been sitting. As the others resumed their seats, he perched on the arm of the sofa next to Bailey and said, "All right, Clark, spill it. What's Catalina really doin' here?"

"I told you, she insisted on coming to see you."

"That's right, I did," Catalina said. "Actually, though, I'd been asking about that for a couple of weeks without getting anywhere."

"Until Maleef got loose," Bill said. He started connecting dots. "You thought the cartel might come after her, didn't you, Clark?"

"There's always been a danger of that," Clark said. "We have every confidence in our ability to keep Señorita Ramos safe, though. Maleef's escape didn't really have anything to do with bringing her here."

Catalina took a long swallow of the cold beer, lowered the bottle, and said, "I want to go with you, Bill."

Even though he'd been halfway expecting that, he frowned at her and said, "What?"

"I want to go with you," she said again. "I want to help you put Maleef and Estancia and whoever else is mixed up in this out of business, once and for all."

Bill came to his feet and barked, "That's the damned craziest thing I've ever heard!"

Bailey and Stillman looked shocked. Catalina regarded all of them coolly and said, "Why? You saw for yourself how I can handle myself in a fight, Bill. I didn't ever hold you back, did I?"

"Well . . . no," he admitted. "But this isn't the same thing. We may be goin' up against hundreds of enemies—"

"All the more reason to have an extra hand on your side," Clark chimed in with a smile tugging at his mouth.

"That's not funny," Bill snapped.

"Look, you're thinking that a Mexican stripper couldn't possibly be any help to you, I know that," Catalina said. "But you know what sort of life I've led.

I've had to survive in some really bad situations. I can handle a gun, and I'm a good driver."

"We've got a driver," Bill said.

Catalina ignored the interruption. She went on, "I've had some MMA training, too. I can fight."

"A little practice to put on a show isn't the same as trainin'," Bill scoffed.

Catalina's eyes narrowed. She set the beer bottle aside on a small table next to the chair, being careful to put it on a coaster. As she leaned forward, she said, "If you want to see what I can do, I'd be glad to give you a demonstration."

"I don't think that—"

She pointed at Wade Stillman.

"Him," she said.

"Me?" Stillman said with a confused frown.

Catalina came lithely to her feet and made beckoning motions with both hands, curling her fingers toward her.

"Come on, amigo," she said. "What's your name?"

"It's, uh, Wade."

"Come on, Wade. See if you can take me down." Her eyebrows quirked up and down. "Unless you're afraid . . ."

Stillman looked at Bill.

"This isn't a very good place for a fight," Bill said.

"Fights pick the place, not the other way around."

"That's true," he said. "All right, Wade." Bill made a little waving motion. "Give the señorita what she wants."

Wade looked pretty dubious about the whole thing, but he unbuckled the belt that held his holstered Colt and handed it to Bailey, who was trying not to grin.

"I notice the girl didn't try to pick a fight with you," Wade muttered.

"She knows better," Bailey said.

Catalina said, "Actually, I thought I'd warm up with the little one, then see what you can do."

"Whoa," Bailey said. "Big talk."

"Not if you can back it up."

Clark crossed his arms and said, "This isn't a banter-off. Are we gonna see any action or not?"

Wade didn't wait for any more urging. He lunged at Catalina, going in low, obviously intending to upend her and put her on the floor.

She twisted out of the way and spun in a half-turn as she whipped her foot around in a kick aimed at his head. Wade recovered in midair, caught her calf, and heaved. With a startled yelp, Catalina went over backward and crashed to the floor.

Wade caught himself on his hands and rolled, but as he came up Catalina had already regained her feet as well. Bill thought she looked a little winded, like the fall had knocked the breath out of her, but she didn't let that stop her as she came at Wade with another kick.

That was just a feint, though, and as he moved to block it Catalina shot out a short, sharp punch that landed squarely on his jaw and rocked his head back. He blinked in surprise, but when she tried to follow that blow with another, he was ready and turned it aside with a forearm.

He had an opening then for a counterpunch of his own, but he didn't take it. That second of hesitation gave her a chance to recover. She wheeled into another kick that landed hard enough on Wade's shoulder to knock him back several feet.

"You had a shot at me!" Catalina said. "Why didn't you take it?"

"I was raised not to hit girls," Wade replied with a grin that he had to know would infuriate her.

Pretty clever, thought Bill. Catalina gave in to her anger and surged toward him with a flurry of blows almost too fast for the eye to follow. Wade was ready for her, though. He gave ground for a second, drawing her in even more, then caught one of her arms and went over backward, executing a perfect throw with a foot planted in her belly for leverage. Catalina sailed through the air and landed on the sofa, bouncing once before she rolled off and landed on the floor.

"That was lucky," Bailey said.

"Luck, hell," Wade said. "I aimed her there."

Catalina scrambled to her feet. She didn't make any excuses. She just attacked again, striking out with swift combinations of punches and kicks. Wade dodged or blocked most of them, but a few of them got through and tagged him. A bruise began to form on his jaw, and one of Catalina's knuckles had opened up a tiny cut above his left eye.

She switched tactics suddenly, going for a wrestling hold instead of punching, and they both went to the floor. Before she could pin him, though, Wade neatly reversed the hold, rolled over, and had her trapped facedown with him on top of her. Her arm was trapped, and all he had to do was put a little more pressure on it to pop her shoulder out of joint.

"This is . . . where you say uncle," he told her, a little breathless from their exertions.

"Go . . . to . . . hell!" she gasped back at him. She

bucked and writhed, trying to break his grip. It was too tight, though, and she couldn't do it.

"That's enough," Bill said.

"No!" Catalina cried. "I can . . . get loose."

"Not in a hundred years," Wade grated back at her.

"Get . . . off me!" She gasped again. "Oh, my God! What's that I feel? Are you getting . . . Oh, God, you are!"

Wade jerked back and exclaimed, "Good Lord! I swear I didn't—"

That reaction gave Catalina just enough room to twist slightly in his grasp, worm her other arm free, and bring the elbow around into his jaw with stunning force. His grip slipped even more. She kicked against the floor and rolled both of them over. The arm he had almost dislocated was loose again. She rammed the heel of that hand up under his chin and forced his head back almost far enough to break his neck.

"John," Bill said.

Bailey had set aside Wade's gun. Now he swooped in, got both arms around Catalina's waist, and straightened, taking her with him. She flailed arms and legs in the air and yelled, "Put me down, you big lummox!"

"Calm down," Bill told her. "We don't want anybody gettin' hurt here."

"Maybe you don't!"

"We're all supposed to be on the same side," he reminded her. "Give me your word you'll stop fightin', and I'll have Bailey put you down."

She looked like she wanted to argue, and more important, she looked like she wanted to keep throwing punches, but after a moment she stopped struggling, glared at Bill, and said, "All right, I give you my word."

Bill nodded to John Bailey, who lowered Catalina until her feet were on the floor again. When he let go of her and stepped back, she whirled and brought up a fist that streaked at his chin.

The punch didn't go very far. Bailey's ham-like hand intercepted it, his fingers closing around her fist and dwarfing it. The blow stopped short, as if her arm had reached the end of a thick chain.

"Looks like your word's not worth much," he said dryly.

"Oh." She was fuming, just about to boil over. "You . . . you . . ."

Wade got to his feet, rubbed his jaw, and looked at Catalina with narrow-eyed anger.

"That wasn't fair," he told her. "You know good and well what you accused me of isn't true. The only thing you felt was the humiliation of getting beat."

Clark said, "Oh, I don't know about that. It looked to me like Señorita Ramos used every weapon she had to *keep* from getting beat."

"Well, yeah, but it was cheating," Wade insisted.

"No such thing in a real fight," Bill said. "There's just winnin' and losin'. And it looked to me like you lost, Wade."

"I didn't," Bailey said.

Catalina sneered at him and said, "That's because you're a freak of nature."

"You children settle down and behave," Bill drawled. "Catalina, you handled yourself pretty good. But you're still not comin' with us to Barranca de la Serpiente. It's just too dangerous."

"Clark tells me you have another woman going with you."

"She's ex–Special Forces."

"Can she handle herself as well in a fight as I can?"

It would be quite a battle, Bill thought. For all of Megan's slim, elegant beauty, she was still tough as nails. If he was being honest with himself, though, he wasn't sure Megan could take Catalina in a fair fight.

"Doesn't matter," he said curtly. "I'm in charge of this team, and I'm not takin' along an amateur, even a talented one."

"Technically," Clark said, "I'm in charge of this team."

Bill looked at him and asked coolly, "Are you gonna try to pull rank on me, after knowin' me as long as you have?"

"I didn't say I was a damn fool." Clark looked at Catalina and shrugged. "I promised I'd try, Señorita Ramos, out of gratitude for the help you gave us before, but I'm afraid Bill's going to have to have the last word on this."

"But I can help," Catalina insisted. "I know the cartel. I know how those animals think. I've been around them for years."

She actually had a point there, thought Bill, but it wasn't enough to change his mind.

"Sorry," he said, and meant it. He liked Catalina, and like Clark, he felt grateful to her for everything she had done so far. But that had to be the end of it.

She sighed and asked, "Can I at least stay here with you while you're getting ready for the mission? Maybe train some with you?"

"Because you're thinkin' about goin' into this line of work?"

Clark said, "That's really not a bad idea. I can usually tell when somebody's cut out for it, and I'm thinking maybe Señorita Ramos is."

Bill considered the suggestion for a moment, then shrugged and nodded.

"I don't reckon it can hurt anything," he said.

"Thank you," Catalina told him. She turned to look at Wade, and her lips curved in a savage grin.

"That means I'll get a chance for a rematch with you," she said.

"Any time you're ready, señorita," he told her.

"And you," she went on, turning her head to glare at Bailey. "We'll see how good you do when you're not grabbing somebody from behind."

"Whatever you say, miss."

This might be an added complication he didn't need, Bill began to realize. But on the other hand, having Catalina around might make the men try even harder.

One thing was for sure: they needed to be as prepared as they could possibly be when they entered the Canyon of the Serpent.

Especially now that Tariq Maleef was on the loose again.

CHAPTER 30

Barranca de la Serpiente

It was easy to see how the canyon had gotten its name. It twisted back and forth between the mountains like a snake before opening up into a wide valley. As they flew over the narrow passage in a helicopter, Tariq looked down and was reminded of his homeland in the Hindu Kush.

"The camp must be easy to defend from a ground attack," he commented.

"Yes, we could hold off an army in there," Alfredo Sanchez replied from the seat next to him. "And we have defenses against an attack from the air as well."

He pointed out several gun emplacements that were cunningly concealed in the rocks so they would be hard to spot.

"There's another way in and out," Sanchez went on, "a tunnel wide and tall enough for trucks. It runs through that ridge behind the valley and was part of an old mine. When we moved in here we widened it so that it could be used to bring in supplies."

"Then you're vulnerable that way," Tariq said.

Sanchez shook his head.

"Not at all. Titanium steel doors close it off when it's not in use. They're strong enough to withstand almost anything." A thin smile curved Sanchez's lips. "Anything short of a bomb like the one you had."

Tariq stiffened in the helicopter seat. Anger flared inside him. The Mexican's words sounded like an insult to him, a reminder of the plan that had failed.

And yet it served no purpose to deny the truth. The plan *had* failed. The device that Tariq had gone to so much trouble to obtain was now in the hands of the Americans, probably locked away somewhere in a secret vault where it would never be seen again.

As he almost had been.

He had been tempted to give in to despair during the long weeks when he was being shuffled back and forth from secret prison to secret prison. He began to think that despite the note that had been smuggled in to him at his first place of captivity, Sanchez and the rest of the cartel had found it too difficult to free him and had given up.

During his darkest hours, he had been convinced that Allah had abandoned him as well and that he would spend the rest of his days being tormented by the infidels.

But then, as three vans, with him shackled to the floor of the middle one, had sped along a lonely back road, the vehicle in the lead had hit a mine of some sort, an IED much like the ones his friends on the other side of the world had used so effectively to fight the invaders of their lands. The blast had toppled the van onto its side and blocked the road, and as the two vehicles behind it skidded to a stop, a rocket had streaked out of nowhere and blown the third van into a million pieces.

The force of that explosion had knocked the van containing Tariq onto its side. As he hung from the shackles, one of the guards had aimed a gun at his head, obviously intending to kill him rather than let him be rescued. That was just the sort of barbaric thing the Americans would do.

Before the man could pull the trigger, though, an automatic weapon had stuttered and stitched a line of bullet holes across his chest. One of the other guards was behind that gun, obviously paid off by the cartel to help free Tariq.

Then other cartel soldiers were there to finish off the remaining guards, and it was done. They found the key to unlock Tariq's shackles, and as soon as his hands were free, he bent down and picked up a fallen pistol.

When they had all climbed out of the overturned van, Tariq went to the guard who had betrayed his fellows and embraced the man.

"Thank you," he said. "Thank you for giving me back my freedom." He stepped back. "How much were you paid?"

The guard, a stocky Hispanic man, looked nervous, like he wanted to be anywhere else but here right now. But he licked his lips and said, "One hundred thousand dollars."

"I wish to give you something else," Tariq said.

With that, he raised the gun and shot the man in the head, two swift shots that bored through his brain and blew the back of his skull off as they exited. As the corpse dropped like a sack of wet sand, Tariq had looked around at the men from the cartel and said, "A man who will betray his friends for money will betray his new friends as well. He could not be trusted."

No one argued with him or even looked particularly shocked. Death was an everyday thing to these men, their stock in trade.

From there Tariq had been taken across what turned out to be the New Mexico desert in a caravan of pickups and SUVs, and when they finally reached an isolated landing strip, a helicopter was waiting there with Alfredo Sanchez standing beside it. Sanchez, as handsome and immaculately groomed as ever, had come forward to meet Tariq and embraced him.

"It is good to see you again, my friend," Sanchez had said. "You never gave up hope, did you?"

"Never," Tariq said, and it was only a tiny lie, not big enough to worry about. And now, since he was free again, he could put it out of his mind entirely and think of only one thing.

Vengeance against the Americans.

After that greeting they had climbed into the helicopter and flown toward the border. Sanchez explained that although the Border Patrol used drone aircraft equipped with cameras to monitor activity along the border, the cartel had enough spies within the American agency that it was no trouble to find out the flight schedule for the drones.

"How have the Americans survived so long, as

weak and foolish as they obviously are?" Tariq had asked. "The rest of the world should be able to have its way with them."

"There are still too many of them who are able to see the truth and think clearly," Sanchez had replied with a shrug. "Although the numbers of those who can are dwindling steadily. The results of their last few presidential elections prove that. Really, all we have to do is wait. It may take another fifteen or twenty years, but then their economy will crash completely and the country will be there for anyone strong enough to move in and take it."

"Destiny will not wait," Tariq had said. "They must be destroyed. Now."

The helicopter reached the end of the canyon and flew over the valley, which was filled with tents, modular buildings, and metal warehouses. There was a landing strip to one side. Another helicopter sat near it, as did several small planes including a corporate jet. A road led toward the cliffs at the far end of the valley, and Tariq assumed that was where the tunnel Sanchez had mentioned was located.

There was also what looked from the air like some sort of large pit with a floor that appeared to be bare dirt. Tariq frowned at that, pointed toward it, and asked Sanchez, "What is the purpose of that?"

"You'll see, amigo," Sanchez answered with a smile. "In fact, we have some entertainment prepared for you. We thought it might lift your spirits after your long captivity."

Tariq had no idea what the man was talking about, nor was he interested in whatever Sanchez's idea of entertainment might be. But the alliance between their organizations was important, so he supposed he would go along with whatever the cartel had planned.

The helicopter touched down. When Tariq climbed out, he saw several of his friends waiting for him, along with some of the cartel men. He embraced his fellow fighters for Islam and nodded to the other men as Sanchez introduced them.

Then the whole group climbed into waiting cars and headed toward the pit Tariq had seen from the air.

One of the men in the car with Tariq was his old friend Anwar al-Waleed. A tall, skinny man with thick glasses and a shock of black hair that tended to fall into his eyes, Anwar had been the mastermind behind the New Sun. It had been his idea in the first place to forge the alliance with the Mexicans, and he had been the driving force behind the establishment of the camp here at Barranca de la Serpiente. Tariq considered himself a fist in the service of Allah, while Anwar fought the holy war with his brain.

"It's so good to see you again, Tariq," Anwar said in his mild voice, smiling as he spoke. "Even though I hoped that the next time we greeted each other, it would be in paradise."

"As did I," Tariq said. "If only Allah had willed it so."

"You will soon have another chance to strike at the godless Americans, my friend. Plans are already in motion."

"Good. The day of holy reckoning for them cannot come too soon."

People were converging on the pit from all over

the camp now and gathering at its edge. There would be quite a crowd, Tariq thought, several hundred, in fact. When the little caravan from the landing strip came to a stop, he and the others got out of the cars and joined the throng. Most of them were Middle Eastern men, although a significant minority were Hispanic. Tariq saw no women, of course; they would not be allowed at a gathering of men like this.

The crowd parted to allow Tariq, Sanchez, Anwar, and the others through to the pit. Many of them reached out to slap Tariq on the back or the arm and shout encouragement to him. He was famous among them, he knew, because he had dared to carry the New Sun into the heart of the American city, but despite the fact that they admired him for his courage, he knew they were also well aware of his failure. That thought put the bitter, sour taste of gall in his throat, and he knew only one thing would take it away.

His own death in the service of Allah, striking a mortal blow into the heart of the infidels.

Most of the men were armed, either with pistols or automatic weapons or both. They would be a formidable army, Tariq thought, but their numbers were still too small. They could not hope to defeat the Americans by conventional means. That was why they had to rely on weapons of mass destruction. Only that would balance the scales and give their holy cause a chance of succeeding.

When they reached the edge of the pit, Tariq saw that a ladder was propped against its wall and several men had descended into it since he had seen the place from the air. The pit was roughly circular, about fifty yards in diameter, and some fifteen feet deep. The walls that had been cut into the hard ground were too sheer for a man to climb.

Two of the men in the pit wore ragged work clothes and bore the marks of rough treatment. Their faces were bruised and streaked with dried blood from an assortment of cuts and scratches. Both were Hispanic, and half a dozen other Hispanic men surrounded them. It was clear that the two men who had been roughed up were prisoners. The others held cudgels and looked quite capable of using them to beat the captives to death if they chose to.

"Are you ready?" Sanchez asked Tariq.

"Ready for what?"

"The spectacle of life and death." Sanchez raised his voice and shouted orders in Spanish to the men in the pit. The club-wielding guards backed off, leaving the two prisoners in the center of the sunken area.

They climbed the ladder and pulled it up after them, ensuring that the prisoners were helpless to escape. Sanchez turned to one of the other men and snapped his fingers. The man stepped up and handed two machetes to Sanchez.

Stepping to the very edge of the pit, Sanchez called down to the two captives, "You know what you must do! May the best man win!"

He tossed the machetes into the pit.

Before the weapons even hit the hard-packed sand, the two prisoners were streaking toward them. A great shout went up from the assembled spectators.

Tariq understood now. He said to Sanchez, "They fight to the death, eh?"

"Exactly," Sanchez replied with a smile.

"Did they transgress somehow against your rules? Is this their punishment?"

"Those two *cabrones*? They are not members of our group. No, we have a whole barracks full of men like them, men we have taken from buses we stopped on their way from one town to another. We take the most able-bodied men, the ones who look like they can fight . . . and the most attractive of the women. They service our men, and some of yours as well."

Tariq nodded. Raping infidel women was allowed. Anything that caused pain to the enemies of Allah was allowed.

One of the prisoners had pulled ahead of the other. He reached the machetes first and tried to snatch up both of them, so the other man wouldn't have a chance. He fumbled one away, though, and didn't have time to reach for it again before the second man tackled him. They rolled across the sand as they struggled. The second man was able to twist the machete free from the first man's grip and chopped at his head with it.

The first man jerked aside, barely avoiding the killing blow, and scrambled after the other machete. He grabbed it and twisted, flinging the blade up just in time to block another stroke from the second man. The machetes clashed with a loud ring of steel against steel, and again the spectators surrounding the pit shouted in bloodthirsty eagerness.

The blades continued to clang against each other as the two men fought their way to their feet. It was a raw, desperate battle, a matter of sheer survival. Neither of the men in the pit was particularly skilled with the machete, but skill played little part in this contest. Speed, strength, stamina . . . and luck. These things would decide who lived and who died.

Long minutes went by as the men hacked clumsily at each other. Some of the blows found their targets and left behind gushing wounds, but none bad enough to put an end to the fight. Big drops of blood spattered on the sand like crimson rain as the combatants circled, lunged, twisted, and darted.

They were tiring before Tariq's eyes. Sweat ran in rivers from their faces and soaked their shirts; their chests heaved wildly as they struggled to draw in enough air to keep fighting.

Then luck played the part it was always destined to play. One of the men slipped, his foot sliding almost out from under him as he tried to avoid a wild swing of the other man's machete. Instinctively, he threw his arms out to the sides in an attempt to catch his balance and keep from falling.

That left him wide open for a split second, and his opponent recovered from the missed swing in time to seize the opportunity. He brought his machete around in a chopping, backhanded blow. The blade struck the other man at the juncture of his neck and right shoulder and bit deep into muscle and bone.

The wounded man screamed and staggered. His right arm wouldn't work anymore, so he couldn't raise his blade and defend himself as his opponent ripped the machete free and struck again, swinging it so hard this time that the blade went halfway through the man's neck and lodged in his spine.

That finished him. Blood gouted in a grisly fountain as the man toppled over to lie twitching while the rest of his life poured out onto the sand. The victor planted a foot on the dying man's chest and wrenched the machete loose.

The shouts from the men around the pit were deafening.

Tariq leaned closer to Sanchez and said, "They fought well, for amateurs."

"They had good reason to fight. Not only were they promised that the victor would have his freedom, but that his wife would be turned loose as well. A man always fights more desperately for his loved ones than for himself."

Tariq nodded. Sanchez was right about that.

A couple of men lowered the ladder into the pit again. Several others descended while the winner of the battle tossed his bloody machete aside and fell to his knees. He covered his face with his hands as he tried to catch his breath. A shudder went through him. As far as Tariq knew, the two men had been friends. But they had been forced to battle to the death anyway.

One of the cartel men picked up the machete that the dead man had dropped. He nudged the victor with the point and spoke to him. Tariq couldn't hear the words, but he saw the horrified expression on the man's face as he looked up at his captors.

"Now he must fight again," Tariq guessed.

"Yes," Sanchez said. "Delicious, is it not?"

Tariq smiled in agreement.

The surviving prisoner suddenly turned and tried

to scramble away on hands and knees. The other men went after him, grabbed him, forced him to his feet, and marched him back to face his new opponent, who stood there patiently tapping the flat of the machete blade against the palm of his other hand.

As the cartel men backed off again, the prisoner looked down at the weapon lying at his feet. Evidently recognizing the inevitability of what was going to happen, he scooped the machete from the ground, let out an incoherent yell, and charged his new opponent.

"If by chance he wins . . . ?" Tariq said to Sanchez.

The slimly handsome man shrugged.

"Then another will test him . . . and another and another, if necessary."

It wasn't going to come to that, however, as Tariq saw almost right away. The prisoner was too exhausted, too weak from his own wounds, too unskilled to match the deadly abilities of the cartel man. The blades rang together several times as the cartel man fended off the ferocious but awkward attack, and then the prisoner's luck ran out. Steel winked brightly in the sun as a fierce, powerful stroke by the cartel man sent his blade shearing completely through the prisoner's neck.

The man's head toppled from his shoulders and thudded to the ground as his body remained on its feet, swaying for several seconds while blood bubbled out of the severed windpipe. Then the headless corpse fell over, too.

The cheering was even more thunderous this time.

"Once more the *hondura de sangre* has drunk deep," Sanchez said.

"I don't know the words," Tariq said.

"It means *pit of blood*," Sanchez explained.

Tariq said, "Ah," and nodded slowly.

He would not be satisfied until all of America was a *hondura de sangre*.

CHAPTER 31

West Texas

Bill was sitting at the desk in the living room of his quarters, a laptop open in front of him as he studied satellite photos of a rugged, mountainous region. Barranca de la Serpiente was located somewhere in that wasteland, according to the sketchy intelligence they had been able to obtain. But they didn't have an exact location, and it would be best to know where they were going before they launched their attack.

Unfortunately, with every day that passed, Bill worried that whatever new hell they were brewing up down there below the border was that much closer to fruition.

A knock sounded on the door. Bill knew how secure the base was, so he didn't hesitate to call, "Come in."

Henry Dixon opened the door and walked in, his gait somewhat deliberate as always but not so much so that anyone would notice it if they didn't know he had lost both legs in Africa. Bill grinned and said, "Henry. Good to see you. I didn't know exactly when you'd get here."

"I came in a little while ago," Dixon said. "Been clearing up a little family business. I could have been here sooner if you needed me, but I figured you'd let me know if you did."

"Yeah, I would have. We're not ready to go yet, by any means. The last two members of the team aren't even here yet. They were supposed to be, but there was some last-minute holdup. Somebody at the DOJ found out that Madigan and Watson were being 'transferred'—" He made air quotes around the word. "—and got a bug up his ass about it. Clark had to do some fast tap-dancin' to get it all straightened out."

Dixon grunted and said, "They ought to call it the Department of Injustice the way it's been run the past dozen years. Whatever happened to upholding the law the way it's written, rather than to suit your own political agenda?"

"Why, that's the old-fashioned way of lookin' at it, Henry. We've all got to be modern and progressive now, not tied down to some moldy ol' Constitution."

Dixon rolled his eyes and said, "You know the wheels are all going to come off one of these days, don't you?"

"Sure. And by the time they do, I plan on bein' so far back in the woods nobody'll ever find me."

"Assuming you live through this mission. Assuming any of us do."

"Yeah," Bill said. "There's that to consider, too."

"Hiram Stackhouse wants me to do this, and I owe that man big-time, so I'm in all the way." Dixon sat down in one of the armchairs. "You might get me a beer, though."

Bill grinned and got up to go into the kitchen.

As he came back with the beer, someone else knocked on the door. He handed the bottle to Dixon, then went over and opened the door.

Megan Sinclair stood there with a sheaf of documents in her hand. She wore jeans and a short-sleeved silk blouse and looked as elegant and lovely as ever. She looked past Bill at Dixon and said, "I'm sorry, I didn't know you had company."

"Henry's not company, he's part of the team," Bill said as he stood aside. "Come on in and I'll introduce you."

"Don't get up," Megan told Dixon as she came into the room. "I know who you are, Mr. Dixon."

"Then you know I was raised to be a gentleman," Dixon said as he stood. He held out a hand to her.

As they shook, Bill introduced them, adding for Dixon's benefit, "Megan is Colonel Sinclair's daughter."

"Old Iron Ba—"

Megan smiled when Dixon stopped short in what he was saying. She said, "It's all right, Mr. Dixon. I know some of his men called my father Old Iron Balls. He deserved the name, too."

"Yes, Miss Sinclair, he did. But he was a helluva commanding officer."

Bill asked, "You want a beer, Megan?"

She shook her head.

"No, thanks. I came across something that's got me thinking."

Bill gestured at the papers in her hand and said, "I figured as much. Why don't we take a look at it?"

They gathered around the coffee table as Megan spread out the documents on it.

"Some of these are news reports," she explained. "Others are intel I picked up from hacking into Mexican law enforcement networks." She said that matter-of-factly, obviously knowing that no one connected with this mission was going to object to a little cyber-piracy in a good cause. "In the past six months, more than a dozen buses have been hijacked in the northern part of the Mexican state of Chihuahua. Passengers have been robbed and sometimes killed, and many of them have been kidnapped, carried off by the attackers. The victims have been both men and women."

"Sounds like somethin' those lowlife cartel hombres would do," Bill said, remembering how that busload of high school students had been kidnapped and held for ransom several years earlier. "Have there been ransom demands?"

Megan shook her head.

"These aren't the sort of people whose families could pay a big ransom, or even any ransom," she said. "They're working people. Farmers and small businessmen for the most part."

"Why would the cartel go to the trouble of kidnapping them if they couldn't make a profit?" Dixon asked.

"I wondered about that, too. In fact, that's what caught my eye and made me see the pattern here. After that it didn't take long to come up with a possible answer."

Bill smiled and said, "You may not know it, but when you were in Special Forces, the CIA tried to steal you away a time or two. Seems they thought you'd make a good analyst for them. They were right."

Megan didn't seem to hear the compliment, but Bill figured she really did. She said, "This ties in with that training camp. If you're going to teach people how to kill, you need victims for your students to practice on."

Bill had already made that same leap of logic. He nodded and said, "Those poor devils taken off the buses would work for that."

"The men would," Megan said. "The female prisoners would be forced to serve as prostitutes for the men being trained at the camp."

Dixon cleared his throat. He and Bill were both of a generation that felt a little uncomfortable at hearing a young woman speak so bluntly about such a thing, but they both had no doubt that Megan was right.

"You're thinkin' that we'd be able to put this to use?" Bill asked.

"I thought it might help us locate this so-called Snake Canyon."

"How can it do that," Dixon said, "if nobody's been able to find those people who were kidnapped?"

"Well, *those* people can't help us . . ." Megan said.

"But if the right fellas were to be on another bus that was hijacked . . ." Bill said.

Dixon frowned.

"Ah. I see now what you're talking about. Walking right into the jaws of a trap."

Bill's brain was working furiously as he turned over the possibilities of using the intel Megan had brought to him. He said, "Nobody would suspect that a couple of poor laborers might have GPS chips implanted under their skin."

"And with satellite tracking we could follow those chips anywhere," Megan added. "I don't see any reason it wouldn't work."

"Other than the fact that no one is going to mistake any of us for Mexican farmers," Dixon said. "Also, how would you know which bus the cartel was going to hit?"

"They're creatures of habit," Megan said. "Nearly all of the hijackings have occurred on the highway between the towns of Dos Caballos and Villa Guajardo. And it's been a couple of weeks since the last incident took place, so there's a good chance that they're running low on . . . practice victims."

She paled a little as she said it. Her background as a thief had been a nonviolent one, other than knocking out a guard now and then, and although she was plenty tough, she had never been exposed to the same levels of carnage that the rest of them had.

"So if we could get a couple of men on that bus in the next few days, there's at least a chance the cartel might stop it," Bill mused.

"Unless they strike again before that," Megan said. "I can be monitoring my sources for any news about that."

Dixon said, "You still haven't said who's going to be the bait."

"Me, for one," Bill said without hesitation. "I can pass for Hispanic, I think, and my Tex-Mex is pretty dang fluent."

"You can't go in by yourself," Dixon protested.

"Stillman's out. Too blond. Bailey might do."

Megan said, "He doesn't really look like a Mexican to me."

"There are gringos in Mexico, too, you know."

Megan leaned back on the sofa where she was sitting and frowned in thought.

"You know, it would help sell the whole thing if you had an actual Mexican citizen with you. A woman, maybe."

Bill's forehead creased as he glared at her.

"You're talkin' about Catalina Ramos," he said.

Megan shrugged. "The rumor is that she badgered Clark into bringing her out here so she could ask you if she can come along on the mission. Maybe that would actually be helpful."

"How well do you know Catalina?" Bill asked.

"We just met for a moment," Megan said coolly. "I don't think she liked me much."

Bill had a hunch the feeling was mutual. It was a cliché to think that a couple of beautiful women would instinctively dislike each other, but like most clichés, it might have a grain of truth to it.

"You know she's not a professional," Bill said.

"I suppose that depends on what line of work you're talking about."

Bill ignored that comment and went on, "She's got no business bein' right in the middle of a covert op."

"And yet that's exactly where she was not long ago. Tell me, how many men did she kill when she was getting that flash drive out of Mexico and into our hands?"

"That's not the same thing," Bill insisted. "She didn't go lookin' for that trouble. It found her."

"But she survived it," Megan said. "If it wasn't for

her, you wouldn't have been able to stop Maleef from carrying out that New Sun business."

Bill couldn't argue with that.

"She can fight, obviously," Megan went on. "And you'd have a few days to train her. Call it a crash course in being an operator."

"That's something you can't learn overnight."

"But if you have an aptitude for it to start with, you might learn enough to stay alive." She paused. "At least until the mission is done. And that's all any of us are really hoping for, isn't it?"

She was right about that, too . . . damn it.

Dixon spoke up, saying, "I don't work with amateurs. Never have and never will."

"If we go along with what Megan is sayin', you wouldn't have to work directly with Catalina," Bill said. "In fact, you probably won't be workin' directly with any of us."

"Even so, I don't like the idea of somebody like that being involved. Amateurs are unpredictable. You can't really prepare for what they might do."

"That's true. And we'd be askin' Catalina to risk bein' kidnapped and forced to do Lord knows what."

Megan said, "I think she's well past the point of worrying about a fate worse than death."

"That's a mighty cold thing to say," Bill told her.

"I prefer to think of it as pragmatic. Anyway, she wants to go. She knows the risks. And sure, there are risks to the rest of us in letting her come along. She might do something crazy that endangers all of us. But I keep coming back to the fact that having her with you on that bus might help you get to Barranca de la Serpiente."

Bill sighed and nodded.

"I don't like it, but I think you're right. I guess I'd better call her over here and tell her that she's goin' along with us after all. If she still wants to when she hears this new angle, that is. This is still a volunteer mission. That's the way it's got to be."

He wasn't going to send anybody to their death who wasn't willing to go. Not convicted murderers, and for sure not a gal like Catalina Ramos.

Bill had a pretty strong hunch how she was going to react, though.

CHAPTER 32

"Are you kidding?" Catalina asked as a smile broke out on her face. "I'm in. You'd better believe I'm in!"

It was the next morning. Bill had changed his mind about asking her immediately and decided to sleep on it instead, but when he got up nothing had changed. Megan's suggestion still made sense. If there was anything that might increase the chances of the mission being successful, they had to do it.

"It's gonna be damn dangerous," Bill warned her as they stood in the shade of one of the hangars beside the landing strip. Bill was waiting for the chopper that would deliver the final two members of the team.

"More dangerous than having Estancia's mad-dog killers after me, like they were back in Cuidad Acuña and Del Rio?"

"There'll be more of 'em," Bill said, "and plenty of terrorists smuggled in from the Middle East, too. They're even worse because they hate all Americans. The cartel just wants to make a profit off of us."

Catalina said, "Well, it's lucky for me, then, that I'm a Mexican and not an American, right?"

"They're not gonna care that much. If you get in their way, they'll kill you, no matter where you're from."

"I'll take that chance. I want to do something to stop those people, Bill." She paused. "Marty wanted to stop them, too, but he can't do anything anymore. He's dead, and they're to blame."

"You were mighty fond of him, weren't you?"

She shrugged and said, "He was a loser in most ways. I hate to say it, but he was. But he really loved me, I think, and that buys him some revenge."

"All right," Bill said. "We've only got a few days to get you ready, though. They're gonna be rough ones."

"Bring them on," she said with a grin. "I'll do whatever I need to."

Bill found himself believing her, too. Before he could say any more, though, he heard the distant *whup-whup-whup* of a helicopter's rotors.

The chopper came into view against the cloud-dotted blue sky. This was one of the bigger jobs, probably because a lot of guards were needed for the two passengers it was carrying. Bill had half a dozen men armed with riot shotguns on hand himself, including John Bailey and Wade Stillman, just in case.

Dust flew as the helicopter settled down to a landing. Bill turned to Catalina and said, "You can go on back to your quarters now. I'll come see you in a little while and we'll get started on your training."

"If you think I'm going to leave now, you're

loco," she said. "I've heard the rumors about these two. I want to get a look at them for myself."

Bill debated making his suggestion an order instead, then decided it wasn't worth making an issue over it. Besides, he saw other people walking toward the landing strip, including Megan, Henry Dixon, Nick Hatcher, Braden Cole, and Jackie Thornton.

It appeared that everybody on the base had heard about Madigan and Watson and wanted to get a look at them.

Several guards climbed out of the helicopter first and set up in a half-circle with their automatic weapons pointing back toward the aircraft. One of them spoke into a radio microphone clipped to his shoulder.

A moment later a massive figure appeared in the doorway and hopped down to the tarmac, landing with a lithe grace and ease that was unusual in such a big man. Bill had seen photos of Ellis "Bronco" Madigan, so he had no trouble recognizing the man. Even in dark blue prison trousers and a faded blue shirt, Madigan was an impressive, unforgettable figure.

So was the man who followed Madigan from the helicopter. He was a black version of Bronco Madigan. Calvin Watson would probably take offense if anyone phrased it that way in his presence, but it was true nonetheless.

Both men wore old-fashioned shackles. Most law enforcement agencies had long since made the change to plastic restraints, but in some cases, steel was just better. Plastic would hold normal human beings, but not Neanderthals like Madigan and Watson.

More gun-toting guards descended from the chopper behind them, so the two convicts were completely surrounded. One of the guards snapped an order, and the whole group started toward the hangar where Bill and the others waited.

"They don't look so tough," Bailey said under his breath.

Bill recognized the tone of competitiveness in the big noncom's voice. He said, "As long as we're all on the same side, John, we won't have to worry about who's the toughest."

"I didn't mean it that way, sir," Bailey said quickly, even though Bill knew good and well that he had.

Nick Hatcher stood in a casual pose with his hands tucked into the hip pockets of his jeans. He said, "They look plenty tough to me."

"Me, too," Jackie Thornton agreed. "I sure wouldn't want to tangle with them." He looked nervous, as if he knew that either of the newcomers could break him in two with their bare hands. Thornton's normal expression was always a little nervous, though, Bill reminded himself.

Braden Cole's face was expressionless. That was normal, too. The explosives expert had about as much personality as a snake.

The guards fanned out a little as they approached so that Bill could confront Madigan and Watson. When the group had come to a stop, he nodded to the two prisoners and said, "You fellas and I haven't met before, but you talked to an associate of mine."

Clark had handled the negotiations with Madigan and Watson, since it was easier for him to get into the high-security federal facility where they were being held. Bill had been busy making arrangements for their staging area to be located here at the old abandoned Air Force base.

Madigan rumbled, "You talkin' about a fella looks like he ought to be an insurance salesman?"

"We killed and ate him," Watson added.

Bill's eyes narrowed. He said, "They told me you two were a couple of badasses who hated each other's guts. Come to find out you're a comedy team."

"You let us worry about who we hate, mister," Madigan said. "Right now I'd say you're on the list."

"Damn straight," Watson said.

"You're gonna hate me even more," Bill said. "I'm your new boss."

Madigan let loose with an obscene tirade that would have scorched the paint off a Sherman tank. When he finished, Watson took the profanity baton and carried on. The cussing started off being directed at Bill, but eventually it came around to Megan and Catalina and what the two convicts would like to do to them.

Bailey had listened with a tight jaw at first, but when the newcomers started verbally assaulting the two women, he stepped forward and snapped, "Shut your filthy mouths."

"Hey!" Catalina objected. "We can defend ourselves, thank you very much."

"Are you kidding?" Megan said. "I'm all for equality and I've taken care of myself for years, but those two are humongous. No way I'm tangling with them. Bailey, you go right ahead and be chivalrous."

Bill stepped forward, moving between Bailey and the two convicts.

"Let 'em spout their filth," he said. "They're just blowin' off steam because they know we've got the upper hand."

"Upper hand, hell," Madigan repeated with a sneer. "You can't make us do anything we don't want to do."

"That's right. If you don't want to cooperate and be part of this, you can climb back in that chopper and it'll take you back where you came from. But you can kiss that deal you agreed to good-bye. No new lives for you fellas."

Watson said, "I don't believe it anyway. That's just one more empty promise from the government."

"Most of the time I'd agree with you. The government's word's not worth a hill of beans, at least not with the people who're runnin' it now. Lyin' comes as natural to them as breathin'."

"Then why do you care what happens?" Madigan asked.

"Because it's not about those worthless sacks o' left-wing shit in Washington," Bill said. "It's about the millions of good people who still live in this country, the ones who try to do something worthwhile with their lives and make the world a better place instead of sittin' around with their hands out for whatever some empty suit promises to give 'em. The deck is already stacked against honest folks like that, stacked by the very people who are supposed to be representin' them. They got enough problems here at home without havin' to worry about a bunch of bloodthirsty relics from the Middle Ages who want to murder 'em in their beds and some slick criminals who want to squeeze every drop of blood and profit out of 'em. That's why I care, Madigan."

Silence followed Bill's words. Watson broke it by saying, "You been workin' on that speech for a while, haven't you, you old geezer?"

"When you call me that . . . smile."

Bill figured it was safe to use the Owen Wister quote. Henry Dixon was the only other person on the base old enough to recognize it.

The only response it got, though, was another flood of curses from both convicts. After a moment Bailey said to Bill, "Let me beat some decency into them. That's the only thing they're going to understand."

Madigan hooted with laughter and said, "Boy, you couldn't beat your own—"

"No, we're not gonna go there," Bill cut in. "They want to be turned loose to settle things man to man. They figure if they pull that trick, they can double-cross us, get their hands on some guns, and fight their way out of here. But this isn't some cowboy movie, gentlemen. This isn't Yuma Prison, and you sure as hell aren't the good guys. You're gonna stay under lock, key, and heavy guard until we get where we're goin'. You don't need any special training. All you need is an enemy, and I'm gonna give you one. And when we get there, *then* you get turned loose. I'm gonna point you in the right direction and say 'Kill,' and you're gonna do it."

Watson sneered and said, "Maybe we'll just cut a deal with that so-called enemy. Maybe we'd rather be on their side than yours."

"A deal goes two ways, and where we're goin', nobody will be interested in makin' one with you boys. They're just gonna try to kill you on sight, and they won't stop to do any talkin'. So you'll fight them or die. Simple as that."

Bill's calm, steady words had an effect. He could tell that, even though Madigan and Watson tried to keep up their façade. They knew he was telling the truth.

"Maybe we don't want to do this anymore," Madigan said.

"Too late. You're part of it. You're goin' along whether you want to or not."

He turned on his heel and walked away, adding over his shoulder an order for the guards to lock them up. The rest of the team followed him, leaving Madigan and Watson behind to shout curses after them.

Now that he had met the two convicts, he was willing to make an exception to his all-volunteer policy. Facing such heavy odds, he needed a couple of killing machines like Bronco Madigan and Calvin Watson.

With any luck, those two would be his own personal weapons of mass destruction.

CHAPTER 33

Chihuahua, Mexico, one week later

The dust and the heat were stifling as Bill swayed slightly on the uncomfortable, thinly upholstered bench seat of the Mexican bus. The upholstery was torn in several places and patched with duct tape. The window beside him was lowered, but that didn't really help much because the air outside was just as hot as that inside the bus.

The breeze coming through the open window didn't dispel the stink inside the bus, either. It just stirred up the various elements of it.

Nor did the noise help matters, starting with the racket coming from the bus's ancient and ineffective muffler. Adding to it was the loud cackling from several crates of chickens resting in the backseats of the vehicle and the strains of *Tejano* music coming from an old-fashioned boom box on the lap of one of the passengers.

"Really?" Bailey had muttered as he, Bill, and Catalina had climbed on board the bus and found places to sit. "Chickens and mariachi music on a Mexican bus?"

"At the next stop somebody will get on with a goat," Catalina said. "You just wait and see. We Mexicans live to fulfill your gringo stereotypes. Anyway, that's not mariachi music. It's *Tejano.*"

"I'm from Brooklyn. It all sounds the same to me."

"Again with the stereotypes!"

Bill hadn't told them to cut out the banter. That was a way of blowing off steam. Knowing what they might be headed into, they had to be a little nervous, especially Catalina. Despite the tough front she put up and the actual dangers she had faced in her life, she had never gone to war, like Bill and John Bailey had.

And war was exactly what they were facing if they made it into Barranca de la Serpiente. A short and bloody conflict, but war nonetheless.

They were about an hour out of the small town of Villa Guajardo, bound for Dos Caballos, which was another two hours away. The day before they had ridden from Dos Caballos to Villa Guajardo, and the trip had been uneventful except for the jolting Bill's spine had gotten from the bus's worn-out suspension. Tomorrow, if they had to, they would make the return trip from Dos Caballos.

Eventually somebody might notice them riding back and forth this way, but the bus driver didn't pay much attention to his passengers. Bill had smelled the pungent scent of marijuana coming from the man's threadbare uniform and figured the hombre was high. He could keep the bus on the road all right—the fact that it was flat and straight for the most part helped—but he didn't care what was going on in the seats behind him.

The highway was narrow and pockmarked with potholes, but they were small ones. It didn't rain enough in this region to cause large potholes. The countryside was semiarid. The people who lived here scratched out livings on small farms, but they weren't good livings.

The mountains of the Sierra Madre Oriental loomed to the west of the road. The terrorist training camp was somewhere up there in one of the valleys hidden among the peaks, Bill knew. Finding it would be almost impossible if you didn't know where you were going.

That was why he and Bailey and Catalina were going to let their enemies take them there.

Bill wore a battered straw Stetson, a faded khaki work shirt with the sleeves rolled up, jeans, and boots that showed plenty of wear and tear. With his craggy face, salt-and-pepper hair and mustache, and weathered skin, he looked like an old farm or ranch hand. He sat by the window and Catalina sat beside him, next to the aisle.

She wore a sleeveless white blouse, jeans, and sneakers. Her thick brown hair was pulled back in a ponytail. She called Bill "*Tio*" when she spoke to him, reinforcing the pose that they were uncle and niece. They were supposedly on their way to the next town to look for work.

Bailey rode in the seat directly behind them, taking up the whole bench himself. Even if he hadn't been so big, nobody would have wanted to sit next to the scary-looking gringo. Dark shades covered his eyes. The sleeves were cut off the blue denim work shirt he wore with a metal-studded leather vest over it. His bare arms were covered with elaborate tattoos. They weren't permanent, but they would last long enough to serve their purpose. He had a revolver stuck in the waistband of his jeans; the vest partially covered the butt, but by design it was visible part of the time, too. He was supposed to look *muy malo*, so people would leave him alone.

If the cartel was really kidnapping men to use in training the Arab terrorists, Bailey would make an irresistible target. He looked like he could actually put up a fight. The kidnappers wouldn't want pushovers.

Bill looked tough enough to take with them, too. And Catalina . . . well, Catalina was still beautiful, even in cheap clothes and no makeup. The cartel wouldn't hesitate to grab her and force her into a life of being a *puta* for their own men and their Middle Eastern guests.

Before they'd left the base in West Texas to make their way unobtrusively into Mexico with forged passports that said Bill and Catalina were Mexican nationals named Hector and Maria Lopez and Bailey was an American named Pete Ericsson, the GPS chips had been implanted under their skin, right at the hairline on the back of the neck so the tiny incisions wouldn't be noticeable.

"The chances of them scannin' us for any sort of signal is pretty small," Bill had said to Megan, "but what if they do?"

"We're the only ones in the world with equipment sophisticated enough to pick up the signal from these transmitters," she had assured him.

"The frequency is so narrow and the bursts are so short that anything else will just scan right past it. Our satellite will stay locked in on it, though."

Bill had looked at Clark and said, "That must've been expensive. How'd you manage to get a satellite like that up there when money for the space program would be so much better spent at social engineerin'?"

"What the blowhard-in-chief doesn't know might just save the country," Clark had replied. "Besides— and this is so far off the record it can't even *see* the record—not all of our funding comes strictly from congressional appropriations anymore. There are individuals in this country who are willing to foot the bill for things that really need to get done that might not otherwise. 'Nuff said?"

"'Nuff said," Bill had agreed. He suspected that Hiram Stackhouse was one of those individuals Clark was talking about, but he wasn't going to press the issue. The fewer details he knew about things like that, the better.

Now, even though he couldn't feel it, Bill knew the chip was there in the back of his neck, and he took comfort in the fact that the rest of his team knew where he was.

Of course, if he got into trouble they were too far away to come and help him right away. He would just have to survive until the cavalry could get there, and that might take hours. Maybe even a day or longer, depending on where they wound up.

Wade Stillman was in Dos Caballos with Megan, Nick Hatcher, Jackie Thornton, and Braden Cole, all of them holed up in the hotel there. Bill worried a little about Wade and Megan having to ride herd on the trio of civilian criminals, but Hatcher and Thornton seemed eager to cooperate and earn their shot at new lives. With Cole it was hard to tell anything about what he was thinking, of course, but Bill knew the man prided himself on his professionalism. Cole had hired on to do a job, and Bill thought he would honor that bargain.

Madigan and Watson were still across the border, being watched over by Henry Dixon and a squadron of guards. When the time came to move, Dixon and the two convicts would be brought in by helicopter. That would mean violating Mexico's airspace, but nobody really gave a damn about that. Mexico was violating common decency by allowing the drug cartels to basically run the country and inviting in a bunch of Middle Eastern lunatics to help them attack the U.S.

The man taking up space in the Oval Office might not like it, but nobody involved in this mission really gave a damn about *him*, either.

Too bad they couldn't just locate the terrorist camp and call in an airstrike on it, Bill mused. A little hellfire raining down from the heavens on the sons of bitches. Something like that took even more juice than Clark had, though. This had to be a surgical strike instead.

And Bill and his team were the surgeons.

Bailey leaned forward and asked Catalina, "Hey, baby, since we got music, you want to dance?"

She turned to look at him and laughed.

"You really should leave me alone, gringo," she told him. They weren't supposed to know each other; they had just made each other's acquaintance on this bus ride. But being slightly obnoxious fit in with the role Bailey was playing, so he kept trying to flirt with her.

Bill wasn't sure how much of it was acting. Back at the old air base, Bailey and Catalina had spent quite a bit of time together. During the several days of training she had gone through, most of it had been spent working with Bailey and Wade Stillman on hand-to-hand combat and weapons practice, and Bill had a hunch a little romantic triangle had sprung up there. Both young men had checked out Megan Sinclair when she arrived at the base, but her cool exterior might as well have been a neon sign reading HANDS OFF.

Bailey said, "Come on, you can teach me some of those *Tejano* dances. Isn't that what you called the music?"

"Where are we going to dance? In the aisle? There's not enough room for that!"

"Well, you could give me a lap dance," Bailey suggested.

From the corner of his eye, Bill saw how Catalina's head snapped around. Bailey had gone too far in his little game. With Catalina's background, that was the wrong thing to say.

Bailey must have realized it, too, because he went on hastily, "Hey, I didn't mean—"

Bill had seen something from the corner of his other eye, too. He said, "That's enough," cutting in on Bailey's apology. "Looks like we've got company comin'."

Off to the west, toward the mountains, a plume of dust rose into the air. Either somebody was driving fast along a dirt road over there, or they were

coming across open country. Either way, they were
going to intercept the bus.

The driver didn't seem to notice, but some of the
passengers did. Frightened cries rang out. All the
people who lived in this area knew about the hold-
ups and the kidnappings, but sometimes they had
to get from one place to another and had no choice
except to take the bus.

Bill could make out several vehicles at the foot of
that dust cloud now. He counted three SUVs and
two jeeps. There was no doubt in his mind that
Megan's intel was about to pay off. A caravan like
that wouldn't be speeding toward the highway
unless it belonged to the cartel.

The driver saw the onrushing vehicles at last and
floored the gas in a futile attempt to get ahead of
the attackers. The bus's engine labored and sput-
tered and sped up a little, but not nearly enough.

The jeeps bounded ahead of the SUVs, reached
the highway first, and whipped into skidding turns
that left them blocking both lanes of the narrow
road. The bus driver turned the wheel a little, like
he was thinking about trying to leave the highway
and go around the jeeps, but he swerved back as
the wheels touched the sand. It was impossible. If
the bus got off the pavement it would either bog
down or turn over.

He had no choice but to stand on the brake and
bring the bus to a shuddering, shrieking, rubber-
burning stop.

One of the jeeps had a .50 caliber machine gun
mounted on the back of it. The passenger leaped
behind the gun and fired a burst that chewed into
the asphalt in front of the bus. Hysterical screaming

filled the bus now as all the passengers realized what was going on.

Bill looked at the machine gun and knew that his earlier musings had been correct. This was war, all right.

And as armed men leaped from the SUVs and charged toward the bus, he knew that the war was on.

CHAPTER 34

The gun-wielding men surrounded the bus and leveled their automatic weapons at it. One of them let off a burst of slugs that shattered several windows on the right side of the vehicle and sent shards of glass spraying over the screaming passengers. Bill, Catalina, and Bailey were on the other side of the bus, so they weren't in any immediate danger. Bill felt anger surge inside him, though, as he saw several people bleeding from the cuts inflicted by the flying glass.

Another man stepped up to the door and tapped impatiently on it with the barrel of his gun. The driver took hold of the lever with both shaking hands and pulled it to the side, opening the door. The man bounded into the bus and slashed at the driver with his gun, driving him cringing back into his seat as the barrel opened a cut on his head. The driver threw up his hands and begged for his life in a loud, terrified voice.

"Everyone down!" the intruder shouted in Spanish. He fired a high burst that shattered the window in the door at the back of the bus and sent the sobbing, shrieking passengers diving for the dirty floor between the seats and in the aisle.

Bill and Catalina weren't crying and screaming, but they got down with the others. Bill twisted his head to look at Bailey and saw that the big man was rising to his feet instead. He kicked Bailey in the ankle. Bailey's instincts told him to fight, but a gun battle right now wouldn't accomplish a damn thing.

Grimacing in frustration, Bailey dropped to one knee, then lowered himself onto his belly like the others. He filled up the aisle next to his seat.

"Open the back door!" the man with the gun commanded. He pointed at one of the passengers. "You!"

The man got shakily to his feet and edged past the crates of chickens to push the bar on the emergency door at the rear of the bus. More of the gunmen were waiting outside. They grabbed the door and yanked it open the rest of the way, then started climbing in. They grabbed passengers and dragged them out. Although the wailing continued, the passengers were too afraid to put up any sort of fight. Once they were out of the bus, more men brandishing guns lined them up, as if for execution.

That possibility was not lost on the terrified prisoners.

While that was going on, more men broke into the bus's luggage compartment and began dragging out everything inside it, going through bags and boxes in search of anything valuable. They were like old-time *bandidos*, joking and laughing as they searched for loot.

When the men came to Bailey, one of them kicked

his foot and ordered him to get up. Bailey pushed himself to his hands and knees. As he did, his vest swung open and the gunman caught a glimpse of the revolver tucked into Bailey's belt. He let out a startled yell and drove a booted foot down into the middle of Bailey's back, knocking him to the floor again. Another man came up and pressed the muzzle of his machine pistol to Bailey's head while the first man slid a hand under the massive torso and retrieved the revolver.

That actually wasn't a bad thing, Bill thought. Now that he was disarmed, Bailey wouldn't have any choice but to cooperate with their captors . . . which had been the plan all along.

When their turn came, Bill and Catalina joined the other captives lined up on the side of the highway. There was no paved shoulder, so they were standing in sand that would make running impossible.

Bill had no interest in running, though. So far everything was going just like he wanted it to.

There were no scheduled stops between Villa Guajardo and Dos Caballos, so Megan or whoever was monitoring the GPS chips at the moment would have noticed by now that the signals were no longer moving. That was a clear indication that the bus had either broken down or been forced to halt. Once the signals began moving again, away from the highway, that would be confirmation Bill and his two companions had been taken off the bus.

Once everybody was off the bus, including the shaking, bleeding driver, the gunman who seemed to be in charge walked along the line of prisoners and studied them. He pointed to all the women between the ages of fifteen and forty, and they were dragged toward a truck that had followed the jeeps and the SUVs at a slower pace. The leader picked out several of the men along the way as well, the ones who were relatively young and well-built.

Bill worried that they might not take him because of his age, even though he still appeared to be hale and hearty. If he had to, he would do something to show them that he could put up a fight.

The leader came to Bailey and said, "This one, for sure. But watch him. He's big like an ox."

"Probably dumb like an ox, too, Jorge," one of the other men said.

"I'll tell you what you can do with your ox," Bailey grated.

The leader, the one called Jorge, smiled.

"So you speak Spanish," he said to Bailey. "So many of you Americans don't. You'll regret that when it becomes the only language spoken there."

"That'll never happen."

"There are already more of us than there are of you, amigo. Can you hold back the ocean's tide by wishing it so?" Jorge jerked his head. "Take him."

Bill wanted to look at Bailey and plead with his eyes for the big man to go along with the plan, but he couldn't risk their captors realizing that there was a connection between them. He kept his eyes downcast and his arm around Catalina's shoulders as she pretended to quiver with fear.

Maybe she wasn't completely pretending, he thought. He wouldn't blame her a bit if she was really scared.

Being prodded by guns, Bailey stalked toward the truck. Bill managed not to sigh with relief when he glanced up and saw that. Everything was still on track.

Jorge stopped in front of Catalina, put the barrel of his gun under her chin, and tipped her head up. He smiled as he looked at her and said, "*Muy bonita.*"

A jerk of his head indicated that the others should take her.

Bill tightened his arm around her protectively and shook his head.

"My niece is young, innocent," he said. "Please, leave her alone."

His Spanish was flawless, the speech of a man who had spent his entire life south of the border.

"Let her go, you old fool," Jorge snapped.

"No, take me instead."

"What we want her for, you would be no help."

Jorge grabbed Catalina's arm and jerked her away from Bill, who didn't hesitate to act.

He swung a punch that cracked sharply against Jorge's jaw and sent the man staggering back a step.

Bill knew he was running a calculated risk. The gunman could fly into a rage and shoot him on the spot. In which case command of the mission would fall to Bailey and he would have to carry on.

But there was a good chance Jorge wouldn't kill him but would pick him to be taken back to the terrorist camp instead. That was what happened, as Jorge shouted an angry curse and swung his gun, smashing it against the side of Bill's head and sending the straw Stetson flying.

"Put this old *viejo* in the truck!" Jorge yelled at his men. "He'll wish he'd let the girl go! He'll die long and hard when we get him back to Barranca de la Serpiente!"

Even through the pain in his head, Bill was glad to hear what the man said. It proved that Megan's intel and the guesses they had made about it were right. When they left here they would be on their way to where they needed to be.

A couple of men grabbed Bill's arms and jerked him to his feet. As they frog-marched him toward the truck, he heard Catalina pleading with Jorge not to hurt her beloved *Tío* Hector.

"Treat me nice, little one, and maybe I'll take it a little easier on him," Jorge said. "But only a little. The old fool struck me, and for that he has to pay!"

The men forced Bill into the back of the truck, which had an arching canvas cover over it. The cover provided some welcome shade, but it also blocked any moving air, meaning that the back of the truck was hot and stifling, filled with the stink of fear sweat and the reek of urine. Some of the men were so scared they had pissed their pants.

The prisoners were sitting on the floor, crowded together like cattle or sheep. Bill spotted Bailey and sank down beside him. Bailey frowned at the sight of the cut on Bill's head and the trickle of blood that wormed from it, but he maintained the pose that they didn't know each other.

"Are you all right, old man?" he asked.

"*Sí, gracias,* I will be," Bill said. He pulled a wadded-up handkerchief from his hip pocket and dabbed at the blood. "I've been hurt worse."

"I'll bet you have," Bailey muttered under his breath.

A minute later Catalina was brought to the truck. Her blouse was disarranged and the top button had been torn off, indicating that at least one of the men, most likely Jorge, had pawed her. Bill felt Bailey stiffen beside him at the sight. He understood the reaction. Rage burned inside him, too. But he had to keep those fires tamped down . . . for now.

A day of reckoning would come, not just for Jorge but for all of America's enemies.

A few more prisoners were forced into the truck, but it appeared that the cartel soldiers were just about finished with their culling. Two guards climbed in and pulled the tailgate closed. They stood at the very back of the truck with their automatic weapons covering the captives. Once the truck got under way, it might have been possible to jump those guards, but Bill could tell from looking at the prisoners that they had no fight left in them. They all sat with their heads down, either crying or just sitting there in numb silence.

The truck's engine started. It lurched into motion. The SUVs must have been leading the way because Bill couldn't see them, but the two jeeps fell in behind the truck to bring up the rear and fight off any pursuit . . . not that there was going to be any.

The highway fell behind them. In the distance, through the opening at the back of the truck, Bill saw the bus start moving again. The passengers who had been left behind were on their way to Villa Guajardo, where they would tell their story of terror and violence. It wouldn't take long for word of what had happened to get around the small town.

Wade, Megan, and the others would hear the news, but they would already know what had happened from tracking the signals of the GPS chips. When those signals stopped moving and stayed stopped, that would be the location of the terrorist training camp. Then the rest of the force could move in, to find with any luck that Bill, Catalina, and Bailey had already struck at the enemy from within and softened their defenses.

Even if everything worked perfectly, the odds would still be overwhelming. But they didn't have to wipe out every low-level cartel soldier and would-be jihadist, Bill mused as he swayed slightly from the truck's bouncing motion over rough ground. The goal they really needed to accomplish was to wipe out the leadership of both factions. That would cripple the operation.

He wondered if they would find Tariq Maleef at Barranca de la Serpiente. It seemed likely that's where Tariq would have gone after he was rescued from custody. In a way, Bill was looking forward to seeing the terrorist again.

If he did, he would make sure to finish the job this time, even if it was the last thing he ever did.

CHAPTER 35

Barranca de la Serpiente

Tariq jerked back with his left arm as it looped around the man's throat. That drew the skin of the neck taut so that the keen-edged blade went in easily and cut deep. The man spasmed in Tariq's grip as blood spurted a good five feet from the severed carotid artery. As the man went limp in death, Tariq let go of him and stepped back to let the corpse fall to the ground with a soggy thud.

"Like that," Tariq said as he held out the knife to one of the killers in training. "Now you try it."

The man took the knife and turned toward the small group of prisoners who had been herded at gunpoint to the training ground.

Tariq heard his name being called and turned his back on the scene as the trainee picked out a victim and moved in on him. Anwar al-Waleed was hurrying toward him from the low, white building that housed the laboratories. Anwar's gangling, bird-like form moved awkwardly and his hair was falling over his eyes, as usual. The tails of his white lab coat flapped around his skinny shanks.

"Good news, Tariq!" Anwar called as he waved a hand over his head excitedly. "The formula is ready to test."

Tariq heard a gurgling sound behind him and knew that another of the prisoners had just had his throat cut. He felt a small surge of pride that his lesson had been successful. The regular instructors could handle the rest of this session. He had just stepped in momentarily as a favor to provide a demonstration.

Tariq went to meet his friend and said with a smile, "You should be careful about running around in this heat, Anwar. You'll give yourself a stroke."

Anwar pushed his glasses up and giggled.

"I know. It's just that I've been working on these spores for quite a while now, and I'm anxious to see if they'll really work like I think they will."

"The Night Flowers? That's what you're talking about?"

Anwar nodded and said, "I thought you might want to observe the test."

"Of course I do." Tariq slapped his friend on the shoulder. "Lead the way."

They went into the lab building, where the air-conditioning felt even colder than it really was after the heat outside. Anwar took Tariq into a darkened room with a large pane of glass set into one wall.

On the other side of the glass was a table. A stocky Hispanic man sat at the table in a straight-backed chair. He wore a pair of handcuffs, and despite the cool air inside the building his face was beaded with sweat. His eyes bulged with obvious fear.

"He can't see us, can he?" Tariq asked.

"No, not at all. He may be intelligent enough to guess that someone is on the other side of the glass, but I don't know about that. It doesn't really matter."

"He's frightened," Tariq said. "What did you tell him?"

"Only that I needed his help to conduct an experiment and that I would be in to see him later." Anwar smiled. "It's true, you know. I couldn't conduct the test without him, and I'll be examining his body once it's over."

"Carefully, I hope."

"Of course. That room is hermetically sealed, and I won't enter it until it's been swept with enough ultraviolet to render the spores harmless."

"All right. Just don't take any chances. We can't afford to lose your genius, my friend."

Anwar ducked his head shyly and clucked in a self-deprecating manner, but he was obviously pleased.

"In the long run, this weapon will kill more infidels than that nuclear device would have. There is a reason Allah decided you should be spared, Tariq. You will carry this to the very heart of their godless government."

Tariq nodded. Anwar was right. The seeds of destruction in the Night Flowers would take root and ultimately wipe out the Americans' capital, and with it their capacity to govern themselves and resist their inevitable destiny.

And the best part about it, Tariq thought self-ishly, was that he didn't have to die in order for this new plan to succeed.

He could live to see paradise right here on earth.

He peered through the glass at the Mexican and asked, "When are you going to expose him to the spores?"

"Oh, I've already done that," Anwar said. "An hour ago. They've had time to implant themselves in his trachea and lungs. Now they're just waiting for the activating agent." He reached down and pressed a button on a control console set under-neath the window. "Which I've just released into the ventilating system in there."

Tariq felt his pulse quickening as he waited to see what was going to happen. For a couple of long minutes the answer seemed to be nothing. The Mexican was still sweaty and frightened, but he ap-peared to be none the worse for it.

Tariq found himself wishing the man would go ahead and die. He didn't know the test subject, didn't know anything about him, not even his name. But he felt nothing but contempt for these Mexicans, even the ones like Sanchez who were working with Tariq and his organization. They were all degenerates, and once Islamic rule was estab-lished over the United States, then they could turn their attention southward and either expand Allah's domain over the Latin countries . . . or wipe out the sinful creatures.

Suddenly Tariq became aware that the man in the other room was breathing harder. The Mexican's chest rose and fell rapidly as he struggled to draw enough air into his lungs. He swallowed hard and lifted his cuffed hands to rub his throat, as if it had suddenly become sore.

"Ah," Anwar said softly. "The spores are activating."

Tariq watched with keen interest as the Mexican quickly grew panicky. The man bolted to his feet so violently that the chair fell over behind him. He leaned forward and rested his hands on the table. His back heaved.

Suddenly the man lunged at the glass and began to pound his open hands against it. His mouth opened wide and the muscles in his throat worked as if he were shouting, but if he made any sound, Tariq couldn't hear it. He didn't know if that was because the other room was soundproofed or if it was impossible for the Mexican to get any words past the grotesque growth clogging his throat and the inside of his mouth.

The white stuff was similar to thistles or spider-webs or strands of cotton. They thickened and braided together before Tariq's eyes to block off more and more of the Mexican's airway.

"The Night Flowers are growing in his lungs the same way?" Tariq asked in a hushed voice.

"That's right," Anwar replied. "Even if he could get enough air down his throat, his lungs couldn't do anything with it. They're already being choked out by the growth. Eventually, if the spores are left unchecked, they'll reproduce exponentially until they fill the entire body to bursting. The tissues won't be able to withstand the pressure."

"He'll explode from inside out."

"Yes. We won't let the process continue that long, however. Once he's dead, we'll deactivate the spores."

"You can do that?"

"Of course, like I said, with UV bombardment."

Tariq stroked his chin as he thought.

"But when the people in Washington D.C. start dropping dead, no one will know to bombard their bodies with UV. The spores will continue to reproduce until the bodies explode, spreading the spores even more."

"Yes, and since the activating agent will already be present in the systems of those who are uninfected because of the aerial spraying earlier in the day, the Night Flowers will quickly find new homes and the process will begin again."

A concern occurred to Tariq.

"What's to stop it from spreading until it wipes out the entire population of the world?"

"We've nano-engineered a limiting factor into the spores. They'll begin to die off quicker than new spores can replace them. Within three days after the initial attack, they'll all be inert and no longer a threat."

"And most of the Americans in the eastern third of their country will be dead."

"If our computer models are correct, yes," Anwar said. When talking about things like this, he wasn't shy or hesitant or gawky. He was in his element when it came to the potential of science to terrorize and kill the infidels. Westerners, in their arrogance, often seemed to forget that the very foundations of science had been laid in the Middle East.

In the other room, the test subject began dashing

back and forth in a frenzy, clawing at his throat. He stopped and hunched over. His body spasmed like he was trying to cough out the thing that was killing him, but of course he couldn't do that. It was in him. It was part of him.

The Night Flowers filled him.

He started running again and slammed into the wall, but there was no way to break out, and it wouldn't have done him any good if there were. He rebounded from the wall and lost his balance, falling to the floor. Tariq moved closer to the glass and craned his neck for a better view.

The Mexican lay with his face turned toward the observation window. He jerked and spasmed. His feet kicked helplessly.

Then a shudder went through him and it was over. His clawing hands fell away from his throat. His eyes stared sightlessly at the glass.

As Tariq watched, the threadlike spores crawled over the man's vacant eyeballs and covered them with an impenetrable white blanket.

Anwar flipped a switch on the console, and the spores seemed to turn a bright, glowing purple. That was because of the ultraviolet light washing over them, Tariq knew.

"Ten minutes of this and it will be perfectly safe to go in there," Anwar explained. "The reproductive mechanism of the Night Flowers will be destroyed."

"Amazing," Tariq muttered. "And you can manufacture this in the quantity we require?"

"Yes. It won't be any trouble. We can have the tanker loaded in less than a week. Then it will be a simple matter to drive it to Washington, turn a single valve, and spend the day driving around the

city. Then a plane flies nearby and takes advantage
of the prevailing winds to spread the activating
agent."

"There's a large no-fly zone over and around
Washington," Tariq pointed out.

"That's why we let the wind do our work for us,"
Anwar said with a smile. "The activating agent is
longer-lasting than the spores themselves. Odorless,
tasteless . . . the Americans won't even know they
have the mechanism of their destruction in their
own bodies."

"When I said you were a genius before, I meant
it, Anwar."

"Please. I just do what I can for our holy cause."

"And Allah will reward you greatly for it. No one
will have more virgins in paradise than you, my
friend!"

And maybe by then, Tariq thought, Anwar would
have figured out what to do with them.

He left the lab a few minutes later. As he walked
across the camp, several vehicles, including a truck
with a covered bed, pulled up near the buildings
where the prisoners were housed. He had known
that some of the cartel men were going to hold up
another bus today and bring back more captives.
Tariq devoted little thought to such matters. It was
up to their allies to keep things running smoothly
around here, to make sure there were men to kill
and women to serve the needs of the flesh.

Tariq turned away without looking back as guards
began to unload the new prisoners from the truck.

CHAPTER 36

Although Bill hadn't been able to see much from inside the back of the truck, he had tried to keep track of where they were going as best he could, making mental notes of any landmarks he'd been able to spot and trying to remember all the twists and turns.

That had proven to be impossible once they entered a canyon with steep walls that he had seen rising behind the truck and the jeeps. It bent and curved back upon itself so frequently that it resembled a snake twisting across the ground.

Barranca de la Serpiente, he had thought to himself with a wry smile. Now he knew how the place had gotten its name.

Eventually the winding canyon had come to an end, opening into what appeared to be a wide valley ringed with mountains. A good place for a stronghold, Bill thought, easily defended against conventional attacks from outside. A few laser-guided missiles dropped into the place would wipe it out, but something like that would also cause a war between Mexico and the U.S.

Once upon a time, the outcome of such a war would have been a foregone conclusion. Now with the anti-American apologists running the government and the news media constantly beating the drums in their favor, Bill wasn't sure the United States could win a war against anybody. The government and a large percentage of the populace simply lacked the will and determination to do what was right in the face of any odds. The statists had almost succeeded in turning America into Europe, a nation of weak-kneed mollycoddlers content to sit back and suckle the teats of Big Government.

Almost . . . but not quite.

Not while men like Wild Bill Elliott still lived.

The truck came to a stop in front of a large prefab building that Bill recognized as a barracks. Such buildings always looked the same, no matter where or when they might be found. Guards opened the tailgate, and the two gun-toters who had ridden inside the truck hopped out.

"Men, stay where you are," one of the gunmen ordered. "Women, come with us."

Catalina turned to Bill and embraced him, exclaiming in apparent fear, "Oh, *Tío* Hector!"

Bill patted her on the back and murmured, "It'll be all right, it'll be all right."

She whispered in his ear, "Can't I kill a couple of the bastards?"

"Later," Bill told her. "You'll get your chance later."

When the female prisoners didn't move fast

enough, some of the guards handed their weapons to their friends and climbed into the truck to drag the women out. One of the men grabbed Catalina, and for a second Bill thought she was going to fight back. He could see her control the impulse, though. She allowed herself to be manhandled out of the truck.

That would have been the end of it for the time being, more than likely, if one of the prisoners, a girl who looked to be about fifteen, hadn't gotten hysterical. She started screaming and struggling in the grip of the guard who held her, and she took him enough by surprise that she was able to jerk free. She tried to run, but she had taken only a couple of steps when another guard tripped her and sent her sprawling on the dusty ground.

His face flushed with anger, the guard she had gotten away from stepped forward and started kicking her. His booted foot had landed twice in her ribs with solid thuds when a figure flashed through the hot afternoon sunshine and tackled him. It was Catalina, of course, and the impact of her collision with him knocked both of them to the ground.

Before anyone could stop her, she had slashed the side of her hand across the brutal guard's throat. As he gagged for breath she rammed the heel of her other hand up under his chin and drove his head back.

The guards were yelling in alarm now. One of them shouted, "Shoot her! Shoot her!" and Bill knew that if any of them lifted a gun, he would have to come flying out the back of the truck and take a hand in this fight. Beside him, Bailey was tensed and ready to do the same thing.

But the leader of the group, Jorge, bellowed, "Hold your fire! Hold your fire! Drag her off of him!"

Several guards leaped to follow the order. They grabbed hold of Catalina, and even though she was a capable fighter she was no match for those odds. They pulled her away from the guard who had kicked the girl, but not before she had hammered a couple more punches into his face. The crunch of cartilage and the way blood spurted from the man's nose told Bill that Catalina had broken it.

He felt a fierce surge of pride in her. Tackling that guard might not have been the smartest thing to do, but Catalina's fighting heart wouldn't allow her to stand by and watch such cruelty. She might have a checkered past, but her heart and her guts still represented much that was good about the human race.

Unfortunately, much more that was evil was on display here in Barranca de la Serpiente. The guards closed ranks around Catalina and hustled her into the barracks. The rest of the female prisoners were prodded inside after her.

"What do you think they'll do to her?" Bailey asked under his breath, so low that only Bill could hear his words.

"I don't know," he said, "but I'm countin' on her to survive until tonight."

He figured it would take at least that long for reinforcements to arrive and the battle to be joined.

With the female prisoners unloaded, the truck moved on to another barracks building. This one was surrounded by a high fence topped with razor wire. There was only one gate in the fence, and it was heavily guarded. A man unlocked the gate and swung it open, and the truck drove through and came to a stop in front of the building.

Bill studied the setup without being too obvious about it. When the time came, he and Bailey needed to be able to get out of here, free Catalina, arm themselves, and carry the fight to the enemy while the rest of their force attacked from the outside.

One thing in their favor was that the guards didn't seem to take their jobs too seriously. The fact that for the most part the prisoners were too scared to fight back had dulled their sense of alertness. While they were filing into the barracks, Bill noticed several moments when he could have jumped one of the guards and taken the man's gun away.

Of course, seizing such an opportunity right now wouldn't really accomplish anything, so he continued being docile and cooperative. Bailey followed suit, although the big man cast dark, challenging glares toward their captors.

The prisoners were taken at gunpoint to a long, low-ceilinged room. There were no bunks, just pallets on the raw wood floor. The only toilet facilities were buckets placed here and there, so the stench in the room was pretty bad. The smell of unwashed flesh didn't help it. An air of gloom hung over the place, too, because the only windows were small, covered with thick layers of wire, and set high in the walls, meaning that it was dark and stuffy inside the building.

When the door slammed closed behind the new prisoners, it was like they had been herded into a dungeon, even though the barracks was above ground.

About two dozen men were already in the makeshift prison, men with ragged clothes and haunted eyes. They sat or stretched out on the pallets and looked up at the newcomers with dull and defeated eyes. None of them voiced a greeting.

Bailey edged closer to Bill and said quietly in English, "I was hoping we could get these guys to fight on our side if we let them loose, but this bunch looks like they've given up."

"Yeah, but things might be different if something happened to give them some hope," Bill replied. "We'll have to wait and see."

He thought Bailey was probably right, though. They couldn't count on much, if any, help from the other prisoners.

They sat down on one of the empty pallets next to another prisoner who glanced at them with a hangdog expression, then quickly glanced away. Bill said, "*Hola, amigo,*" then asked the man in Spanish, "How long have you been here?"

At first he thought the man wasn't going to answer him, but then with a sigh he said, "Three weeks. My time is almost up."

"What do you mean?"

"All those who were brought here at the same time I was are . . . are gone already. My luck is bound to run out soon."

"What are they going to do to us?"

The man looked at Bill again and asked, "You do not know?"

"I know only that we were taken off the bus we

rode to Dos Caballos. And my niece, she was taken as well, along with some of the other women."

The prisoner made the sign of the cross and said, "Then you should say a prayer for her, amigo, because she is as doomed as we are. The women who are brought here, they are used as . . . as . . ."

"You don't have to say it," Bill told the man grimly.

"They are subjected to terrible things," the man went on, "and then when the devils incarnate who run this place grow tired of them, they are taken out and put to the same use as the rest of us."

"And what use is that?"

"They practice killing. They slaughter us like animals. I have seen it with my own eyes. I was taken out once before and thought my time was up then, but they stopped for the day before they got around to my group. But I watched as they turned men loose and made them run so they could be shot down as moving targets. I saw other men have their throats cut or be chopped to pieces with knives. Some were turned loose and told to run across a field, not knowing that bombs were buried there, bombs that blew them into bloody pieces of meat. They call this place the Canyon of the Snake, but it is really hell on earth."

What Bill had just heard shook him to his core. He wasn't really surprised, though. The Mexican cartels had long been known for their cruelty, and of course those Middle Eastern fanatics knew no limits on their evil.

"What would you do if you had the chance to fight back, amigo?" Bill asked the man.

"You mean in the Pit of Blood?"

Bill frowned. This was the first time he had heard that phrase. He asked, "What's the Pit of Blood?"

The prisoner pointed at Bailey and said, "That one will soon know. They will take him there. They will make him fight . . . fight or die."

Bailey understood enough Spanish to know what the man was saying. He took a deep breath, glared, and said, "Bring it on."

CHAPTER 37

Dos Caballos

Megan Sinclair pointed to the image on the laptop's screen and said, "That's it. They've stopped moving again."

Wade Stillman leaned forward to look over her shoulder.

"Lay in the grid over it," he told her.

Megan tapped keys and did so, resulting in longitude and latitude lines appearing on the screen, overlaid on the satellite imagery it was already displaying. Three tiny red dots also were visible on the screen, so close together they looked almost like one. When Megan moved the cursor over those dots, a pop-up window appeared displaying their coordinates.

"We know their location, almost right down to the foot," she said. Her voice shook a little, betraying the depth of the emotion she felt. "Let's go get them."

"We can't yet," Wade said, "and you know it. We have to figure out exactly what we're doing."

From the chair where he sat on the other side of the hotel room, Braden Cole said, "That's right. Planning is everything."

Megan took a deep breath. She didn't like Cole. None of them did. He was about as cuddly as a copperhead. But she knew he was right. She had always planned out her jobs as thoroughly as she could.

Of course, in the end, when she was caught, it hadn't really helped . . .

Nick Hatcher moved to Megan's other side and looked at the screen.

"What's the best way in there?" he asked. As a getaway driver, he always studied all possible routes in and out of a place.

The brightly painted nail on Megan's slender index finger traced a path on the screen.

"This is the canyon that leads into the valley where Bill, John, and Catalina are right now," she said. "Despite its name, the camp must actually be in the valley, not the canyon. But you can see how the name came about. Look at how the canyon writhes around."

"Like a snake," Wade said.

"Yes."

"This image isn't real-time, is it?"

"No, it's archived and must be several months old, because you can see there are no buildings or any other visible signs of the camp. We know it must be there, though, otherwise Bill and the others wouldn't be."

"Can we get a real-time satellite feed?" Wade asked.

"Maybe off one of the DOD or NSA sats. Let me work at it for a few minutes."

She hunched over the laptop's clicking keys while Wade and Nick stepped back. They joined Jackie Thornton, who stood at the window of the second-floor room, looking out at the town of Dos Caballos. The population was maybe two thousand people, and the town had a dusty, run-down look about it, as most places did in this rugged, mostly semiarid region of northern Mexico.

"I don't think you guys are gonna need me," Jackie muttered. "I can fight a little, I guess, but Bill said he wanted me along in case he needed a spy. Not gonna be any spyin' done on this mission, from the sound of it."

"We didn't know that when we started," Wade said. "Anyway, there's no tellin' what might come up before we're finished."

"Maybe you should say 'before we're done'," Nick suggested. "'Before we're finished' sounds so . . . final."

Wade shrugged. They all knew there was a good chance none of them would be coming back. As long as they wiped out the men behind the camp, and as many of their followers as they could, that was all that mattered.

"All right, take a look," Megan said from the table where her computer was set up. All four men gathered around her, even Braden Cole.

The image on the screen was different and didn't have the GPS signal visible on it. Megan explained, "This is a real-time satellite feed, Wade, like you wanted, and I had to go through a different server for that so I can't access the GPS feed at the same time. But it doesn't really matter anymore since we know where they are."

She tapped the screen with her fingernail.

Wade's eyes narrowed as he studied the image. He said, "How come we never picked that up when we were looking for the camp earlier? I can see the buildings all right."

"That's because you know they're there, despite the camouflage on the roofs," Megan said. "You're looking for them. And I had to zoom in to a high degree of magnification to see as much as we're seeing. Maybe we would have found the place eventually using just the satellite imagery, but it might have taken weeks or even longer. Bill was afraid we didn't have that much time."

"Is there a road through the canyon?" Nick asked.

"Yes. See that line? It doesn't look like much of a road, though. More like just a dirt track."

"Doesn't matter. I can drive it."

Megan smiled at the confidence in the man's voice, then she said, "Now, here's something interesting. There looks like another road here, in this basin west of the valley. See it? But where does it go? It appears to end at the mountains."

"Maybe it does," Wade said. "There could be an old abandoned mine or something up there."

"There could be, but in that case the road would have deteriorated more than it has. It looks to me like it's been used recently."

She knew that was a hunch, but she had learned over the years to trust her gut. Bill had mentioned to her that the CIA thought she would have made a good analyst. People like that had almost supernatural ability to take the tiniest indicators and put them together to make a meaningful picture. That was what she did now, as she continued, "The range of mountains that closes off the western end of the valley is about a mile wide, and there's no pass where a road could go through it. But if there was a tunnel, this road over in the basin could lead to it."

Wade scratched his chin and frowned in thought.

"They would have needed a way to bring in building materials and supplies," he said. "That would be easier than trying to come up the canyon with them."

"Yes, but if it's a back door in and out of the place, they must have it heavily secured. We probably don't have the firepower to breach it. The canyon is still our best way in."

"Then that's the way we'll go," Wade said. "Tonight?"

Megan shook her head.

"No. Tomorrow."

"That means leavin' Bill, John, and Catalina in there overnight," Wade said with a frown.

"I know. But they'll just have to hang on until then, because I have an idea." Megan turned to look at Jackie and Cole. "And it all depends on the two of you."

Barranca de la Serpiente

The afternoon was a long one in the hot, crowded, stuffy barracks. Bill had been in plenty of tight situations before and knew how to handle the strain, but even he felt his nerves growing taut. Sitting and waiting was one of the hardest parts of the job.

Bill could tell that Bailey was struggling with it. The big man wanted to strike back at their enemies. He was worried about Catalina, too, as he mentioned in several muttered comments to Bill during the day.

"That gal can take care of herself," Bill said. "She'll be all right."

He wanted to believe that, but given the odds against them, he had his doubts. All they could do for the moment was hope he was right.

Finally, as the light of day began to dim, guards entered the barracks and forced the prisoners to crowd together on one side of the big room. More guards came in, these bringing loaves of bread, hunks of meat, and plastic bottles of water that they threw on the floor. When they all withdrew, the prisoners swarmed on the food and water, fighting with each other like animals to claim their fair share . . . or more.

Bailey's size and speed enabled him to grab a couple of bottles of water and enough food for both him and Bill, who stayed out of the melee. He came over to the spot they had claimed against the wall and shared the meal.

"Pretty smart," Bill commented. "They pit these fellas against each other so that it's every man for himself. That way they're used to fightin' with each other."

"For when they get thrown into the Pit of Blood, you mean," Bailey said.

"Yeah. Men like the ones who work for the cartel, it's got to be somethin' pretty brutal to entertain 'em. So the prisoners who look like the best fighters, they turn 'em into gladiators."

"That's why that guy said I'd wind up there."

"It won't come to that," Bill said. "We'll be out of here before then."

"Or dead."

Bill didn't argue with that statement.

Darkness settled over the room after the crude supper, and soon most of the men were asleep. Bill tried not to doze off. He didn't know exactly when the rest of his team would show up. It might be any time now.

Exhaustion finally took its toll, though. Bill slept, and so did Bailey. When they woke, it was morning.

"What the hell?" Bailey muttered as he sat up and knuckled his eyes. "I thought—"

"I know what you thought," Bill broke in. "So did I."

"You think something happened to them?"

Bill had every confidence in the world in Wade Stillman and Megan Sinclair. But it was possible that one or all of the other three had double-crossed them. They were in a foreign country, after all, where enemies were a lot more common than allies.

"Either they got delayed somehow," he said, "or they're takin' their time because Megan's got some plan in the works. She's a tricky one, that gal. Smart as a whip."

"Yeah, and pretty, too. Too bad she's such a cold fish."

"Maybe you just don't know her well enough."

"And it's starting to look like I won't get the chance to."

Bill couldn't argue with that, either. All he could

do was wonder where the others were and when they would get here.

If they didn't, the job would be up to him and Bailey and Catalina. What was the old saying? *The difficult we do right away . . .*

The impossible takes a little longer.

CHAPTER 38

Catalina hadn't spent a more nerve-wracking night since the time she had dodged the cartel killers back in Ciudad Acuña, after Marty was killed. Nothing happened, though. Some of the women were taken out of the barracks, then brought back later, and it wasn't difficult to guess what had happened to them while they were gone, but Catalina wasn't among those singled out.

That wouldn't last. As a newcomer, she knew her services would be in high demand.

If that happened before the others showed up, she wouldn't give in. In the past, she might have, figuring that with everything else she had done in her life, it didn't really matter anymore. But the time she had spent with Bill, Bailey, Stillman, and the others had taught her that some things were worth fighting for. The past couldn't be changed, but the way people lived their lives every day was still up to them. They didn't have to allow their past mistakes to rule them. Human dignity meant something to her again, and she wouldn't let anyone take it away from her.

So she would fight. It wouldn't be hard. None of the guards considered the female prisoners a threat. Catalina could tell that by looking at them, watching the careless way they acted around the women. They believed that all the women were too beaten down and terrified to ever fight back.

When the time came, they would find out how wrong they were about her.

In the canyon

"Are you sure this is a good idea?" Jackie Thornton asked nervously as Cole steered the jeep along the rutted track that barely qualified as a road.

"Of course it's not a good idea," Cole said. "We're headed right toward a whole training camp full of cartel killers and bloodthirsty terrorists who want to murder as many Americans as they can. But you knew this job was going to be dangerous when you agreed to it, didn't you?"

"I didn't like prison," Jackie said. "I never could sleep much. And when I did sleep, I had nightmares about all the bad things I done."

"Well, there you go. You have a chance now to make up for those things, and either way, you won't be going back to prison, my friend."

"If that's supposed to make me feel better, Cole, I ain't sure it does."

"I don't care if you feel better or not. Just do your job."

"Which is what, exactly?"

Cole smiled thinly.

"Helping me blow the hell out of that camp."

He wasn't sure how far along the canyon they had come. The way it twisted around, judging distances was practically impossible. But it seemed like they ought to be getting to the camp soon. Eyes had been watching them for a while, Cole was sure of that.

So he wasn't surprised when he steered the jeep around another bend in the canyon and found two jeeps waiting for them, both with machine guns mounted on them and filled with men carrying automatic rifles. As the weapons were leveled at them, Cole slammed on the brakes, brought his jeep to a skidding stop, and thrust his hands in the air as a smile broke out on his face.

"Whoa," he said. "Take it easy, fellas. We're not looking for trouble. We just want to do a little business."

At least one of the men spoke English. He stalked forward, menacing Cole and Thornton with his rifle, and said, "Business? What sort of business would we have with the likes of you, gringo?"

"I have something to sell. It's in the back. Show them, Jackie."

Thornton started to get out of the jeep. Instantly more of the rifles pointed at him. He held up his hands in plain sight and said quickly, "Don't shoot. I'm just followin' orders, like you."

The leader of the cartel gunmen gestured with his rifle, jerking the barrel toward the tarpaulin-covered object behind the seats of the jeep.

"Uncover it," he ordered. "Carefully."

"Trust me, I'm gonna be mighty careful with this thing."

Thornton untied a couple of pieces of rope and pulled the tarp back, revealing a large metal case.

"I have to open it to show you what's inside," he said.

The leader hesitated, then jerked his head in a nod.

Thornton flipped the latches and raised the lid. Cole waved a hand at the cylindrical object inside the case and said, "Just in case you don't know what you're looking at, gentlemen, that's a tactical nuclear weapon. A suitcase nuke, if you will."

Alfredo Sanchez joined Tariq in the dining room of the building that housed their quarters and those of the other upper-level occupants of the camp. Sanchez smiled and said, "You slept well, I trust, amigo?"

Many times, Tariq had been tempted to explain to Sanchez—forcefully, even—that the two of them were not friends. But let the man think whatever he wanted to. Their association was almost over.

Tariq and Anwar were leaving Barranca de la Serpiente later today, and as far as Tariq was concerned, it would be just fine if they never returned. The camp could continue its operation without him.

And it would be needed, no doubt about that. With the United States in a shambles from the devastating biological blow that was about to be unleashed upon them, well-trained, ruthless men would be required to move in and complete the job of taking over the country, bit by bit.

Next they would strike at what was left of the U.S. communications industry, crippling it. The left-wing politicians who ran things in America just thought they knew what it was like to have a captive media. They would soon learn how pathetic their grip really was.

The power transmission grid would follow, going down in a series of precisely timed strikes. Some Americans liked to tar his people with the brush of being stuck in the Middle Ages; soon, cut off from each other, huddling in the dark, afraid, the infidels would learn what the Middle Ages had really been like.

In two months, maybe three, the United States would be ruled by a strict but benevolent Muslim government, and sharia would be the law of the land. The citizens who were left would embrace their new destiny, since it promised peace, at least, and a degree of security. Those who could adapt successfully to this new order would be taken in. Those who couldn't would be . . . eliminated.

The idea that a relative handful of warriors could win such a decisive victory against what was still a military power was amazing, Tariq knew. But that was the way wars would be fought in this new age.

The New Sun might not have risen in San Antonio, but it was a new day, nonetheless.

With those thoughts in his head, was it any wonder that Tariq paid little attention to whatever it was that Sanchez was babbling about?

"What did you say?" he asked the Mexican.

"I said we're going to have some entertainment again today," Sanchez replied. "The Pit of Blood will once more be a battleground of life and death."

"I'm leaving," Tariq said curtly. "Anwar and I have things to do."

Tariq hadn't told Sanchez or any of the other savages about the Night Flowers. They didn't need to know. The camp could continue in operation even though the Mexicans were ignorant of what was about to happen. It was enough that Tariq and a few of his trusted associates were aware of the truth.

"You can stay long enough to watch the fight, surely," Sanchez said. "There was a man among the prisoners we took yesterday . . . a gringo, from the looks of him, probably down here looking to buy drugs . . . but such a fighting man we have not come across in quite a while. It will be a special battle."

Tariq found such spectacles only mildly entertaining. He would rather kill infidels than watch them kill each other. But Sanchez seemed so determined, and Tariq supposed it wouldn't hurt. Anwar wouldn't have everything packed up and ready to go until later in the day, anyway.

"All right," Tariq said. "We will pay a visit to the Pit of Blood. But you had better not disappoint me, Sanchez."

Sanchez smiled and said, "Trust me, amigo, when you see this monster, you will not be disappointed."

Bill wondered if today was some sort of crazed killer holiday. The camp didn't seem to be as active. Nobody came to the barracks to haul out any of the prisoners so they could "practice" on them. The men huddled together and talked quietly among themselves, glad to be spared for even an extra few hours of life.

That changed late in the morning when several

guards came in and brandished their automatic weapons, causing the captives to cringe and shrink away from them.

"You!" one of the men said as he jabbed the barrel of his rifle at Bailey. "On your feet!"

Bill recognized the man as Jorge, the leader of the group that had held up the bus the previous day.

Bailey climbed to his feet, not getting in any hurry about it. He wore an insolent sneer on his face.

"What do you want?" he demanded.

"You'll find out soon enough, gringo," Jorge said. He looked around the room at the other men, then pointed out two more, both fairly well-built. "You and you. You will come with us, too."

The men couldn't argue, not with half a dozen automatic weapons trained on them.

Bill didn't want them taking Bailey out of here without taking him, too. With contempt dripping from his voice, he said, "You're brave men, when you have all the odds on your side."

Jorge had been about to leave, but he paused to glare at Bill.

"I remember you," he said. "The *viejo* who gave me trouble yesterday." A leer stretched across Jorge's face. "The one with the oh-so-pretty niece. I think I will take her to my bunk tonight, old man. What do you think of that?"

Bill leaned forward and spat, narrowly missing Jorge's boot.

The man swung that foot at him in a kick that grazed Bill's shoulder. Bill made it seem like the blow had landed with more force than it really did and fell to the side.

"Get up," Jorge snarled. "You're going to the Pit of Blood, too, old man!"

Holding his shoulder to make it appear that he was hurting, Bill climbed awkwardly to his feet. Jorge clubbed him between the shoulder blades with the rifle butt, driving him toward the door. Bill stumbled outside into the blinding sunlight with the other prisoners.

Jorge had called him a fool, but *he* was the dumb one, Bill thought. Jorge had played right into his hands.

Whatever happened, he and Bailey were still together, ready to fight side by side.

The guards marched the four prisoners across the camp. Bill saw a crowd gathering in the distance, and as they came closer, he saw that it was a mixture of the cartel gunmen and the terrorists who had come here from all over the Middle East to refine their skills at killing Americans.

Along the way they passed within about fifty yards of a long, low, white building. Several jeeps had just pulled up in front of it, leaving a cloud of dust hanging in the air behind them to swirl slowly and disperse. Men got out of the jeeps to go into the building, and Bill noticed that a couple of them seemed to be under guard.

A shock went through him as he recognized Braden Cole and Jackie Thornton.

At least, he thought the two men were Cole and Thornton. At this distance, with the dust in the air, it was hard to be sure. Also, the guards hustled the men inside the building so quickly that Bill didn't get more than a glimpse of them.

His heart pounded. He tried to control the

reaction and stay calm. But if Cole and Thornton really were here, that meant some sort of operation had to be under way. Once the GPS signals told them for sure where the camp was located, Wade and Megan had the responsibility of planning the team's next move. Bill had no way of knowing what that was, but he felt reasonably sure of one thing.

Hell would be popping in Barranca de la Serpiente before too much longer.

CHAPTER 39

Tariq was watching Anwar pack containers of the deadly spores in a case cooled by dry ice when Alfredo Sanchez hurried into the lab. The Mexican looked excited about something.

"Our guards just captured two Americans," he announced.

Tariq frowned and asked, "Were they spying on the camp?" Everyone involved in establishing this place had been sworn to secrecy, but such a high level of security was difficult to achieve in practice, even with the threat of death hanging over the heads of those who might break it. It was possible the American intelligence apparatus had gotten wind of Barranca de la Serpiente and sent someone to check it out.

Of course, they wouldn't be able to do anything to stop what was going to happen, Tariq thought.

"No, they weren't spies," Sanchez said. "They were driving boldly right up the canyon. They *wanted* to be taken prisoner and brought here."

Tariq's frown deepened.

"Why would they want that? Surely they know we kill Americans."

"They claim to be arms dealers who want to do business with us. And as proof of that . . ." Sanchez apparently couldn't resist a dramatic pause. "They have brought a nuclear weapon with them."

Anwar hadn't been paying any attention to what Sanchez said. He'd been too caught up in the preparations to move his lethal little creations.

But at the mention of a nuclear weapon, he straightened from the case where he was packing the spores and turned around sharply.

"What was that?" he demanded.

Sanchez nodded and said, "Yes, a suitcase nuke like the one that was supposed to blow up San Antonio. These men claim to have gotten it through connections in the Russian military and *Mafiya*, the same way you got the other one."

That was crazy, Tariq thought. Yet he had no doubt that other such devices existed. It was impossible to know how many objects of destruction the collapse of the Soviet empire had set free upon the black market more than thirty years earlier. Many of them still had to be unaccounted for.

"Can you bring it in?" Anwar asked eagerly.

"Wait a minute," Tariq said before Sanchez could answer. "How did these men know where to find us?"

Sanchez shrugged. He said, "We've had to obtain a great deal of weapons and ammunition, for your men as well as ours. You know there's always a grapevine. There are always rumors, no matter how hard you try to prevent them. And when it comes to dealing in death, the men at the top of that chain are a small group. Word gets around."

That explanation didn't really satisfy Tariq, but he had to admit that what Sanchez said was true.

"Men such as you speak of would not simply drive in as if they were door-to-door salesmen."

"They might if they believed they have a strong enough hand to play," Sanchez said. "There is nothing stopping us from looking at what they've brought to us. If something is not right, we can always kill them."

"Yes, I suppose," Tariq agreed, although it was with some reluctance. "Have them brought in."

"And the bomb," Anwar added.

"And the bomb," Tariq said with a nod.

A moment later, ringed by armed guards, the two Americans came into the lab. Both were smallish men, and rather weaselly in appearance, Tariq thought. One appeared to be nervous, while the other exuded a confidence that bordered on arrogance. That annoyed Tariq, but he kept the feeling in check.

The confident one stepped up to Sanchez and said, "I'm Braden Cole. Are you the man in charge here?"

"No," Tariq said as he moved forward. He ignored the angry glance Sanchez gave him. "I am."

"It's good to meet you, then," Cole said with a nod. He didn't offer to shake hands. Instead he nodded at the other man and went on, "This is my associate, Mr. Thornton."

"What do you want?" Tariq asked coldly.

"I think we're in a position to do each other

some good," Cole said. "You need weapons, and we can supply them."

"Look around you. Do you see any shortage of weapons?"

"I see men armed with rifles and pistols," Cole replied with a smile. "I'm talking about something on a much larger scale." He half-turned to sweep a hand toward the case that a couple of Sanchez's men had just brought in and placed on a lab table. "I'm talking about being able to unleash hell on your enemies."

Tariq thought rapidly. The Americans had covered up the fact that a suitcase nuke had almost gone off in downtown San Antonio several weeks earlier. So Cole wouldn't be aware that Tariq had already had his hands on such a device. If Cole and Thornton were trying to put something over on him, they would soon learn what a bad mistake that was.

"Let's have a look," Tariq said coolly.

Anwar crowded forward in excited anticipation as Cole went to the case and snapped the latches open. He lifted the lid, and as the object inside was revealed, Tariq's heart slugged a little harder in his chest. The carrying case was the same sort that had housed the other bomb, and the cylindrical shape was similar, too, if not exactly identical. Tariq supposed there might be slight differences in the weapons, depending on where and when they were manufactured.

"My friend needs to take a closer look at it," Tariq said.

"By all means." Cole stepped back and waved for Anwar to come closer.

After several minutes of scrutiny, Anwar looked at Tariq and nodded.

"It appears to be real. It would take more detailed examination to be sure, though. One thing concerns me."

"What's that?" Tariq asked.

"There doesn't appear to be a triggering mechanism."

Tariq glared at Cole.

"What good is a bomb that can't be detonated?"

"Don't worry, there's an internal triggering mechanism," the American said. "In fact . . ." He glanced at a watch strapped to his wrist. "If I don't call my people in another five minutes, they'll transmit a satellite signal to it and set it off, and this whole valley will cease to exist." Cole's face hardened. "We're not fools, you know. We didn't just waltz in here trusting in your good will."

Anwar's eyes widened at the threat, and Sanchez's elegantly casual posture vanished as he stiffened.

Tariq remained as stonily expressionless as Cole himself did. He said to the American, "You're bluffing."

"I never bluff where two million dollars is concerned. And my life."

"Two million dollars?"

"That's the price. And here's how the deal works. I call my people and tell them that we have an arrangement. Then you come with me back down the canyon. We leave the device here. Once Mr. Thornton and I are out of danger, you make a call—I know you have sat phones, just like we do—and have your people transfer the two million. As soon as I receive word that the transfer has gone through, we part ways. You come back here, and my friend and I leave. Simple enough?"

"How do we make the bomb operational?"

"You'll get an email detailing the procedure. It'll be waiting for you when you get back."

"But in the meantime you still hold the threat of a nuclear explosion over this camp."

Cole shrugged and said, "At some point you have to trust the people you're doing business with."

Tariq remembered saying much the same thing to men he had later betrayed. But that was for his holy cause, and these Americans had no such cause, only an unholy lust for wealth and power.

He looked at Sanchez, who said coldly, "You claimed to be in charge, amigo. The decision is yours."

Tariq drew in a deep breath. He said to the Americans, "All right. We have an agreement." He glanced at Anwar's work with the Night Flowers, which was not yet complete. He saw no reason not to carry on with the packing as planned. The suitcase nuke could remain here in the camp to be used later as they finished the work of taking over the United States. "But we can't leave yet. It will still be an hour or more."

Cole quirked his thin lips and shrugged.

"As long as we have a deal, we're in no hurry. I need to make that call, though."

Tariq nodded and said, "Go ahead."

Cole reached in his pocket and took out a slender satellite phone. Anwar said, "You may not get reception on that in here."

"Our signal is strong enough," Cole said confidently. He punched numbers into the phone, waited a moment, and then went on, "This is Cole. We have a deal. Proceed as planned." He broke the connection and put the phone away again. "All right. Now we have all the time in the world."

"Then perhaps you'd care to join us," Sanchez suggested, as cool as ever again now. "We're about to indulge in some entertainment."

"What sort of entertainment?" Thornton asked, the first time the man had spoken.

Sanchez smiled and said, "Tell me, have either of you gentlemen ever heard of the Pit of Blood?"

CHAPTER 40

Henry Dixon's legs hurt like the very devil. Phantom pain, of course, since his legs weren't even there anymore, and he wasn't thinking about the stumps where the prostheses attached, either, although those ached considerably after hours of climbing around in the mountains. It was the legs themselves, the ones he'd left behind in Africa. Stubborn little bastards.

It would be nice to be young and whole again, but of course, that was never going to happen.

He had moved in during the night, when he was less likely to be seen, and once it was light he began working himself into position with all the stealth at his command. Now he was perched on a high ledge overlooking the valley. He could see every building in the camp with the naked eye, and when he looked through the scope attached to his rifle, details sprang into sharp relief.

The rifle was resting in a cleft between two rocks where the sun couldn't reach it and strike reflections that might be spotted by the enemy.

All the surfaces of the weapon had been dulled to minimize that danger, as well. The sun might still glint on the scope's lenses, though, if he allowed that to happen.

He wouldn't.

Dixon liked being in a position like this. He was content. He had no delusions of grandeur, but the comparisons to God were unavoidable: he sat in a high place, seeing all, ready to reach down and smite the evildoers, delivering death to them from above.

God didn't have a satellite phone in His pocket, though. Dixon did. When it buzzed, he took it out and opened it.

"Dixon."

"Are you ready?" That was Megan Sinclair's voice.

"I am."

"Twenty minutes."

"All right," Dixon said. He broke the connection and put the phone away, then leaned forward and nestled his cheek against the smooth wood of the rifle's stock.

It felt good to be home.

The SUV looked like a beat-up old American vehicle, but really it was heavily armored and all the glass was bulletproof. Clark had delivered it to Dos Caballos the night before, along with its "cargo": Bronco Madigan, Calvin Watson, and a lot of big guns and ammunition.

Wade was a little surprised to see Clark. The boss of the whole operation should have been back across the border somewhere. Somewhere safe, because this part of Mexico was fixing to be anything but.

Clark had come in person, though, because he had news. Worrisome news.

"Using the intel we developed from that flash drive Catalina brought to us, we've been able to track some of the email traffic between high levels in the terrorist organization," Clark had explained. "Something's coming out of that camp today, something bad. I don't know what it is, but they call it the Night Flowers."

"The New Sun didn't sound all that bad, either," Megan had said, "but it would have been if they'd gotten away with it."

"Yeah, I know, that's why we're concerned. It's a good thing we're able to make this move now." Clark had looked around at Megan, Wade Stillman, Nick Hatcher, Madigan, and Watson. "Wade, when you and your men get in there, try to find out what the Night Flowers are, and do something to neutralize them, okay?"

"You mean while we're tryin' to kill as many of those varmints as we can and keep from gettin' killed ourselves?"

"I know it's a lot to ask, but stopping this new operation may be the most important thing you ever do."

Wade had shrugged and nodded.

"Sure. Sounds like a piece of cake."

"It'll be easier if you leave most of the killing to us," Madigan had said. "That's what we're best at."

Watson had nodded in agreement.

Wade was struck by the change in the two convicts. They still looked tough and scary as hell, but they seemed to have reached some sort of truce between themselves. The seething anger ready to explode just under the surface was still there but it wasn't as strong. He didn't know what had caused the change, but if he didn't have to worry about the two of them being completely loose cannons, that was a considerable improvement.

Nick was at the wheel of the SUV, of course. Madigan had shotgun, Watson was behind him, and Wade and Clark were in the back. Megan had argued that she ought to come along, too, insisting that she could fight, but Wade and Clark had both vetoed that idea.

"You may think that your father's disowned you," Clark had told her, "but I'll still be damned if I'm gonna let Old Iron Balls' daughter get herself killed in one of my operations."

"It's not fair. Bill promised me excitement."

Madigan had growled, "This kind of excitement, you don't need, lady."

In the end, they had left her in Dos Caballos.

Nick brought the SUV to a halt when it was still a mile from the entrance to the Canyon of the Serpent. Wade turned to Clark and said, "You can get out now. One of your fellas ought to be along to pick you up in a little while."

"Who said I was getting out?"

Wade frowned.

"No offense, sir, but this is a field operation. You're in charge of puttin' these things together, not taking part in them."

"I was right there in downtown San Antonio

helping Bill stop Maleef from blowing it up. And I was doing fieldwork while you were still in diapers, sonny."

"I don't care," Wade said stiffly. "Bill left me in charge of this part of the deal, and it's supposed to be just the four of us. You know what the odds are against us."

"Yeah, and I know you wouldn't be risking your lives like this if those ass hats in Washington would just realize the world's still a dangerous place and there are people out there who have to be stopped before they kill us all. I'm coming along, Stillman, and you might as well get used to the idea."

"He's the boss," Madigan said with an ugly grin. "You can't argue with him."

Wade saw that it would be a waste of time and sighed.

"All right," he said to Clark. "But when you get your butt shot off, old man, don't blame me."

"I won't," Clark said. "But I'll remember that 'old man' crack, buddy-roo."

The phone in Wade's pocket buzzed. He took it out and said, "Yeah?"

"It's a go," Megan's voice said in his ear. "And Wade . . . ?"

"Yeah?"

"Come back if you can."

That took him by surprise. He hadn't seen any sign that Megan cared for him in any way other than as a comrade-in-arms in a dangerous game. And maybe that's all it was he was hearing now, to be honest. But maybe not, he thought.

"Do my best," he told her. He closed the phone and put it back in his pocket. To Clark, he said, "Last chance to get out."

"Are you kiddin'? Let's get this rodeo started!"

The gathering crowd around the pit parted to let Bill, Bailey, and the other two prisoners walk through, followed by Jorge and the rest of the gunmen. Jeering shouts came from the cartel men. The terrorists-in-training looked at the prisoners silently but with cold hatred in their eyes. Bill had dealt with their sort enough to know that they considered anyone non-Islamic to be barely human, even their so-called allies.

The Mexicans didn't know what they were letting themselves in for by partnering up with those fanatics. It was like the old folktale about the scorpion crossing the river on a frog's back and stinging it halfway across so they both drowned.

Death and treachery were just in their nature.

Someone had placed a ladder in the pit. Jorge jerked the barrel of his gun toward it and ordered, "Get down there. Now."

One of the other prisoners shook his head and started backing away. He said in a panicky voice, "No, no, no—"

A guard struck him in the back with a rifle butt, driving him to his knees. Jorge said, "We'll throw you in if we have to, and then you might break an arm or a leg. You'd be easy prey. Climb down and at least you'll be able to fight."

The prisoner was sobbing silently in fear, but he struggled back to his feet, stumbled over to the ladder, and started to descend. The second man started forward, ready to climb down as well, but Jorge stopped him.

"The old man next," Jorge said with a sneering grin directed at Bill.

"Sure," Bill said. He made himself move awkwardly as he went down the ladder, as if his shoulder where Jorge had kicked him was still bothering him.

"Now you," Jorge told Bailey.

Bailey sneered right back at Jorge, climbed halfway down the ladder, then jumped the rest of the way to the bottom of the pit, landing as easily as if he had just stepped down from a curb. The fourth man came down behind him.

As the ladder was drawn up, the crowd closed in again so everyone would have a good view. Jorge stood at the edge of the pit and said, "This is how it will work. The three of you," he pointed at Bill and the other two prisoners, "will fight the gringo. He's so big, three against one will only make it fair."

"I don't care how many there are," Bailey said. "I'll fight you all, one at a time or all together. Come on down, you bastards. I'm not afraid of you."

"You will learn to be afraid," Jorge told him. "But not for long, because then you'll be dead. But if you kill these three, there will be more opponents for you, don't worry about that. You can stay down there as long as you kill those we send against you, even if it takes all day."

Bill saw Bailey swallow hard. Bailey didn't want to kill any of the prisoners. Neither of them did. How were they going to avoid it, though?

If help was going to show up, soon would be a mighty good time.

Jorge took a handful of machetes from another man and held them above his head. Only three machetes, Bill saw. Somebody in the pit was going to be the odd man out. Just one more way of ensuring that blood would flow down here and the damned pit would live up to its name.

"As soon as our leader and our special guests arrive, we will begin," Jorge went on.

"Ah, hell, let's get it over with," Bailey said. "The sun's hot and I'm tired of waiting."

"I said, as soon as Señor Sanchez and Señores Maleef and al-Waleed get here," Jorge snapped. "This entertainment is being staged for them before they leave."

Bill didn't let the reaction he felt show on his face. So Tariq Maleef was here, he thought. And he knew from briefings with Clark that the man called al-Waleed had to be Anwar al-Waleed, another leader of the terrorist organization who was supposed to be some sort of scientific genius.

According to Jorge, Maleef and al-Waleed were about to leave Barranca de la Serpiente. There had to be a good reason for their departure, and a chilling possibility occurred to Bill.

Maybe they were setting out on some new operation, a new strike against the United States that would bring death and destruction if it wasn't stopped in time.

With that thought in mind, each second that ticked past took on a whole new importance. He and Bailey had to get out of here, Bill thought. They had to find Maleef and al-Waleed and kill the two men. That was the surest way of stopping whatever deviltry they were about to get up to.

Bill's instincts told him that the lives of millions of people might be riding on this.

But the ladder was up now, and he and Bailey were stuck in this pit, and if Maleef came to watch the bloody show, he might recognize Bill from San Antonio. He might order his killers to machine-gun them without mercy and leave them here in this damned hole in the ground. The breaks were going against them, and Bill felt what little control he had of the mission slipping away from him.

The crowd stirred, parted again. Three newcomers stepped up so they could see. Bill kept his head lowered and his eyes downcast, hoping Maleef wouldn't get a good enough look at his face to recognize him.

That brief glance had been enough for Bill to recognize the terrorist leader, though. Maleef had a serene look on his face, as if he were confident that everything was going his way again.

And his way meant death to Americans.

Jorge threw the machetes into the pit and yelled, "Fight!"

CHAPTER 41

The other two prisoners leaped for the machetes, but Bailey was too fast for them. With almost supernatural speed for such a big man, he grabbed their shirt collars and jerked them back, then swung them together like they were nothing more than rag dolls. Their heads cracked against each other with a resounding thump. When Bailey let go of them, they both fell limply to the sand, out cold.

Well played, Bill thought.

Bailey bounded over to the machetes and scooped them up. He slid one behind his belt and held the others, one in each hand, as he faced the wall of the pit, tilted his head back, and bellowed at Jorge, "What now, you son of a bitch? What now?"

"Kill the old man," Jorge ordered coldly.

Bailey spat contemptuously.

"The hell with that," he declared. "That's not a challenge. Give me a challenge."

Rage flushed Jorge's face. The slim, elegantly dressed man at his side, who had to be Alfredo

Sanchez, looked angry as well. Sanchez snapped, "Give the gringo what he wants."

"But señor—" Jorge began.

"Did you not hear me? Send four of our best men down there. They are not to come out of the pit until those two are dead!"

Jorge shrugged eloquently and said, "I will be one of the four."

"Suit yourself," Sanchez said.

Guards lined their rifles on Bill and Bailey while the ladder was lowered into the pit again. Armed with machetes as well, Jorge and three more of the cartel soldiers descended.

Bailey turned and tossed one of the machetes to Bill, who caught it deftly. He didn't mind fighting for his life against cartel goons. He could kill them without any stain on his conscience.

That didn't come any closer to getting him and Bailey out of this damned hole in the ground, though.

The last of the cartel men reached the bottom of the ladder and stepped off it. As he did, two more men edged up beside the trio of Sanchez, Maleef, and al-Waleed. Bill's heart pounded harder as he recognized Braden Cole and Jackie Thornton. So he'd been right about seeing them earlier, he thought. But what—

Cole slid his hand out of his pocket and turned it so that Bill could see what he was holding. It was just a little box with a red button on it, but Bill knew what it was. Cole smiled, the first sign of genuine warmth Bill had ever seen on the man's face, as he pressed the button.

The ground shook as a huge explosion rocked the valley.

Bailey didn't waste any time. He leaped forward, holding two machetes again as his arms whirled in a deadly windmilling motion. Jorge's face still wore a shocked expression as his head leaped from his shoulders, sheared cleanly off by one of the razor-sharp machetes. Two more of the cartel men went down in a shower of blood before the lethally whirling blades.

Bill finished off the fourth man, driving the machete into his belly with such force that the tip tore out through his back. Bill ripped the blade loose as he shoved the body away. He had moved so fast and agilely that he had taken the cartel soldier completely by surprise.

Even holding the two machetes, Bailey swarmed to the top of the ladder like a monkey going up a coconut palm, before the riflemen surrounding the pit could bring their weapons to bear on him. The explosion had shocked them and made them turn toward it, and that delay gave Bailey the time he needed to get out of the pit.

Bill scrambled toward the ladder, but by now a couple of the gunmen had recovered their wits and opened fire on him. Bullets kicked up sand around his booted feet as he ran. He would be an easy target as he climbed the ladder, he knew, but he couldn't stay down here.

Bailey bulldozed into the crowd, knocking several men over the edge. They toppled yelling into the pit. That disrupted the shooting long enough for Bill to make it to the top. In the distance he saw a huge cloud of smoke and dust billowing into the air from the spot where the long, low white building had been. He had no doubt that Cole was responsible for that blast.

That wasn't all Cole was doing. He chopped the edge of his hand across a cartel gunman's throat, then ripped the machine pistol out of the man's grip. Spinning, Cole squeezed the gun's trigger and sent a hail of lead slicing through the crowd.

A few feet away, Jackie Thornton scooped up a fallen pistol and opened fire with it. One good thing about being so outnumbered: anywhere you turned there was an enemy waiting to be shot down. Several of them spilled off their feet as Thornton's slugs ripped through them.

While that was going on, Bill and Bailey used the machetes to chop down several more cartel soldiers and would-be terrorists. They fought their way to the side of Cole and Thornton. The four Americans had done an amazing amount of damage in a matter of a minute or two, but they were still surrounded by bloodthirsty killers. So far, surprise and momentum had kept them alive, but they couldn't hope for that to hold true for more than another few moments.

They needed help, and they needed it now.

Dixon had been upset when the cartel thugs put Bill and Bailey into the pit. From this angle, and with so many men crowded around, he couldn't see them anymore. If he couldn't see them, he couldn't help them. He couldn't see who to shoot.

Then he'd spotted Cole and Thornton among the crowd, and for a split second, he had thought that the two men must have double-crossed the team. He settled his sights on Cole's head, the crosshairs resting on the hit man's temple. It would have been easy to take up the slack on the trigger . . .

That was when one of the buildings on the other side of the camp blew into a million pieces, and Dixon realized that Cole had just carried out the main part he had to play in the plan. That phony suitcase nuke might not have been a nuclear device, but it was packed with enough regular explosives to take out that building, anyway.

And now Bill and Bailey were out of the pit, Dixon saw, fighting with machetes, mowing down the cartel men and the Middle Eastern terrorists while Cole and Thornton armed themselves and contributed to the carnage.

Tracking the scope to the side, Dixon settled the crosshairs on one of the terrorists and stroked the trigger. The man's head exploded in a grisly spray of pink as the high-velocity round blasted through it. Before the body could hit the ground, Dixon had shifted his aim and was ready to fire again. A cartel gunman's skull burst open like a melon.

Head shots, one after the other, continued. Death from above, Dixon thought grimly. It was what he had been born to do, and he felt a deep gratitude to Wild Bill Elliott for giving that back to him.

Catalina heard the explosion and knew the battle was starting. Some of the guards would probably rush toward the trouble to try to help, while the others would make sure the prisoners were secure.

She was waiting behind the door when a couple of men carrying automatic rifles burst in. A kick broke one man's knee; clubbed fists to the side of the head sent the other to the floor. Both men were still dangerous, though. Catalina bent and jerked a holstered Colt .45 from one man's hip and shot them both in the back, their bodies jerking as the heavy slugs hammered them into the floor.

The rest of the women shrieked in terror and cowered against the far wall of the barracks. Catalina shoved the .45 into the waistband of her jeans and picked up one of the automatic rifles. She yelled, "Shut up!" at the women and had to repeat it before they started to settle down a little.

Then she went on, "I'm getting out of here. There are two guns left." She pointed at the other guard's pistol and rifle. "Anyone who wants to fight for your freedom, grab a gun and follow me."

She whirled through the open door as bullets stitched across the wall beside it. Spotting the guard who had opened fire on her, she squeezed off a burst that punched into his body, spun him around, and dropped him to the ground as a bleeding sack of meat. Catalina didn't see anybody else. From the looks of it, the other guards on the women's barracks had run off to join in the battle on the other side of camp.

Catalina did the same.

The explosion was their signal to go. Nick tromped the gas and sent the SUV surging along the crude trail that followed the winding canyon. He had sent it careening around a couple of bends before bullets began thudding into the vehicle's armored body.

"They're up on the rim!" he called to the men behind him.

"My job!" Calvin Watson yelled. He stood up, reached to the ceiling, and rolled back a specially designed sunroof.

Then he picked up a huge, air-cooled machine gun so big it took a man with massive strength to handle it. Watson had that strength and more. He stepped onto a firing platform bolted to the floor of the SUV. His head, shoulders, and arms extended up through the sunroof opening. He thrust the machine gun's barrel toward the canyon rim on the right and bellowed as he began firing. The gun swung back and forth as he hosed the guard positions on the rimrock with lead.

"Leave some of them for us to kill, you black bastard!" Madigan yelled at him.

"There'll be plenty, you damn redneck cracker!" Watson shouted back.

Bucking and rocking over the ruts, the SUV kept going. Hatcher was driving faster than any sane person would have on such a rough road, but somehow he kept the vehicle under control. Dust and grit sprayed from under its madly turning wheels and left a cloud filling the canyon behind them.

Bodies of guards shot to pieces by the storm of bullets from Watson's gun plummeted from the rocks to smash onto the canyon floor. Whenever a dead man fell in the road, Nick didn't try to avoid the corpse. He just plowed right over it and kept going. The cartel bastards couldn't get any deader, after all.

Suddenly Watson's gun fell silent. Wade heard it and thought at first that the convict must have fired the gun dry and run out of ammunition.

But Watson slumped back against the edge of the opening and started to slide down. Legs braced wide against the motion of the SUV, Madigan stood up and grabbed the gun as Watson dropped it. Watson slumped heavily to the floor, blood pumping from a gaping wound in his upper chest.

"Madigan . . ." he croaked.

"What?" Madigan snapped as he knelt beside the other convict, holding the gun.

"I still . . . hate you," Watson gasped out.

"I hate you, too, you black son of a bitch."

"If I . . . gotta die . . . you better not . . . live through this. Wouldn't be . . . fair . . . Freakin' . . . racist . . ."

Watson sighed and died.

That was the first one, Wade thought, the first one of their team to die, at least as far as he knew.

But he was mighty damn sure that Watson wouldn't be the last.

CHAPTER 42

When he saw the terrorists and cartel thugs dropping around him from head shots, Bill knew that Henry Dixon was taking a hand. Dixon had to be up high somewhere, maybe as much as half a mile away.

Those lethal strikes from above demoralized some of the enemy. They started to run for cover. As the ranks thinned around the four members of the team at the edge of the pit, the tide of battle turned. Bill buried his machete in the chest of a gunman who was about to shoot Bailey, then left it there as he scooped up a couple of fallen pistols and went to work like old Wild Bill Elliott the cowboy movie star.

This was no soundstage, though, and the guns weren't firing blanks.

Jackie Thornton grunted and doubled over as a bullet tore into his midsection. He clamped his free hand to the wound. Blood welled over his fingers as he struggled to stay on his feet and keep fighting. He failed in that effort and fell to his knees.

One of the terrorists, screaming something about Allah, had gotten hold of one of the machetes. He rushed at Bill from behind, who barely caught a glimpse of the man from the corner of his eye. He tried to swing around, but the machete was already slashing through the air at his head.

Thornton squeezed off a last shot and put the bullet in the middle of the terrorist's forehead. The man stumbled, already dead on his feet, and dropped the machete before the deadly blow could land. Bill said, "Thanks, Jackie," and started to reach toward the man to help him up.

Before Bill could do that, though, the gun slipped from Thornton's nerveless fingers. He looked up at Bill, smiled slightly, laughed, and pitched forward on his face to lie still.

Their gazes had met for that split second, and for the first time since Bill had known Jackie Thornton, he hadn't seen guilt lurking in the man's eyes. Thornton had finally found a measure of peace and redemption, here at the end of his life.

Now there were three of them battling side by side, and although things had swung their way for a moment, the odds were still too heavy against them. Too many bullets buzzed through the air around them like angry hornets. They needed another tide-turner.

They got it in the form of a racing, careening SUV that burst out of the canyon and roared across the camp with Bronco Madigan firing a huge machine gun from the opening of a sunroof. The vehicle turned and skidded to a stop, kicking up even more dust, and Wade Stillman, Nick Hatcher, and another man spilled out, firing automatic weapons. Bill's eyes widened slightly as he recognized the third man. Clark had no business being here . . .

But Bill was glad to see his old friend anyway.

More help came from another direction. Bill heard the shots and swung in that direction to see Catalina Ramos coming toward them, firing a Colt .45 in one hand and an automatic rifle with the other. She was a warrior woman, a true Amazon . . . or maybe, given her heritage, more like an Aztec goddess of war.

She had followers, too, as several of the female prisoners were right behind her, also spraying lead toward the cartel soldiers with guns they had liberated from men they had killed.

Most of the men in the camp had gathered to see the spectacle in the Pit of Blood, and now the three-pronged attack was scattering them, mowing them down, sending panic coursing through them. He and his companions might actually win this battle, Bill thought.

Beside him, Braden Cole coughed and stumbled. Bill looked over and saw Cole pressing a free hand to a wound in his chest. Bill's left hand gun was empty, so he looped that arm around Cole's shoulders to hold him up.

"No," Cole choked out. "Let me go." He shrugged out of Bill's grip. "Damn it . . . I won't ever collect . . . that million-dollar bonus . . . but I might as well . . . earn it."

He lunged forward, still firing, and jerked as more slugs pounded into his body. He emptied his gun, though, bringing down several more cartel soldiers before he collapsed in a bloody heap.

"Come on!" Bailey yelled. "We all need to link up!"

Bill knew the big former noncom was right. Their ranks were thinning. They might not be able to wipe out all the enemy—that would be a feat almost beyond belief—but they had to keep the battle going until Sanchez, Maleef, and al-Waleed were all dead. Bill had been looking for their bodies among the bloody shapes sprawled on the ground, but he hadn't spotted them. They might have slipped away when the fighting started.

The two terrorists were the biggest threats in this entire valley. They couldn't be allowed to escape.

If they did, all the dying here might be for nothing.

Anwar was almost hysterical. He had never been under fire before. His efforts on behalf of their cause had never been in the front lines but rather in secret hideaways where the infidels couldn't get to him. Tariq knew that, so he kept a firm grip on his friend's arm as he hustled Anwar toward the jeep into which the cases containing the spores had been loaded.

"Come on!" he urged. "We have to go! None of these other men matter!"

"They're shooting," Anwar babbled. "They're going to shoot me."

"Nobody's going to shoot you if you keep your head down and *move*!"

Tariq didn't know what had happened to Sanchez and didn't care. The man was meaningless now. All the Mexicans were. Their boastful "security" had proven to be less than nothing. A mere handful of Americans had thrown the whole valley into havoc and chaos. It was impossible . . . but it was playing out right before Tariq's eyes.

The jeep was up ahead, only a few yards away. They were going to make it.

Then Sanchez somehow got ahead of them and vaulted into the jeep's front seat. He twisted the key and started the engine, even as Tariq shouted, "No!"

The jeep leaped ahead with a spurt of gravel.

Suddenly a woman dashed in front of it. A woman, a shameless woman with her head uncovered and the shape of her body blatantly displayed in her clothing and most important . . . a gun spitting fire and death in her hand.

The jeep's windshield shattered under the onslaught of lead. Sanchez's head jerked back as a bullet broke his expensive sunglasses and bored on through his brain before exploding out the back of his skull and ruining his carefully arranged hair.

His foot was still heavy on the gas, though, and the woman who had just killed him couldn't get out of the way in time. The jeep's grille slammed into her and sent her flying through the air like a broken toy.

As Sanchez finally toppled out the side of the open vehicle, it slowed to a stop.

Tariq dragged Anwar toward it.

"Come on! We can still get away!"

Wade, Nick, and Clark reached Bill's side. Bailey flanked Bill on the other side. Bailey's bare arms were gory to the elbows, and blood dripped from the machetes he held. He looked like some ancient

barbarian standing on the field of battle with heaps
of corpses strewn around his feet, surrounded by
his fallen enemies.

"Where are the others?" Clark shouted above the
din of gunfire.

"Thornton and Cole are dead!" Bill replied.
"Catalina was on her way here a minute ago, but I
don't see her now!"

"Son of a bitch!" Bailey exclaimed. "Look at
Madigan!"

The massive convict had climbed out of the SUV,
bringing the heavy machine gun with him. A long belt
of ammunition trailed behind him. The weapon's
barrel glowed red from heat as he continued firing
while holding it cradled in his arms.

He strode through the throng of killers, laying
waste to them. Bullets struck him again and again,
but he didn't go down, didn't even slow his pace.
He ignored the blood flowing like crimson rivers
from his wounds and kept fighting with a savage
grin on his ugly face.

He looked like he had never been happier in
his life.

Men could stand up to a lot, but not to a seemingly indestructible engine of destruction, at least
not for long. Cartel thug and terrorist alike broke
and ran in sheer terror from Madigan's onslaught,
and Madigan continued gunning them down from
behind. Wade, Nick, and Clark dropped some of
them as well.

Madigan was starting to sway, though. No man,
no matter how big and strong, could absorb as much
punishment as he had and not begin to weaken. The
machine gun's barrel drooped. Gritting his teeth

and grimacing, he forced it back up and fired a long burst that finished off the rest of his ammo and chopped another dozen men into raw meat. Then Madigan dropped the empty weapon and stood there swaying like a tree in the wind.

When he finally fell, it was like a giant redwood toppling.

Bill spotted a jeep spurting toward the canyon. He recognized the man at the wheel as Tariq Maleef. The skinny, wild-haired man beside him had to be Anwar al-Waleed.

"Damn it!" Bill exclaimed. "Maleef's gettin' away!" He grabbed Nick's arm. "Can you catch him?"

"Not in that SUV," Nick said, "but there's another jeep! Come on!"

"Go after them," Bailey urged Bill. "We'll mop up here!"

Bill left Bailey, Wade, and Clark to do that. He and Nick sprinted toward the other jeep. He hoped the blasted thing had the key in it. No reason why it wouldn't have. Nobody was going to steal it here in the camp.

Until now.

Nick leaped behind the wheel. The key was in the ignition. He twisted it, and the engine roared to life. Bill piled into the passenger seat and they were moving before he could even get settled.

The other jeep had already reached the entrance to the canyon. Bill and Nick were about two hundred yards behind. Catching up would be difficult on the rough, twisting trail, but they had to try.

Bill took Nick's pistol and checked to see how many rounds were left in it. Only half a dozen, he saw to his regret. His own gun held just four rounds. Ten shots in all, so he couldn't afford to waste any.

"Get me as close as you can," he urged Nick.

"Will do!" the driver said.

As the chase led into the canyon, the jeep took some of the turns at such high speed the wheels came off the ground for a second on one side, then the other. Sometimes it hit such a rough spot that the whole vehicle went airborne for an instant before slamming back down on its tires. Nick kept it moving somehow without wrecking them, and they were drawing steadily closer to the jeep up ahead. Maleef wasn't the wheelman that Nick Hatcher was.

He had a gun, though, and as he continued wrestling with the wheel one-handed, he twisted in the seat and fired back at the pursuers.

Bill didn't think it was very likely that Maleef would be able to hit anything from such an unsteady platform, but flukes could always happen. The terrorist might get off a lucky shot. Bill leaned to the side, braced his gun arm as much as he could, and squeezed off two shots. He was going for the tires on the other vehicle, but he must have missed because Maleef's jeep didn't slow down.

Nick suddenly said, "Oh!" and when Bill glanced over at him he saw the crimson stain spreading rapidly across the front of Nick's shirt.

"How bad is it?"

"You keep shooting and I'll keep driving," Nick said through gritted teeth. He pressed down harder on the accelerator, and the jeep surged closer to the other vehicle.

A fluke, Bill thought grimly. A lucky shot. Or unlucky, depending on how you looked at it.

Nick clung tightly to the wheel, though, and kept the jeep moving at a dangerously high rate of speed.

Bill leaned out to try another two shots.

He never knew if he hit the jeep's right rear tire, or if it struck a sharp rock or something else that made it blow. But blow it did, and just like that the jeep was in the air, turning crazily, throwing Maleef and al-Waleed free, and then crashing back down to the canyon floor to roll over and over before coming to a skidding halt on its side.

Hatcher hit the brake and sent their jeep into a sliding stop. Bill leaped out while it was still moving and ran toward Maleef and al-Waleed. His gun was empty now, but he still had the weapon he had taken from Nick. It was a Browning Hi-Power 9mm, a good gun. Bill switched it to his right hand and covered the two men lying on the ground as he approached them.

Al-Waleed came up off the ground with no warning, shrieking in hate and hysteria. He had a rock in his hand and clearly intended to smash Bill's brains out with it.

Bill shot him before the terrorist even got near him. He came close to putting a bullet through al-Waleed's head, but he changed his aim at the last second and shattered the man's shoulder instead. A man like Anwar al-Waleed might have a lot of useful information in his brain, to go along with the crawling snakes of his fanatic evil.

Al-Waleed went down hard, whimpering in agony. He was out of the fight. The same wasn't true of his companion, Tariq Maleef. The man who had almost blown up San Antonio wasn't going to give up. He scrambled onto hands and knees and threw himself at the pistol lying on the ground a few yards away. Bill fired but missed, his bullet kicking up dirt only inches from Maleef.

The terrorist's hand slapped down on the gun. He rolled, fired on the move. Bill felt like a giant hand had punched him in the side as the slug plowed a furrow through his flesh. He stayed on his feet and triggered the Browning again as Maleef came up on his feet. Maleef jerked back as the bullet punched into his chest. He fired yet again, the bullet whining past Bill's head.

The Browning roared and bucked against Bill's palm as he fired a final time. This bullet drove Maleef off his feet. Maleef's pistol slipped from his fingers and flew off to the side.

Bill stalked up to the fallen terrorist. Blood flowed warmly on his side, but he still felt strong enough, although the wound might catch up to him later. He kicked Maleef's gun even farther out of reach and covered the man as he stood over him.

Maleef's shirt was soaked with blood. He blinked pain-wracked eyes against the sun's glare as he looked up at Bill.

"You . . . again," he gasped. "Who . . . are you?"

"Wild Bill Elliott. And I reckon you can call this the showdown at Snake Canyon."

He could tell Maleef didn't understand. The terrorist husked out, "I go . . . I go to . . . paradise."

"No," Bill said. "You go to hell."

He put the last round in his gun through Maleef's brain.

Bill left the broken body where it lay and went to check on the other terrorist. Anwar al-Waleed had passed out, probably from shock and loss of blood, but he was alive. Bill hurried back to the jeep to see about Nick. The driver was still alive, but his face was pale and drawn.

"Did you get 'em?" he asked.

"Maleef's dead," Bill told him. "The other one's wounded and passed out but alive. Reckon he'll be lookin' at a lot of interrogation somewhere down the line. How about you?"

"I think I'll be all right," Nick said. "Sure wouldn't mind . . . having somebody take a look at this wound, though. And I don't think . . . I can keep driving, Bill. Sorry."

"That's all right, I can handle it."

"But you're . . . wounded, too. I just noticed . . ."

"Just a scratch," Bill insisted. "Let me help you over into the other seat."

Between the two of them, they got Nick over into the passenger seat. Then Bill went back to retrieve al-Waleed. He dragged the senseless terrorist/scientist to the jeep and hoisted him into the area behind the seats.

Then he went to the wrecked jeep to see if he could find what the two of them had been so desperate to get away with.

Several metal cases had been tossed out during the crash. Bill gathered them up and put them in the back of his jeep with al-Waleed. As he started to set the last case on the floorboard, he looked at the latches and thought about opening it to see what was inside.

Then he shook his head, said, "Nah," and added that case to the rest of the cargo.

A minute later they were headed back to the camp with Bill at the wheel. He didn't hear any more shooting coming from the valley.

That was either a very good thing . . . or a very bad thing.

Only one way to find out.

CHAPTER 43

Del Rio

"And in other news, there are reports from Mexico of a pitched battle between two rival drug cartels earlier today, at a remote location in the Sierra Madre mountains that one of the cartels was using as a drug distribution center. Oddly, a number of Mexican nationals who were being held prisoner and forced to work at the compound have claimed that several Americans were involved in the incident, as well. The State Department has vehemently denied this. A spokesperson said that it's possible some expatriate Americans were working for one of the cartels but that Washington has no knowledge of such matters."

Clark pushed a button on the remote to shut off the hotel room's TV and said, "The guy should have just stopped after that line about how Washington has no knowledge."

"How much do they know?" Bill asked from where he sat propped up in bed. Bandages were wrapped tightly around his midsection. The bullet that had grazed him hadn't done much damage, but he would still have to take it easy for a few days.

"Who can say how much they know?" Clark replied with a shrug. "There's nothing on the books officially. The help we got from your friend and his friends made it easier for us to keep the whole thing dark."

Bill nodded, knowing that Clark was talking about Hiram Stackhouse. The multibillionaire was continuing to pay for much of the operation's fall-out. Nick Hatcher was in a private hospital and would be for several weeks, before he was strong enough to claim that new life he'd been promised. A life that Nick had promised would be lived on the straight and narrow from here on out.

Stackhouse would foot the bill for the private funerals of Braden Cole, Jackie Thornton, Ellis Madigan, and Calvin Watson, too. All four of them would be laid to rest under false names, but Bill didn't figure that would have bothered any of them. They had lived their lives as they saw fit, done plenty of bad things, but in the end had served a higher purpose, regardless of their motivations for doing so. Let 'em rest, Bill thought. Just let 'em rest.

The hard one was Catalina. She was the one he'd shed tears for as he cradled her broken body in his arms. Her life had been filled with hardship and she had known little joy in her time on earth. She had ended it by killing Alfredo Sanchez, a man who thoroughly deserved to die, and Bill figured she would have taken a little comfort in that, but her life could have been so much more, if only she'd been given the chance to make something of it.

She would be buried under her own name in a cemetery in Ciudad Acuña, next to Martin Chavez.

Counting Catalina, he had lost half of his team, Bill reflected. Actually, looking at it in the cold light of reality, that wasn't bad, considering that all of them had gone into this job believing that it was a suicide mission. But really, that wasn't the right thing to call it and never had been, he thought. Sacrificing your life to protect your country and save the lives of innocent people wasn't suicide. Not hardly.

It was the highest form of honor and duty, and it was within the reach of anyone with the courage to grasp it. Catalina Ramos was the proof of that.

"What about those cases Maleef was tryin' to get away with?" Bill asked. "Any word on what was inside them?"

"They went on a jet back to Langley already, to the deepest, most secure labs we've got. What I'm hearing is that it was some new sort of biological weapon, and a particularly hellish one at that. You may have done more than just save the country, Bill. You may have saved the whole damned world."

"The world's not damned," Bill said. "Not yet, anyway. Seems like we're workin' on it . . . but it's not damned yet."

Keystone, Colorado, six months later

Jake Costigan came into the diner, pushed his cap to the back of his head, and sat down at the counter. A nod to the waitress was enough to let her know that he just wanted coffee. Costigan had lived in Keystone for only four months, but that was long enough for folks to get to know him, and like him.

He was a tall, muscular man, bigger than anybody else in the diner. He worked mostly as a hunting and fishing guide but was also an excellent carpenter and handyman, and his wife Sarah was the town librarian, having taken the job when the previous librarian retired after thirty years on the job. They were a nice young couple, a mighty fine addition to the community, everybody agreed.

A few minutes later another man came into the diner and took the empty stool next to Costigan. He was older, with a shaggy thatch of mostly gray hair and a mustache. As he sat down he said to the waitress, "Reckon I could get a cup of coffee and a slice of that apple pie, miss?"

"Sure," she said. She was about twenty years old, a pretty, rosy-cheeked blonde who had probably been the head cheerleader at Keystone High School a couple of years earlier. A little bulge under her uniform showed that she was expecting. "I don't remember seeing you in here before, sir."

"That's because I've never been here before," the stranger said with a smile. "Just passin' through."

Costigan looked over at him and extended a big hand.

"Jake Costigan," he introduced himself.

"Call me Bill," the older man said as he shook hands.

"Good to meet you. You're not staying around here?"

Bill shook his head and said, "Nope. Just checkin' in on a couple of friends of mine who moved here a few months ago."

"My wife and I just moved here not that long ago ourselves," Costigan said. "It's a really nice place. We love it here. I hope your friends do, too."

"I've got a feelin' they do," Bill said. The waitress put the pie and coffee on the counter in front of him, and for the next few minutes he concentrated on them.

"Actually, Sarah and I got married here, right after we moved to Keystone," Costigan mused. "A buddy of ours was the best man. To be honest with you, I think he was sort of sweet on Sarah himself for a while, but he got over that when the two of us got together. He's a good guy, this buddy of mine. Drives a truck, so he gets to see the whole country. I hear from him now and then, and he seems happy."

"I'm glad to hear it, even though I don't know the fella." Bill took a sip of his coffee, then said, "The friends of mine I was looking for, I really wanted to see 'em because I heard about a job they might be interested in. Seems like it'd be right up their alley."

Costigan's eyes narrowed. He said, "If I lived in a beautiful place like this and had a good life here, I don't think I'd be interested in any other job, no matter how good it was. Hey, I do live here, don't I? It's a good thing I'm not looking for anything else."

Bill sighed and said, "Yeah, now that I think about it, I've got a hunch my friends would feel the same way. I don't think I'll even bother 'em about it."

"Maybe you should stop by their house and have dinner with them anyway," Costigan suggested.

"Naw, I don't really have time. Anyway, this

pie'll tide me over." Bill took the last bite of his pie, drained the rest of his coffee, and stood up. "But it was nice talkin' to you . . . Jake, was it?"

"Yeah. Nice talking to you, too, Bill. Take care."

Bill laid a twenty on the counter and nodded.

"You, too," he said. He walked out of the diner, not seeming to hurry but not wasting any time, either.

The blond waitress wandered back over and said, "That seemed like a nice old man."

"Yeah, I guess," Costigan said.

"Hey, would you tell Sarah that I'll come by and help her with Story Time at the library tomorrow?" The waitress patted the little bulge on her belly. "I want to get used to reading to kids, so I'll know what I'm doing when my own little one gets here."

"Sure," Costigan agreed. "I'd be glad to."

He finished his coffee a few minutes later, paid for it and left a nice tip, and started out of the diner. As he stepped through the door, a man coming the other way bumped heavily into him.

"Hey, watch where you're going," the man said gruffly. He shouldered on past Costigan and went inside.

He never noticed the way Costigan's muscles bunched and tensed, or the way the big man's eyes narrowed as he calculated just where and how hard to strike to break the rude son of a bitch's neck.

Then Costigan took a deep breath and told himself to calm down. The guy was just an asshole, not worth doing anything about. Anyway, those days were far behind him now. He was content just to live out his days here in this peaceful little Colorado town where nothing ever happened, just him and his beautiful wife . . .

And he wouldn't even tell Sarah about running into that talkative old-timer in the diner. He made that decision as he got into his pickup and drove away.

He made it almost a mile before he pulled over to the side of the road. It was starting to snow a little, but it would be a while before the roads got bad enough to keep them from getting to the airport in Denver.

The flakes sure were pretty, though, floating and dancing on the air currents as they drifted down.

He sighed, took a cell phone from the pocket of his hunting jacket, and punched in a number that only half a dozen people in the world knew. When the familiar voice answered, he said, "It's me. Damn it, Bill, what's the job?"

THE ASHES SERIES BY
WILLIAM W. JOHNSTONE